I0847053

LOVE AND LUMINOL

GEORGE WESLEY SCOTT

LOVE AND LUMINOL

This book is dedicated to my family:
To my amazing wife, whose vision and dedication to our true crime
podcast inspired this story.
To my children, without whom this book would have never been
conceived.
To the memory of my father, who recently passed away. He supported
me in everything I did, even when he didn't fully understand it.
To my mother, who continues to be my unwavering support each and
every day.
And to our beloved Maybelle, our faithful feline companion who has
been part of our podcast since day one and whose memory lives on in
these pages.

THANK YOU ALL.

Copyright © 2025 by Love & Luminol
All rights reserved. No part of this book may be reproduced in any manner
whatsoever without written permission except in the case of brief quotations
embodied in critical articles and reviews.
First Printing, 2025

CONTENT WARNING

This novel contains themes and scenes that some readers may find disturbing, including:

- Graphic violence involving both adults and children
- Detailed depictions of gore
- Portrayals of experimental abuse
- Religious imagery and symbolism
- Anti-religious themes and rhetoric
- Occult practices and witchcraft
- Fictional political figures who may resemble real individuals, portrayed in villainous roles

Reader discretion is strongly advised. If you are sensitive to any of these elements, you may wish to reconsider proceeding with this book.

"MONSTERS ARE REAL, AND GHOSTS ARE REAL TOO. THEY LIVE INSIDE US, AND SOMETIMES, THEY WIN."

—— Stephen King

ⵔⵔⵔ

PROLOGUE

1666

Seven figures stood in perfect formation around the mouth of the well. Their heavy cloaks—adorned with symbols that blended Christian iconography with far older signs—hung motionless despite the autumn breeze that stirred the forest around them. Each wore a medallion crafted from materials not found in any colonial settlement: metals with peculiar luster, stones that seemed warm to the touch even on cold nights, crystals that captured lantern light in unsettling ways.

They had gathered in this remote clearing of the New World, drawn by sensations that none could properly explain but all could feel—a vibration that resonated not just through air but through the very fabric of God's creation. What they had discovered beneath this virgin soil would alter the course of the colonies, though no official record would ever acknowledge their covenant.

The First Elder raised his hand, and perfect silence fell across the gathering. When he spoke, his voice carried a resonance that seemed to make the very air shudder like a plucked string.

"For generations uncounted, our Brotherhood has safeguarded the boundaries between the world of men and the realms unseen," he intoned. "Tonight, those boundaries have grown thin as parchment."

The Second Elder stepped forward, her face obscured by shadow though women rarely held such authority in colonial matters. The gemstone of her medallion caught moonlight in ways that revealed patterns too profound for untrained eyes to comprehend.

"The prophesied alignment of heavenly bodies has revealed what lies beneath," she said, gesturing toward the well. "Not merely a source of water, but a doorway to realms beyond mortal comprehension."

From the perfect circle cut into bedrock, a presence emerged that made the Council members' bones ache with recognition. Ordinary settlers would have perceived nothing—just common darkness, common stone. But these seven had been chosen through carefully maintained family lines, their blood preserved across generations for this very moment.

"Is it as the ancient texts foretold?" asked the Third Elder, his voice betraying the first hint of godly fear.

The First Elder nodded solemnly. "The Great Devourer stirs beyond the veil. And with it, the Divine Protector has awakened."

At his words, blue light began to emanate from the well—not rising from below, but manifesting within the air itself, forming symbols that recorded holy truths no mortal tongue yet possessed the words to name.

"It speaks to us," whispered the Fourth Elder, her hands trembling despite her Puritan discipline.

"Not in words," corrected the Fifth Elder, the physician among them whose face remained half-hidden beneath his wide-brimmed hat. "In signs and wonders. The divine language from before Adam's fall."

The seven Council members moved closer to the well, their bodies automatically arranging themselves into the formation that would please the powers below. They had practiced this sacred geometry in secret for decades, waiting for this moment when stars and earth reached the harmony foretold in texts far older than the colonies.

"We must decide our course," said the Sixth Elder, the wealthy merchant whose ships had carried more than mere goods across the Atlantic. "What we have uncovered here is beyond mortal capacity to contain. If knowledge of this spreads among the settlements—"

"It cannot spread," interrupted the Seventh Elder, the oldest among them whose accent suggested origins far from English shores. "You all sense what I sense. What waits beyond that threshold hungers for the souls of mankind. For the divine spark God placed within us."

The First Elder nodded, his face illuminated by blue symbols still forming in the air above the well. "The Divine Protector has granted me visions of what would follow. Eternal damnation would be a mercy compared to what the Great Devourer would inflict upon our kind."

"Then we must seal it," said the Second Elder. "We establish our Brotherhood as its eternal watchers, passing knowledge only to those with the proper bloodlines, the proper gifts of second sight."

"Not merely watchers," corrected the First Elder. "The Divine Protector has shown me more. We must be shepherds as well—guiding the colonies through generations, shaping the divine spark itself to strengthen the barriers between worlds."

"You speak of arranging marriages and births as though we were breeding horses?" The Fourth Elder's voice held cautious curiosity beneath her horror. "You suggest directing the mixing of bloodlines across generations?"

"Precisely." The First Elder's face was suddenly illuminated by blue light, his eyes reflecting patterns matching those flowing from the well. "The Divine Protector requires sacred vessels—humans with the gift to hear its holy music, capable of channeling powers that strengthen the boundaries when they grow thin."

"And the Great Devourer will seek the same," added the Seventh Elder. "It will call to those who can hear its unholy whispers, trying to create vessels of its own."

"A war fought through blood inheritance," murmured the Third Elder. "Through divine music that shapes the very soul."

The First Elder raised his hands, and the blue light above the well intensified, forming symbols that burned themselves into the Council members' souls. "Tonight, we establish the twin Orders that will guide this conflict through countless generations. The Shepherds of Light to serve the Divine Protector, and the Shepherds of Transcendence to walk the dangerous path of studying the Great Devourer."

"Why establish two Orders?" asked the Fifth Elder, the physician's scientific mind seeking clarity. "Why not focus all our efforts on containing the evil below?"

"Because balance must be maintained," explained the First Elder. "The Divine Protector has shown me that the whispers of the Great Devourer cannot be simply silenced—they must be understood, channeled, redirected. Both Orders will believe they serve mankind's highest purpose. Both will be correct, in their way."

The seven Council members joined hands, forming the first circle of what would become the most influential secret society in the New World. Above them, stars pulsed in patterns that mirrored the blue light still emanating from the well.

"From this night forward," intoned the First Elder, "we dedicate ourselves to shaping the destiny of this New World through subtle influence. Through carefully guided bloodlines. Through divine harmonies that will echo across generations."

"And when the time comes," added the Second Elder, "when the proper sacred vessels have finally been born through our careful guidance—"

"They will either save mankind from eternal darkness," finished the First Elder, "or usher in its final transformation."

The blue light pulsed once more, forming a symbol in the air above them—three perfect interlocking circles, each one bisected by a vertical line. The Council members stared in reverent silence, committing every detail to memory.

The First Elder drew the symbol in the earth with his staff, carving it deep into the soil. "This shall be our sign, our protection, our purpose. Through it, we shall communicate across generations, marking safe havens and warnings alike."

"And our covenant?" asked the Sixth Elder. "What shall bind us to this sacred duty?"

"Blood," replied the First Elder simply. "As it has always been."

Each Elder approached the carved symbol, drawing a knife across their palm and allowing seven drops of blood to fall upon the interlocking circles. As the last drop fell, the blue light intensified, seeming to absorb the blood offering before fading into the night air.

"It is done," the First Elder declared. "The pact is sealed. May God have mercy on what we have set in motion this night."

The Council departed before dawn, scattering to establish the foundations of their twin Orders across the colonial settlements. They left behind only a stone well, sealed with the symbol of three interlocking circles carved deep into its cover—a mark that would remain hidden for centuries, waiting to be rediscovered.

The Divine Protector settled into its eternal vigil beneath the sealed well. The Great Devourer pressed against the boundaries that held it at bay. And the bloodlines of the chosen families began their long, carefully guided journey through the generations, seeking to produce vessels that could hear the divine music that flowed between worlds.

The three circles. The twin Orders. The battle for mankind's soul.

It had begun.

Chapter 1: Wes

"Dad, do you think ghosts are real?"

Xander's gaze remained fixed on his soggy cereal, milk pooling around the edges of his bowl. This wasn't one of his typical ADHD-sparked questions that ricocheted around our breakfast table like stray bullets. I glanced at Cynthia, watching as she methodically packed lunches, her obsidian hair cascading over one shoulder, occasionally catching glimpses of her jade eyes as she worked. Even in these mundane moments, she had a way of stealing my breath.

"That's a complicated question, bud—"

A sharp ping from my laptop interrupted us. The subject line sent ice through my veins:

"URGENT: The Hallows' Whispers - More Lives at Stake"

On any other morning, I'd have dismissed it as another piece of digital detritus cluttering my inbox. I'd earned my reputation as our household's resident skeptic—forever searching for rational explanations behind the inexplicable. "Not everything needs a scientific explanation, baby," Cynthia would tease, usually moments before something occurred that defied my carefully constructed logic.

But after last night's episode of Love and Luminol—our true-crime podcast that plays on our surname, Lumin, and the chemical that illuminates blood at crime scenes—I couldn't simply ignore it. The unexplained interference that had sliced through our recording at precisely 3:33 AM, the crystalline whisper we'd captured—too pristine to be random noise, too distinct to be imagination—still echoed in my thoughts: "The hallows know your names."

I'd spent hours trying to find a technical explanation. I'd checked the wiring, searched for interference patterns, even interrogated the boys about potential pranks. Yet nothing explained why our quartet of cats had simultaneously snapped to attention, their fur bristling as they stared, transfixed, at that empty corner of our recording space.

"I know that look," she murmured, her silver pentagram catching the morning light like a trapped star. "Still can't figure out what happened last night?"

"Someone's got to be the voice of reason around here," I replied with a half-smile as she traced another protection symbol in the air.

Ben slouched into the kitchen doorway, his gangly teenage frame awkwardly propped against the wall, backpack dangling from one shoulder. "What're you guys talking about?" he asked, grabbing the final piece of toast. Upstairs, Casey and Tyler's voices rose in their typical morning argument.

"Nothing important, honey," Cynthia said, though her fingers instinctively sought her pendant. Her eyes met mine, a silent warning passing between us. "Just stuff for the podcast."

After Ben's footsteps retreated upstairs, I opened the email. The timestamp made my stomach lurch—3:33 AM. The message was sparse:

"You heard us. We've been trying to reach you. The Hallows' Whispers isn't just a legend - it's a warning. Many families have vanished in Johnson. Families with children. If you don't help us, yours will be next. Check your latest recording again. Listen for the names."

"Babe," I whispered, "you need to see this."

She drifted behind me, her palm warm against my shoulder as she leaned forward. The attached image showed our Victorian home from across the street. At first glance, nothing seemed amiss, but the longer we stared, the more wrong it felt. The brass numbers above our door read 333—not our actual address of 2947.

Each window—the boys' bedrooms, our recording studio, even the unused circular attic window—contained pale faces pressed against the glass. They weren't merely watching; they were anticipating. Their features stretched and distorted in ways that defied human anatomy. But the recording room window chilled me to my core: there we were, hunched over our equipment, while behind us, seven translucent figures formed a perfect circle, their ethereal hands reaching toward our oblivious forms.

Her grip tightened. "Look at the boys' windows..."

I zoomed in, my hands trembling slightly. The faces weren't random apparitions—they were our sons, but wrong. Their features were twisted, eyes transformed into bottomless voids, mouths stretched into impossible grins. "Christ," I breathed.

"Mom! Can't find my shoes!" Casey's voice shattered the moment, jarringly ordinary against our mounting horror.

"Check by the back door!" Cynthia called back, her voice steady despite her grip betraying her fear. "Baby," she whispered, "I know you don't believe in this stuff, but..."

"I believe what I'm seeing right now," I said, quickly shutting the laptop as thundering footsteps announced the arrival of our brood.

They filtered into the kitchen—Tyler helping Casey with his shoelaces, Brayden pushing his glasses up while quietly spooning cereal, Xander still hung up on my unanswered question about the supernatural. Seven families had disappeared in Johnson. Seven families just like ours.

Maybelle, our aging matriarch of a cat, suddenly erupted in a low growl, her matted fur rising like a gray tide. The other three quickly joined her chorus, all fixated on the same empty corner of our kitchen.

"Dad?" Xander's spoon hovered between bowl and mouth, his emo-styled hair partially obscuring his orange and black frames. "About those ghosts..."

Cynthia's fingers intertwined with mine beneath the table. "Let's talk about it after school, okay?" she said to Xander, though her attention remained locked on the cats' focal point. "You guys need to get going."

"But—" Xander protested.

"Baby," I interrupted, squeezing her hand as the kitchen air grew inexplicably frigid. "Can you help Casey with his shoes while I finish up the lunches?"

She caught my meaning instantly. The boys didn't need to witness Patches, our rotund orange and white tabby, arching like a Halloween decoration, or Penny, our perpetually irritated ginger, retreating beneath the table, or even little Nala, our black and white princess, bristling at some unseen presence.

"Alright, time to move it," she announced, managing to keep her voice light as she herded them toward the door. "You're gonna miss the bus." Her smile, usually bright enough to light up the room, looked strained at the edges, worry creeping into the corners of her mouth.

I continued packing lunches, trying to ignore how my breath now misted in the kitchen air. The numbers 3:33 pulsed in my mind: the email's timestamp, the whispered message's arrival, the impossible house number in that unsettling photograph.

A thunderous crash from our recording room shattered the moment. Equipment toppling, though we'd meticulously secured everything after last night's session.

"Just gotta check something real quick!" I called out, trying to sound casual. "Have a good day at school!"

"Love you guys!" Cynthia added, still shuffling them toward the exit. A chorus of "Love you too!" and "Bye!" mixed with the usual chaos of zipping backpacks and scuffling shoes. The moment the door clicked shut, she appeared beside me.

"Baby," she said, moving toward the recording room. "Tell me that wasn't—"

Another crash interrupted her, followed by the distinctive hiss of static—identical to last night's disturbance.

"Maybe it's just the cats," I suggested weakly, though Maybelle remained frozen in her corner vigil, while Patches and Penny huddled by the back door. Nala had vanished entirely.

"Right," she replied, clutching her pentagram. "Because cats love messing with recording equipment."

The static intensified, more aggressive than before, as if fighting to break through some unseen barrier. As we approached the recording room, the temperature plummeted further.

"Got any science for this one, baby?" she asked, her voice wavering. I reached for her hand.

The recording room door stood closed—we'd left it open the previous night.

"Maybe we should—" I began, but then we heard it. Through the static, voices emerged. Not a single voice this time, but many, overlapping like a ghostly symposium. Beneath them all, barely perceptible but unmistakable, were children's voices.

Our children's voices.

"They just got on the bus," I said, more to convince myself than anything else. Through the window, I watched the empty street where the bus had pulled away moments ago.

"Something's in there," she whispered, her free hand still gripping her pendant as she mouthed protection rituals. For once, I didn't question her beliefs. I welcomed any shield against what awaited us.

The whispers ceased abruptly. In the deafening silence, we heard our recording equipment activate with a decisive click.

"The hallows know your names," the voice from last night repeated. Then, in perfect synchronization, every screen in our recording studio blazed to life, each display flashing the same haunting sequence:

3:33

Chapter 2: Cynthia

The white candle felt heavy in my hand as I traced another protection symbol above Ben's door frame, my fingers moving with practiced certainty even as my mind raced through the morning's events. I'd already lined every window with salt and hung bundles of dried rosemary and sage in each corner—familiar protections that suddenly felt desperately important.

Beyond the windows, clouds drifted lazily across the afternoon sun, casting shifting shadows that had me startling at nothing. Or maybe it wasn't nothing. The house felt darker than usual, a deep chill settling into the rooms. Probably just the AC acting up again, but I couldn't shake the feeling that something was off.

"Keep an eye out, girls," I murmured to the cats as I moved to Xander's door. The candle's flame wavered—just the air vent above, I told myself, even though the air felt completely still.

Over my years of practicing, I'd drawn these protection symbols countless times, usually with my skeptical husband watching. Wes would lean against the doorframe, torn between fascination and disbelief, running his fingers through his long dark blondish-red beard or adjusting his black rectangular frames. But today he hadn't questioned a single ritual. Hadn't even raised an eyebrow when I pulled out my emergency altar kit.

I spread my black altar cloth on the hallway floor between the boys' rooms, the triple crossroads symbol embroidered in silver thread catching the light. Three black candles formed a triangle, with a single deep red one in the center. My silver pentagram, adorned with onyx stones, felt unusually warm against my skin as I knelt before the makeshift altar. A small bowl of moon water sat before me, alongside sprigs of lavender and cypress—Hecate's chosen plants.

Lighting each candle counterclockwise, I tried to focus on the ritual instead of that disturbing photograph. My eyes burned from hours of staring at screens—maybe that's why those twisted faces seemed to float in my vision. My third cup of coffee sat untouched beside me, long since gone cold.

"Hecate," I whispered, watching the flames dance, "Dark Mother, Queen of the Crossroads..." My voice grew stronger with each word. Now wasn't the time for doubt. "I call to you in our hour of need. My children are in danger. Something walks between worlds, threatening our family. I ask for your guidance, your protection—"

A floorboard creaked upstairs. Just the old house settling, I tried to convince myself. But why had all four cats suddenly turned to stare at once?

I grabbed my phone, pulling up the research I'd been doing since the boys went to school. The Hallows' Whispers. It appeared in old Johnson folklore—whispers heard in the historic district, especially around the oldest houses. But most mentions were buried in ancient newspapers, wedged between ads for miracle tonics and fortune tellers.

Then I found something solid: an article from exactly thirty-three years ago. The journalist seemed credible, though the paper had folded years back. Property records confirmed the basics—seven families had vanished without a trace. Seven investigations had gone cold.

Nala jumped into my lap, her tiny dictator mustache momentarily breaking my dark mood. The article filled my screen, showing a familiar street. Our street, back when the houses were new and Johnson was just becoming a real town.

I rubbed my tired eyes, trying to focus on the blurring text. The psychic's account was relegated to a sidebar, the yellowed newsprint making it nearly illegible. She'd claimed the whispers were warnings, but also invitations. "They take those who seek truth," she'd said—or was it "those who speak truth"? The scan was too degraded to be certain.

The patterns emerging were more disturbing. Every missing family had been investigating previous disappearances. Journalists, cops, private investigators—all trying to solve the mysteries that came before. The exact kind of stories we covered on Love and Luminol.

Something caught my eye: the Vernon case file. Their address was listed as 333 Maple Street. I frowned, reaching for my coffee. Maple Street... wasn't that what they used to call—

The mug slipped from my hand, cold coffee splashing across the floor. Maple Street was the old name for our street. Which meant...

Unless... was I seeing connections that weren't there? Sleep deprivation could do that, make patterns seem more significant than they were. The house creaked again, making me jump. The AC kicked on, the sound suddenly ominous.

My hands trembled as I checked the time: 3:28 PM.

The static started so quietly I almost missed it. Just a faint hiss from down the hall—probably interference from someone's phone, or the neighbors' wifi, or any of the dozen logical explanations Wes would suggest. But it was growing stronger.

Through the static, fragments of whispers emerged. They sounded like children, but not our children. Older. From another time. Or was my exhausted mind playing tricks, finding voices in white noise like seeing shapes in clouds?

"...three times three..." "...the hallows between..." "...they took us all..."

3:33 PM.

The candles went out.

No—not all at once. I blinked hard, trying to clear my vision. The first one had flickered out from a draft I must have missed. The others followed because... because...

Something changed in the air—a heaviness that pressed against my chest. Or maybe it was just panic, my imagination spiraling after hours of reading about missing families and mysterious whispers. At the end of the hallway, near the attic access, a figure appeared. It was child-sized but wrong—like a photograph that had been stretched and twisted. As it began moving toward me, each floorboard creaking beneath invisible weight, I noticed something that made my heart stop.

It was wearing Xander's favorite Pokemon t-shirt.

My phone lit up with a text from Wes: "Baby, the school just called. Xander never made it to his afternoon classes."

The figure took another step closer. Then another. The static built to a crescendo, and the whispers became a chorus of children's voices, all speaking at once: "Join us... join us... join..."

3:34 PM.

The temperature suddenly returned to normal. The static cut off mid-crescendo. I pressed my palms against my burning eyes, blinking hard. When I looked again, the figure on the stairs had vanished. My phone showed its normal background—the boys laughing in the Bahamas surf from last fall break. No text from Wes. No distorted article numbers.

Only the extinguished candles proved anything had happened at all. Or had the AC finally kicked on, like I'd been telling myself all afternoon?

With shaking hands, I called the school. "Hi, this is Mrs. Lumin, Xander's mom. Just checking..."

"Oh, hi!" The secretary's cheerful voice jarred against my nerves. "Xander? He's in math right now. Everything's fine."

I released a breath I hadn't realized I'd been holding. Whatever this was—supernatural, psychological, or just exhaustion—it knew our fears. Knew how to use them against us.

And it was only getting stronger.

Or maybe I was just getting more afraid.

My phone's ring made me jump. This time it was real—Wes's contact photo lighting up the screen.

"Baby," he started, his voice tight. "I've been looking at the specs for our recording equipment—"

"If you're about to give me a logical explanation for all this," I said, trying to keep my voice steady, "maybe wait until after I tell you what just happened."

A pause. "What do you mean, what just happened?"

I opened my mouth to explain, then stopped. How could I describe what I'd seen on the stairs when I wasn't even sure what was real anymore? The candles were still unlit, but had they gone out simultaneously, or had my tired mind just registered them that way?

"I—" The words caught in my throat as movement caught my eye. The article I'd been reading was still open on my phone, but the text was changing. Not just the numbers this time. Names were appearing in the middle of sentences that hadn't been there before.

Benjamin. Xander. Brayden. Tyler. Casey.

"Baby?" Wes's voice seemed distant. "What's wrong?"

The names vanished as quickly as they'd appeared. Another hallucination? I looked at my phone screen again, but now it showed only the original article. No names. No distortions.

"Cynthia?" Wes tried again. I could hear the worry creeping into his voice.

"I think..." I swallowed hard, trying to organize my thoughts. "I think we need to look into the history of our house. The actual history, not just the bits we used for the podcast."

"What did you find?" I could hear him already typing at his computer.

"Nothing concrete yet," I admitted, suddenly feeling foolish about how I'd let my imagination run wild. "Maybe I've been staring at these old articles too long. Getting spooked by creaky floors and shadows."

"Want me to come home early?"

"No," I said, managing a weak laugh. "No, I'm fine. Just tired. But baby? When you have time, could you look into something about a house at 333 Maple Street? No rush. Just... curious about something I read."

"Of course, babe. Love you."

"Love you too, baby."

After we hung up, I started cleaning up my makeshift altar. The practical tasks helped ground me—storing candles, sweeping salt, opening windows to clear the lingering smell of sage. Normal things. Real things.

But I kept the article about the Hallows' Whispers open on my phone. Just in case.

The screech of bus brakes yanked me from my thoughts. 3:50 PM. Right on schedule. Within seconds, the front door burst open with our usual after-school chaos.

"Mom! Tyler's lying about the lunch trades!" Casey's voice carried up the stairs, his blonde hair flopping over his ears—the ones his brothers never stopped teasing him about.

"Am not!" Tyler shot back, shoving his black hipster glasses up his nose, his blonde hair swaying as he stomped in.

Ben trudged in last, already lost in his headphones, his short blonde hair hidden under that ratty hoodie he refused to wash. Xander and Brayden were bickering about something from math class, their voices mixing with their brothers' as they raided the kitchen for snacks.

Just our normal, noisy family. No whispers, no apparitions, no mysterious texts. I caught myself touching my pentagram again and forced my hand down.

As Brayden yelled at Xander through a mouthful of chips, my phone buzzed with a text from Wes: "Baby, be home around 4:30."

The afternoon settled into its familiar rhythm. Casey and Tyler's argument dissolved into giggles over something on Tyler's phone. Ben disappeared into his room, music thumping through his door. Xander spread his math homework across the kitchen table while Brayden sprawled on the couch with his book.

Normal. Safe. The morning's events felt distant, almost silly in the warm afternoon light and familiar chaos of our family. I was about to start dinner when something caught my eye. The boys' backpacks were lined up by the door—all five of them, arranged perfectly by age.

But my boys were chaos incarnate. They never lined up anything. Their bags should be scattered across the living room like always. And I hadn't heard anyone organize them. "Hey," I called out, trying to sound casual, "who lined up the backpacks?" Five voices called back various versions of "Not me!" from different parts of the house.

I stared at the perfectly arranged bags. Ben's worn black backpack with its band patches. Xander's cyan one with the fraying strap we kept meaning to fix. Brayden's black and yellow bag with his folder poking out slightly. Tyler's red backpack with its Demon Slayer keychain. Casey's newer black one with last week's juice box stain.

Each one exactly where it shouldn't be.

Chapter 3: Wes

"The hallows know your names."

I'd replayed the recording so many times the words had lost meaning. Now it could just as easily be "The hollows need the names" or "The shadows know their names." Or nothing at all—just random static our sleep-deprived minds had shaped into words, searching for patterns in noise.

The frequency analysis software displayed its familiar peaks and valleys across my screen. There was definitely a pattern to the static, regular pulses that could be interference from—

My phone buzzed. Mom had been trying to reach me all morning, probably worried after our latest podcast episode. Despite her evangelical Christian beliefs and Cynthia's practice of witchcraft, we'd found a way to make it work. It hadn't been easy at first, but she'd come to understand that different beliefs didn't have to divide us. These days, she focused on being a loving grandmother to the boys, keeping her concerns to herself and respecting our choices in raising them.

I hesitated before declining the call. She meant well, but whatever was happening in our house, I needed to focus on the evidence in front of me first. I'd call her back once I had something concrete to share. The interference pattern matched the frequency of local radio towers. Except those towers wouldn't have been broadcasting at 3:33 AM. And they definitely wouldn't have triggered every piece of equipment in our recording room simultaneously.

A chat notification popped up from one of our podcast listeners: "Hey, loved the episode about the Vernon family disappearances. Have you guys ever looked into the original name of Johnson? There's this weird pattern with—"

I closed the message. We had enough weird patterns to deal with right now. Besides, our listeners loved spinning elaborate theories.

A strange crackle came through my headphones—similar to last night's recording but not quite the same. I adjusted the audio levels, watching the waveforms spike and dip. There had to be a logical explanation. Bad grounding in the old house wiring. Interference from nearby electronics. Even weather could affect sensitive recording equipment.

But that didn't explain what Cynthia had texted about the backpacks.

The crackle shifted, becoming more rhythmic. Almost like speech, but stretched and distorted. I ran it through another filter, trying to clean up the signal. Years of podcasting had taught me how to pull clear audio from the worst recordings, but this was different. Every adjustment made the sound more unclear, not less.

My second monitor displayed the security footage from the recording room. We'd installed cameras when we first set up our podcast space, mainly for safety after covering some unsolved cases that had gotten a little too close to home. I hadn't told Cynthia yet, but I'd been reviewing the footage from last night. Right before the 3:33 AM incident, there was a frame—just one—where the camera caught something behind us.

I hadn't been able to bring myself to look at it again.

The static in my headphones suddenly cleared, replaced by a single, clear tone. A woman's voice, thin and distant: "Ask your mother about Hallows Creek."

I yanked off my headphones, heart pounding. That voice hadn't been in the original recording—I was certain. A quick check of the waveform showed nothing unusual in that segment. Just the same garbled static we'd caught last night.

My fingers hovered over my phone. Ask Mom? She'd moved to Johnson not long after we did, wanting to be close to the boys, and she'd thrown herself into learning everything about the town's history since then. She might have come across something about Hallows Creek in all her research. But involving her meant potentially dragging her into whatever was happening. After all the progress we'd made with accepting each other's beliefs, did I really want to risk frightening her with what was going on in our house?

Especially when I wasn't even sure what I'd tell her. That we were hearing voices in our podcast recordings? That something impossible was happening in our home? No, better to have something concrete before worrying her.

The security footage caught my eye again. That single frame...

I minimized the audio software and pulled up the video file. 3:32 AM showed Cynthia and me hunched over the equipment, reviewing our latest episode. At 3:33 AM, the static began. Then, between one frame and the next, something appeared behind us. A figure? A shadow? The video quality made it impossible to be certain.

But it seemed to be reaching for us.

I played the footage frame by frame, willing my hands to stay steady. The figure was there for exactly one second—fifteen frames—before the video dissolved into static. When the picture cleared, everything looked normal again.

Except...

I leaned closer to the screen. In those fifteen frames, something else had changed. The whiteboard behind us, where we kept our episode notes and research timeline, showed different writing. Not our usual neat organization, but a single line scrawled across everything else:

MAPLE STREET 333

The same numbers that kept appearing. The same ones Cynthia had mentioned in her text about the backpacks. I reached for my phone to call her, then stopped. She'd had enough supernatural revelations for one day. Better to verify a few things first.

I opened our podcast research folder, scrolling through old episode notes. The Vernon family disappearance, local haunted houses, unsolved mysteries in Johnson... we'd covered dozens of stories, but something about this felt connected. Like we'd been circling around it without realizing.

The time on my computer caught my eye: 4:15 PM. Time to head home. I reached for my mouse to close everything down—

The video player suddenly sprang to life. The footage began playing backward, fast, then faster. Days of recordings whipping past in seconds.

I scrambled to close the window, but nothing responded. The footage kept rewinding, the timestamps blurring: last week, last month, our first episodes in the new house. The motion finally stopped on a specific date: exactly thirty-three days after we'd moved in.

The frame showed Cynthia and me setting up our equipment for the first time. But something was wrong with the image. The camera angle was different—higher, looking down at us from the corner of the room. We'd never mounted a camera there.

I hadn't even installed the security system yet.

My fingers flew across the keyboard, trying every command I knew to stop the playback. The video began to distort, colors inverting, then splitting like a prism. Through the digital noise, I could make out movement in that corner of the room. Something shifting in the shadows.

Then every monitor in my office went black.

For three seconds, nothing.

Then, in green text like an old computer terminal: THEY FOUND YOU THROUGH THE PODCAST JUST LIKE THEY FOUND THE OTHERS 33 DAYS YOU HAVE 33 DAYS

The monitors snapped back to life as suddenly as they'd gone dark. Everything looked normal—files intact, video player closed, audio software still running. If it weren't for my racing heart, I might have convinced myself I'd imagined it.

I checked my phone: 4:17 PM. Two minutes lost. Or had the timestamp on that warning been wrong? I pulled up the system log, searching for any evidence of what I'd just seen. Any trace of an intrusion, a hack, a glitch—anything.

The log showed nothing unusual. Just like the security footage from last night, just like the audio recording. No proof except what I'd seen with my own eyes.

I took the stairs two at a time, mind racing through possibilities. Someone could have hacked our systems—we'd made enough episodes about cold cases and unsolved mysteries to have attracted attention. The hidden camera could be explained by previous owners, urban explorers, anyone really.

But none of that explained what I'd seen in the footage, or why that specific date thirty-three days after we moved in seemed significant.

I pushed through the lobby doors into the late afternoon sun. A group of kids played on the sidewalk, their laughter echoing across the parking lot. Normal. Ordinary.

My phone buzzed again. Unknown number: "THE HALLOWS HAVE WAITED 33 YEARS FOR THE RIGHT FAMILY"

I blocked the number, then blocked it again when the same message appeared from a different one. By the time I reached my car, I'd blocked five variations of the same number sequence. Each one ending in 333.

My podcast app launched automatically when I connected my phone to the car's bluetooth—something it had never done before. Instead of our latest episode, there was dead air. Then static. Then—

I jabbed the power button. The radio fell silent, but my phone lit up with a new message. Wifey: "Baby, did you ever figure out what that interference pattern meant? The one from the recording?"

Before I could respond, another text appeared beneath it: "Because it's happening again. Right now."

The drive home usually took twenty minutes. Today, I'd make it in fifteen. Traffic crawled along Main Street, past the old library where we'd researched our first episodes. A man stood on the steps, staring at my car as I passed. He lifted his hand in what might have been a wave.

He wore the same shirt I'd seen in the security footage. The same shirt I'd seen standing behind us at 3:33 AM.

I whipped my head around for another look, but a bus blocked my view. When it passed, the library steps were empty. I pulled over, throwing the car into park and rubbing my eyes. Sleep deprivation could make you see things. That's what I would have told Cynthia if she'd mentioned seeing a mysterious figure. That's what I'd been telling myself all day.

My phone lit up again. Wifey: "The boys are doing homework. Everything's fine here. But baby... remember how you said the recording was probably just interference?"

Three dots appeared as she typed. Then: "I don't think interference can explain what I'm looking at right now."

She sent a photo. My hands trembled slightly as I opened it, expecting to see something supernatural, something impossible. Instead, it showed our normal recording room. Empty. Ordinary.

Except for the whiteboard.

Where our episode notes had been, someone had written a single word. Not in Cynthia's flowing script or my messy scrawl, but in precise, mechanical letters:

"SOON"

I started the car, fingers already dialing Cynthia's number. No signal. Of course.

Movement caught my eye—my podcast app cycling through old episode titles at impossible speed. It stopped on our very first one: "The Vernon Family Vanishing: Johnson's Oldest Cold Case."

The episode summary began to change, text rearranging itself: "A family investigating previous disappearances... found nothing but empty rooms..."

My grip tightened on the wheel. We'd been investigating disappearances too, through our podcast. Just like the Vernons. Just like those other families...

My phone suddenly reconnected, notifications flooding in. Missed calls from Wifey. Text messages from numbers I'd already blocked. And one voicemail from an unknown caller.

The timestamp: 3:33 PM.

I hit play, knuckles white on the steering wheel as I pulled back into traffic. Through the static, a child's voice—or something trying to sound like a child:

"Welcome to Hallows Creek."

Three blocks from home, my podcast app displayed one final message: "Episode 333: The Lumin Family Disappearance - PREVIEW"

Chapter 4: Cynthia

"Mom, is Dad almost home?" Xander called from the kitchen table. "I need help with this math problem."

I stared at the whiteboard, that single word "SOON" somehow more threatening than any of the whispers or shadows we'd encountered. "He's on his way, honey. Try asking Brayden—he's good with algebra."

"Dad probably wouldn't understand it anyway," I added, earning snickers from the boys. They loved their father, but his struggles with anything beyond basic math had become a running family joke.

My phone displayed the photo I'd just sent to Wes. The whiteboard looked different in the image than it did in person. In reality, the word seemed to shimmer, like heat waves rising from hot pavement. In the photo, it was stark. Clinical. Like it had been typed by a machine.

"Thanks, Mom!" Xander shuffled his papers toward Brayden, who was already reaching for his brother's worksheet.

Normal complaints. Normal afternoon. I could almost pretend everything was fine, if I ignored how cold the recording room had gotten. Or how none of the cats would come near it anymore.

The sound of pencils scratching against paper, pages turning, Casey humming while he worked on his reading—ordinary sounds that should have been comforting. Instead, they reminded me of what we had to protect.

My phone stayed stubbornly silent. No response from Wes.

The doorbell rang, making me jump. I wasn't expecting anyone, and something about the timing felt wrong. Through the front window, I caught a glimpse of badly bleached orange hair and a smile that never quite reached the eyes.

Great. Just what this day needed.

"Is that Amber?" Tyler asked, his nose wrinkling. Even the boys knew to dread her visits.

"Pretend we're not home," Ben muttered without looking up from his history book.

The doorbell rang again, more insistent this time. I touched my pentagram for reassurance before opening the door. Behind me, I heard Brayden explaining an equation to Xander, their normal voices a stark contrast to the tension I felt.

"Cynthia!" Amber's voice carried that familiar artificial sweetness, her plastic smile stretched across her face like she'd practiced it in a mirror. "I just had to stop by. I heard the most interesting thing about your latest podcast episode."

Of course she had. She never missed a chance to criticize our work. Ever since her true crime blog had failed to take off, she'd appointed herself the unofficial "fact-checker" of Love and Luminol. Every minor detail, every slight inconsistency became fodder for her social media rants.

"We're actually in the middle of something, Amber." I started to close the door, but she stuck her foot in the gap.

"I just thought you should know what people are saying." Her smile widened, showing too many teeth. "About the Vernon case? There are some... concerning similarities. The investigation they were doing before they vanished... the types of cases they were looking into... quite similar to your podcast, isn't it?"

The temperature seemed to drop. Or maybe that was just the effect Amber always had on a room.

"And you felt the need to come tell us this in person?" I kept my voice level, though my hand tightened on the door frame. Through the house, I could hear the boys still working on homework, blissfully unaware of the tension at the front door.

"Well, as a concerned member of the community..." She pulled out her phone, screen already loaded with what looked like old newspaper clippings. "I've been doing my own research. Did you know—"

"Mom!" Casey's voice carried from the kitchen. "Nala's acting weird again!"

Thank the goddess for interruptions. "I need to check on my son," I said firmly, finally managing to edge Amber back from the doorway.

But before I could close the door completely, she called out, "Just be careful what energies you're inviting in with that podcast of yours. We wouldn't want history to repeat itself, would we?"

The door clicked shut, but her words hung in the air. How much had she actually discovered about the Vernon case? About the house? And why did she choose today of all days to bring it up?

My phone buzzed with a notification: "New Message from Wes." But when I opened it, the sender showed as my own phone number—something that shouldn't be possible.

"THE VERNONS WEREN'T THE FIRST. ASK AMBER ABOUT 1957."

I stared at the text, my mind racing. 1957—the year after the Vernons disappeared. The message vanished as I watched, leaving my text history normal, as if it had never existed.

Back in the kitchen, the boys had spread their homework across the table—math worksheets, history books, English essays. Xander and Brayden still huddled over the algebra problem, while Ben had finally removed his headphones to help Casey with his reading.

Just an ordinary afternoon. Through the wall, I heard the familiar crackle of static from the recording room—faint, almost routine now. Like something settling in, making itself at home.

I'd grown almost used to these little reminders—the static that came and went, the occasional cold spot, the feeling of being watched. They were almost comforting compared to this morning's events. At least nothing was trying to actively frighten us.

The podcast schedule nagged at the back of my mind. With everything happening, I'd almost forgotten about our regular upload timeline. Listeners would be expecting the new episode, and we couldn't exactly tell them we were taking a break because something was wrong with our recording room.

Or worse, we'd end up with Amber posting another one of her "investigative" pieces about our unprofessionalism.

I glanced at my phone. No new messages from Wes. The static crackled again, softer this time. Almost like laughter.

Through the kitchen window, late afternoon sunlight cast long shadows across the homework-covered table. Normal shadows. Unlike the ones from this morning.

I should start dinner soon, she thought. Keep things routine. Act like this was just another Thursday, like I hadn't spent the day researching disappeared families. Like Amber's visit hadn't left me wondering what else she might know about our house.

The static came again, a soft hiss that barely registered. But this time, it was followed by the distinct sound of footsteps from upstairs. Heavy ones, like an adult walking across the floor.

Ben's music thumped faintly through his headphones. Brayden was still explaining something about equations to Xander. Tyler and Casey had moved to the living room, their voices drifting in as they argued about a video game.

All accounted for. All downstairs.

I stood at the bottom of the stairs, listening. The footsteps had stopped. Probably just the house settling. Old houses made noise—that's what Wes would say. And he'd be right, most of the time.

My phone buzzed. Finally, a real message from Wes: "Almost home, baby. Traffic's awful on Main."

Something creaked overhead, but I forced myself to ignore it. Instead, I headed to the kitchen to start dinner prep. Thursday meant tacos—the boys' favorite. Though I'd need to cook some pepperoni for Brayden. That kid would live on pepperoni alone if we let him.

"Hey Mom?" Xander looked up from his math. "Is Amber going to write another weird article about us?"

"What do you mean, honey?"

"I saw her taking pictures of our house from her car last week. Ben saw her too."

The static crackled, louder this time. My phone lit up—another message appearing to come from my own number:

"CHECK THE VERNON CASE FILE"

I frowned at my phone. The Vernon file was locked in the filing cabinet upstairs in the recording room, but after those footsteps, there was no way I was going up there alone. I pulled up our digital backup files on my phone instead, but when I opened the Vernon case folder, something was wrong. Instead of our usual research notes, there was a single image of a weathered manila envelope I'd never seen before.

The label read: "HALLOWS CREEK POLICE DEPARTMENT - 1957" And below that, in faded red ink: "Property of Amber Sullivan"

Her maiden name. From thirty-three years ago?

But Amber couldn't be more than forty.

The static cut off abruptly. In its place, I heard Wes's voice through the recording room speakers: "Baby? Something's wrong."

My phone buzzed with a text from the real Wes: "Still stuck in traffic on Main. Be home in ten."

Chapter 5: Wes

Main Street hadn't changed much since we moved to Johnson. The same brick buildings lined both sides, their faded signs hinting at decades of different businesses. I drummed my fingers on the steering wheel, watching the sun sink behind Anderson's Hardware—still using the sign from 1962, still run by the same family.

Traffic crept forward another few feet. Some accident up ahead had everything backed up past the library. The old limestone building loomed over the street, its windows catching the late afternoon light. Cynthia and I had spent countless hours in there, poring over archived newspapers and old town records for our early episodes. Back when our biggest worry was finding enough interesting cases to cover.

My phone sat silent on the passenger seat. No more mysterious messages, no more strange numbers. Just that last text from Cynthia about the recording equipment acting up again. Part of me wanted to call her, but what would I say? That I'd seen impossible things on my office computer? That something about the Vernon case was starting to feel uncomfortably personal?

The line of cars inched forward. Through the library's iron fence, I caught a glimpse of someone watching the traffic. For a moment, I thought—but no. The man in the familiar shirt was gone, if he'd ever been there at all.

The cars edged past the library, giving me a clear view of Johnson's historic district. Kelly's Diner still anchored the corner, its neon sign flickering to life in the deepening afternoon. Three generations of Kellys had served breakfast there, though none of them had ever managed to make their eggs as runny as they liked to claim.

Past the diner, the old movie theater's marquee stood dark. Another victim of streaming services and multiplexes. We'd covered a story about a disappearance there back in '73—one of our most popular episodes. The building had been empty ever since the last owners gave up trying to sell it.

The traffic light at Cedar Street finally changed, letting a few more cars through. To my right, St. Michael's Episcopal reached toward the sky, its weathered spire a constant landmark for lost tourists. Mom used to remind me weekly that their doors were "always open for salvation." Now the church just marked the halfway point of my drive home.

The business district gave way to residential streets, where hundred-year-old Victorians sat shoulder-to-shoulder with post-war ranches. Each house had its own story, its own history. After two years of producing Love and Luminol, Cynthia and I knew more of those stories than most people would be comfortable hearing.

Finally clear of downtown, I turned onto Oak Drive. Our street was lined with old growth trees, their branches meeting overhead to form a natural tunnel. Most of these houses dated back to Johnson's early days, their elaborate trim and wraparound porches testament to more optimistic times.

Our Victorian stood about halfway down the block, its dark green paint and white trim setting it apart from the other houses. The late afternoon sun caught the beveled glass in the front door—the original door, according to the realtor, though I sometimes wondered if anything about this house was really "original."

The porch swing Cynthia insisted we keep from the previous owners swayed slightly in the breeze. Two years of Halloween decorations had left permanent hooks in the eaves, and the boys' bikes lay scattered across the front lawn despite my constant reminders to put them away.

Normal. Familiar. Except...

I killed the engine, studying our home. Something about the angle of the shadows seemed wrong. Or maybe it was just knowing what I'd seen in that security footage, knowing what had happened in the recording room this morning.

From the outside, you'd never guess this house had a history. The flower beds Cynthia had planted last spring lined the walkway, black-eyed susans still hanging on despite the cooling weather. The brass numbers beside the door caught the sunlight: 2947.

I grabbed my laptop bag from the passenger seat, trying to shake off the memory of those green numbers on my office monitors. The walk to the front door felt longer than usual. Past the oak tree where we'd hung the boys' rope swing. Past the window to the living room where I could see Casey and Tyler arguing over a video game controller. Past the porch steps that always creaked on the third board up.

Movement caught my eye—a flicker in one of the upstairs windows. But when I looked again, there was nothing there but late afternoon shadows.

My key stuck in the lock. It always did when the weather changed, another quirk of an old house settling. The door swung open to the sound of homework complaints and the smell of taco meat cooking.

"Dad!" Casey abandoned his video game controller. "Tell Tyler he has to let me play the next round!"

Dinner was its usual chaos—boys talking over each other, Brayden eating his plate of pepperoni while the rest of us had tacos, Ben trying to sneak his headphones back from where Cynthia had stashed them. The normal routines helped push the day's strangeness to the back of my mind. For a while, I could almost pretend everything was fine.

Evening chores, showers, teeth brushing, and the usual bedtime negotiations followed. Three separate water requests, two bathroom breaks, and one monster check later, the house finally settled into evening quiet.

The house always felt different after the boys went to bed. Quieter, but not exactly peaceful - especially not tonight. Cynthia curled against me on the couch, her head resting on my chest while I absently played with her hair.

"So," she said finally, "want to tell me what really happened at the office?"

"Only if you tell me why Amber showed up today." I felt her tense slightly at the mention of Amber's name. "That bad, huh?"

"Baby, you have no idea." She shifted to look up at me. "But you first. What happened with the recording? And don't give me that interference theory again - I know that look you get when you're trying to rationalize something."

"I don't have a look," I protested, but we both knew I did. Just like I knew her tell - the way she touched her pentagram when something genuinely spooked her. Like she was doing right now.

"Fine, I have a look," I admitted. "But you have to admit, some of this could be explained by technical issues. The timestamps, the audio interference—"

"The message telling us we have thirty-three days?" She raised an eyebrow. "The security footage you still haven't told me about?"

I pulled her closer, buying time. The warmth of her body against mine helped ground me, made the impossible things I'd seen today feel less threatening. "How do you always know when I'm holding something back?"

"Baby, we've been doing this dance long enough." Her finger traced lazy patterns on my arm. "You try to find logical explanations, I follow my intuition, and somewhere in the middle is the truth. So spill it."

"The footage showed something behind us in the recording room. Last night, at exactly 3:33." I felt her hand pause its tracing. "But that's not the weird part. There was a camera angle we never installed, showing us setting up equipment thirty-three days after we moved in."

She was quiet for a moment. Then, "Well, that explains what I found in the digital files."

"Remember how I said Amber stopped by?" She sat up slightly, reaching for her phone. "Right after she left, I found this image in our system. Where the Vernon file should have been."

Even on the small screen, the manila envelope looked old. The label made my stomach tighten: "HALLOWS CREEK POLICE DEPARTMENT - 1957."

"Baby," I said slowly, "why does this have Amber's maiden name on it?"

"That's the thing." Cynthia settled back against me. "Amber Sullivan. But she'd have been, what, negative seven years old in 1957? And I grew up here - I've never heard of any other Sullivans in Johnson."

"Could be her mother's family?" I offered, but even I didn't believe it. Something about that envelope felt wrong.

"Maybe," she said, in that tone that meant definitely not. "But that's not even the strangest part of today. The boys' backpacks—"

A soft thud from upstairs cut her off. Probably just one of the kids getting up for water. But we both froze, listening.

Neither of us moved. The house creaked - normal settling sounds we'd heard a thousand times before. But after today, nothing felt normal.

"Probably just Ben with his headphones on again," I said, not quite believing it.

"Ben's headphones that I confiscated at dinner?" Cynthia's hand found mine in the dark. "Baby, there's something else I haven't told you about today. About what the house used to be called."

Another soft thud, followed by footsteps. Too heavy to be one of the boys.

"The Vernon house?" I asked, though I already knew that wasn't it.

"No," she whispered. "Before that. When it was 333 Maple Street. When they called this whole area Hallows Creek instead of Johnson."

The footsteps stopped directly above us. Right over the spot where seven shadowy figures had stood behind us in that security footage.

"Baby," I said, trying to keep my voice steady, "I think it's time you told me everything you found today."

"You're not going to like it," she said, but there was no playful edge to her voice now. "And for once, I don't think even you can find a logical explanation."

The footsteps started again, moving toward the stairs. We both stared at the darkened hallway, waiting. Nothing appeared. After a moment, the steps retreated.

"Try me," I said, pulling her closer. "I've already had my computer tell me we have thirty-three days before we disappear. Kind of hard to explain that one away."

"Speaking of computers..." She shifted to face me. "Did yours show you anything about 1957? About what happened after the Vernons vanished?"

"No, just the countdown and that weird camera angle. Why?"

"Because according to what I found, seven families disappeared in 1957, right after the Vernon case. All of them had been looking into what happened to the Vernons." She touched her pentagram. "And baby? They all reported hearing static and voices, just like we are now."

The sound of static whispered from upstairs, so faint we might have imagined it.

"But here's the weird part," she continued. "This keeps happening. And every single time, there's a Sullivan connected to the case."

"A Sullivan like Amber?" I asked, pieces starting to click into place. "Who just happened to show up today, asking about our podcast?"

"And taking pictures of our house." Cynthia's hand tightened in mine. "The boys saw her last week, watching from her car."

The static upstairs grew louder for a moment, then faded completely. The sudden silence felt heavier than the noise had been. "Baby," I said slowly, "what exactly did Amber say to you today?"

"That's just it - she tried to warn me. About the house, about the podcast. Said we needed to be careful what energies we were inviting in." Cynthia sat up straighter. "But she said it like she knew something was coming. Like she's seen it happen before."

The lamp beside us flickered once, and in that brief darkness, we both heard it - the distinct sound of our recording equipment powering up.

"Should we—" I started. "Check it? Yeah." She stood, pulling me up with her. "But baby? Whatever we find up there... I don't think we can explain this away anymore."

I thought about the strange camera angle in the footage, the countdown on my computer, that envelope with Amber's name from 1957. For once, I didn't try to find a logical explanation.

As we headed toward the stairs, my phone buzzed. A new message from an unknown number:

"THE HALLOWS HAVE CHOSEN. 32 DAYS REMAIN."

Chapter 6: Cynthia

The stairs creaked under our feet as we climbed toward the recording room. Each step felt heavier than the last, like the air itself was pressing down on us. The static had stopped, replaced by something worse - complete silence.

The protection symbols I'd drawn earlier seemed to pulse faintly in the darkness, or maybe that was just my imagination.

"Ready?" Wes asked, his hand on the doorknob. I gripped his arm, grateful for his solid presence despite his skepticism.

"Let's find out what we're dealing with," I said, trying to sound more confident than I felt.

He pushed open the door. The recording equipment hummed softly. All the screens were active, cycling through our old episode thumbnails at impossible speed. They stopped suddenly on a new one - an episode we hadn't recorded yet. The title made my blood run cold.

"The Lumin Family Legacy: A Love and Luminol Special Report by Amber Sullivan."

The thumbnail showed our house - not as it looked now, but as it must have appeared in the 1950s. A date stamp in the corner: 33 days from today.

"Baby," Wes started, but I was already moving toward the computer. The episode description below the title seemed to be writing itself:

"In this special episode, we examine the tragic disappearance of the Lumin family, following their investigation into Johnson's darkest mystery. Join guest host Amber Sullivan as she pieces together the final days of Love and Luminol, and the curse that claimed seven families..."

The cursor blinked at the end of the text like it was waiting to write more.

I reached for the mouse, but the screens went black before I could click anything. For a moment, our reflections stared back at us in the dark monitors. Then text began appearing, one letter at a time:

"FOUND THE FILE YET?"

I looked at the filing cabinet near our recording equipment, my skin prickling. Something told me I knew exactly where to look.

"Should we?" I asked Wes, though I already knew the answer. Whatever game Amber was playing, she wasn't the only one who could investigate.

The screens flashed once, and our regular desktop returned. Everything normal. Everything familiar. I moved to our filing cabinet, pulling open the drawer where we kept our research files. The Vernon file was missing, but in its place sat a weathered manila envelope that made my stomach tighten. The same one from the mysterious image that had appeared on my phone earlier - now here, somehow real and solid in our filing cabinet.

"Let's take this downstairs," Wes said quietly. "I don't think we want to open it here."

The equipment powered down on its own as we left, the soft hum fading to silence. But I could have sworn I heard something else just as Wes closed the door - the sound of a recording starting up.

Back on the couch, the manila envelope sat between us like a living thing. The label "HALLOWS CREEK POLICE DEPARTMENT - 1957" seemed to catch every shadow from the lamp.

"You know what's weird?" I said, running my finger along the edge of the envelope. "Amber's only been in Johnson for what, five years? Shows up right after we start the podcast, acting like she's the local expert on everything."

"Six years," Wes corrected. "Remember that article she wrote criticizing our first episode? Called herself a 'lifelong resident.'"

"Right." I studied the document more closely, half expecting more strange messages. Instead, what I saw looked like standard police reports. Incident logs. Witness statements. But something about the arrangement caught my eye.

The paperwork was organized too perfectly, like someone had wanted these specific pages to be found in this specific order. Red marks dotted the margins - not corrections, but some kind of notation system.

"Baby," I said, adjusting the screen brightness. "Look at how these markings line up."

"Does this look like code to you?" I asked, tilting my head to see the pattern better.

Wes leaned in closer. "Could be. But why would police reports from 1957 use—"

He stopped suddenly, pointing at one of the pages. "Look at the officer's signature."

The name at the bottom of the report: Alexandra M. Sullivan.

Not Amber, but the connection was impossible to ignore. Especially with those deliberate marks in the margins, forming some kind of pattern across the pages. Like breadcrumbs left for someone to follow.

"Baby," I said, studying the way the red marks seemed to flow from one page to the next. "Remember what you said about finding patterns where there might not be any?"

"Yeah?"

"I don't think these are random marks. Look how they connect when you view the pages chronologically instead of by case number."

I leaned closer to the documents, following the flow of the red marks. My grandmother used to talk about codes her family passed down, ways of hiding messages in plain sight. These marks reminded me of that somehow - deliberate but disguised as casual notation.

"Here," I pointed to a sequence that repeated across several pages. "See how these dots and lines create a pattern? And look at the dates on these specific reports."

The pages we'd singled out were all from thirty-three days before each disappearance. And each one had a similar note in the margins: "Subject claims audio disturbance." Below that, those strange red marks.

"It's like..." Wes started sketching the pattern on a notepad. "Like they're meant to be read together, but not in the way you'd expect."

The marks did seem to shift and change meaning depending on how you arranged the pages. Almost like—

A loud thump from upstairs cut through my thoughts. Then another. Like footsteps, but not from the recording room this time.

They were coming from the boys' rooms.

Wes was already halfway to the stairs before I could move. The thumping had stopped, but something else replaced it - the sound of whispered voices, too faint to make out words.

"I'll check on the boys," he said quietly. "You keep working on those marks."

I watched him take the stairs two at a time, trying to focus on the scattered police reports instead of my racing heart. The red marks seemed to blur together in the dim light, but there was definitely a system to them. Alexandra M. Sullivan hadn't just been taking notes - she'd been documenting something specific.

Three short marks, followed by a longer one. Repeated across multiple pages, but slightly different each time. Like she was recording changes in whatever she was tracking.

The sound of Wes checking each bedroom door carried down the stairs. Tyler mumbling something in his sleep. Casey rolling over. Normal nighttime sounds that somehow felt wrong tonight.

I arranged the pages in a circle on the coffee table, the way the marks seemed to want to flow. That's when I saw it - the pattern wasn't just moving across the pages, it was creating something when viewed as a whole.

A sequence emerged from the marks, clearer now that I could see them all at once. Not just random notation, but a deliberate circle of symbols. Some looked like ancient letters, others like mathematical symbols, but arranged this way they seemed to tell a story.

The footsteps above had stopped. I heard Wes's voice, soft and reassuring, probably soothing one of the boys back to sleep. But I barely registered it, too focused on what was forming in front of me.

In the center of the circle of images, the marks seemed to point to specific words in the reports. "Audio." "Signal." "Frequency." Each one tagged with those strange red symbols.

My fingers traced the pattern on the screen, following Alexandra Sullivan's hidden message. Whatever she'd discovered about the disappearances, she'd wanted someone to find it. But why hide it in police reports? And why was this file in our system?

The sound of Wes's footsteps on the stairs pulled my attention away from the pattern.

"Boys are all sound asleep," he said, settling back beside me. "What did you find?"

"Look at this." I shifted the papers so he could see the circular pattern. "Each report mentions some kind of audio disturbance, and these marks..." I traced the sequence again. "They're not random notes. They're recording something specific about each incident."

Wes leaned in closer, his skepticism momentarily forgotten. "These symbols here," he pointed to a repeated sequence, "they almost look like old radio frequencies."

He was right. The marks did have a mathematical precision to them, despite their hand-drawn appearance. And the way they connected from page to page...

"Baby," I said slowly, "what if Alexandra Sullivan wasn't just documenting the disappearances? What if she was trying to track whatever was causing them?"

The documents suddenly felt heavier, more significant. This wasn't just a cold case file - it was a warning. Or maybe instructions.

"There's something else," Wes said, pulling up one of the report images. "Look at the location listed for each incident."

The addresses jumped out immediately. Each disappearance had happened in buildings that still existed in Johnson, places we passed every day. Kelly's Diner. The old movie theater. Even St. Michael's Episcopal.

"They're all in a pattern too," I said, sketching the locations quickly on a notepad. When I connected them, they formed a shape across the town map. And at the center...

"Our house," Wes finished my thought. "Back when it was 333 Maple Street."

I started to respond, but my phone buzzed. A text from an unknown number: "GETTING WARMER. CHECK THE DINER AT MIDNIGHT."

The message disappeared as soon as I showed it to Wes. But the implications were clear - someone was watching us piece this together. Someone who knew what Alexandra Sullivan had hidden in these reports.

"We're not really considering going to Kelly's at midnight, are we?" Wes asked, though we both knew the answer.

The red marks seemed to pulse in the laptop's glow, waiting for us to decode their full message.

"Wouldn't be the strangest thing we've done for the podcast," I said, but my attempt at humor felt flat. "We need to figure out what these marks mean before we go anywhere."

I took several photos of the arranged papers with my phone, trying different angles to capture all the details. The pattern was clearer in the photos somehow - the way the marks created a series of concentric circles, each one pointing to specific details in the reports.

"You know what's weird?" Wes said, comparing dates across the pages. "Every incident report was filed thirty-three days after someone reported hearing static. Just like—"

"Just like what's happening to us," I finished. A chill ran through me despite the warm room. "But why would Alexandra Sullivan encode this information? And why would Amber have her file?"

The grandfather clock in the hallway chimed once - 11:15 PM. If we were going to check out the diner, we'd need to decide soon.

"The boys," we both said simultaneously.

We couldn't leave them alone, not after everything that had happened today. But Kelly's Diner might hold answers we needed - answers about Alexandra Sullivan, about these reports, about why Amber seemed to be playing some twisted game with us.

"Mrs. Martinez next door," Wes suggested. "The boys love her, and she's always offering to help."

He had a point. Our elderly neighbor had practically adopted our whole family, constantly bringing over cookies and fussing over the boys. Plus, her house was close enough that we could be back in minutes if anything felt wrong.

"Forty-five minutes," I said firmly. "We check out the diner, then come straight back."

I took another photo of the arranged papers with my phone, just in case they mysteriously vanished like everything else today. The pattern was clearer when I looked at it through my phone screen somehow - the way the marks created a series of concentric circles, each one pointing to specific details in the reports.

I carefully gathered the papers back into their original order, making sure none got mixed up. Something told me we'd need to study this pattern more closely.

A few minutes later, Mrs. Martinez was settling onto our couch with her knitting, shooing us toward the door. "Go, go. The boys are sleeping, I have my shows, everything will be fine."

But as we headed for the car, something made me look back at our house. The porch light caught the beveled glass in the front door, creating patterns that seemed to mirror the red marks in Alexandra's reports.

The drive to Kelly's was quiet, both of us lost in thought. Downtown Johnson looked different at night - the empty storefronts, the dark windows of St. Michael's looming over Main Street, the old movie theater's blank marquee. Places we passed every day transformed into something almost unrecognizable.

Kelly's neon sign flickered ahead of us, the only bright spot on the block. The diner looked closed, but a single light burned in the back.

Chapter 7: Wes

Kelly's hadn't changed its hours in thirty years - "6AM to 10PM, just like God intended," according to old man Kelly himself. So seeing that single light burning in the back kitchen well after midnight didn't sit right.

"Could be the cleaning crew," I said, but Cynthia's expression told me she wasn't buying it either.

We sat in the dark parking lot, engine off, watching. The diner looked different at night, its usually cheerful neon casting strange shadows across the empty booths inside. Our regular spot by the window, where the boys always fought over who got to sit next to the jukebox, seemed darker than the rest of the interior.

The police file lay heavy in Cynthia's lap, those red marks still visible even in the dim light. I couldn't shake the feeling that we were being led here, each step carefully planned by someone. Or something.

"Baby," Cynthia whispered, "look at the windows."

At first, I didn't see it. Then the pattern emerged - tiny marks etched into the corners of each pane. The same marks that dotted the margins of Alexandra Sullivan's reports.

"They look old," I said, leaning closer to the windshield. "Like they've been there for years."

How many times had I eaten here, stared out these windows, never noticing those marks? They were subtle - you'd have to be looking for them to spot them at all. But now they seemed obvious, like a message written in plain sight.

Movement caught my eye - a shadow passing behind that lit kitchen window. Then the light went out.

"We should—" I started to suggest leaving, but Cynthia was already opening her door. The sound seemed too loud in the empty parking lot.

Main Street stretched silent in both directions. The dark windows of Anderson's Hardware watched us from across the street. St. Michael's spire cut a stark line against the sky. Everything familiar made strange by darkness and what we now knew.

A soft click came from the diner's side door - the one Kelly used for early morning deliveries. It swung open an inch, though no one stood in the doorway.

My flashlight beam caught something as we approached the door - more marks, carved into the metal frame. These were different from the window etchings, more like the mathematical symbols in Alexandra's notes.

"Could be graffiti," I said, not believing it even as the words left my mouth. After everything we'd seen today, coincidences were getting harder to accept.

The door creaked as Cynthia pushed it wider. The kitchen lay in darkness, the same darkness we'd watched fall when that shadow moved past the window. The familiar smell of coffee and grease hung in the air, mixed with something else. Something metallic.

Our footsteps echoed on the checkerboard tiles. My flashlight caught the edge of the serving window, the row of coffee cups lined up for morning service, the ancient register that Kelly refused to replace.

"Over here." Cynthia's voice came from near the prep station. She was studying something on the wall behind where the daily specials board usually hung.

The flashlight beam revealed more marks - dozens of them, arranged in concentric circles. At the center, carved deeper than the rest: 333.

"They've been painted over," I said, running my fingers across the marks. "Multiple times. But they keep showing through."

Cynthia compared the wall markings to Alexandra's file. "They match. Not just similar - they're exactly the same pattern. But these were carved decades before these reports were written."

A sudden burst of static made us both jump. The ancient radio on Kelly's shelf had switched itself on, red power light glowing in the darkness. Through the white noise, I could almost make out—

The overhead lights flared to life.

"Well, well." Amber's voice came from behind us. "I was wondering when you'd figure it out."

She stood in the doorway, that badly bleached orange hair almost luminous under the fluorescents.

"Baby," Cynthia said quietly, her hand finding mine. "Someone really needs to tell her that shade of orange isn't found in nature."

"Maybe she's trying to match her fake tan," I replied, just as quietly. "Though with the way her husband's been begging for 'loans' around town, I'm surprised she can still afford the salon."

Amber's practiced smile faltered. "You two think you're so clever with your little podcast—"

"At least we do this because we love it," Cynthia said, squeezing my hand. "Not because we're desperate to be famous. Or need to cover last month's credit card spree at the mall."

Everyone in town knew about that incident - the awkward scene at Designer Outlets when multiple cards were declined. Hard to maintain that perfect image when you're being escorted out by security.

"Besides," I added, "aren't you supposed to be busy with that 'exclusive story' you've been promising your readers? The one about... what was it this time, baby?"

"Oh right, the secret government base under the library," Cynthia played along. "Or was it the alien conspiracy at Anderson's Hardware?"

Amber's face reddened beneath her obvious spray tan. "Mock all you want, but I know things about this town—" "Let me guess," I cut in. "Things you can't reveal yet because you're 'protecting your sources'? Just like that exposé you promised about the Vernon case?"

"The one that mysteriously never happened," Cynthia added, "right after Kelly mentioned he might stop letting you run up a tab here?"

That hit a nerve. Amber's smile disappeared completely. "You have no idea what you're dealing with. These marks, the house, all of it—"

"All of it what?" Cynthia asked. "Another wild theory you're going to post about without fact-checking? Like that 'breaking news' about the mayor that got you sued last year?"

"At least I'm trying to expose the truth," Amber snapped. "While you two play ghost hunters and—" She stopped suddenly, her eyes fixed on Alexandra's file in Cynthia's hands. The practiced confidence drained from her face.

"Interesting reaction," I said quietly. "For someone who claims to know so much about the town's history, you look pretty surprised to see these old reports." "Where did you get that?" Her voice had lost its usual fake sweetness. "That's not— you shouldn't have those."

"Why?" Cynthia's tone was lighter now, but I could feel her tension. "Because they prove you've been making up your 'insider knowledge' about the Vernon case?"

Static burst from the radio again, making all three of us jump. When it cleared, Amber's smug expression had returned. "You really think this is about some old case?" She laughed, but it sounded forced. "Check your podcast feed. I left you a little preview of what's coming."

But Cynthia was already pulling out her phone. Her grip on my hand tightened. "Baby," she said softly. "Look at this."

Our podcast feed showed a new episode had been uploaded three minutes ago. The thumbnail was that same old photo of our house, but the title made my stomach turn: "The Last Episode: A Love and Luminol Finale."

"Tampering with someone else's podcast," I said, keeping my voice steady. "That's a new low, even for you, Amber." The jab hit home, but Amber's smirk didn't waver.

"Go ahead, listen to it," she said, backing toward the door. "Oh, and you might want to call your babysitter. Mrs. Martinez always did have trouble staying awake during her late-night shows." "Baby," Cynthia's voice had that dangerous edge I recognized - the one that meant someone had gone too far. "Did she just threaten our fucking kids?"

But Amber was already out the door, that fake laugh trailing behind her. Through the window, I watched her practically run to her car - not quite the dramatic exit she'd probably planned. My phone was already dialing Mrs. Martinez. Each ring felt like an eternity.

"Hello?" Maria's warm voice came through clear, if a bit groggy. "Wes? The boys are fine, still sleeping. Though the oddest thing... the recording room door keeps opening by itself. I've closed it three times now."

I met Cynthia's eyes in the darkness of Kelly's kitchen. The marks on the wall seemed to shimmer, like they were trying to tell us something. Behind us, the radio crackled to life again.

Through the static, we heard our own voices. A recording from this morning's podcast session - the one that had caught that first whisper at 3:33 AM.

"We need to get home," Cynthia said, already moving toward the door. But she stopped suddenly, staring at the file in her hands. "Baby, look at this."

The red marks in Alexandra's notes had shifted somehow. Not forming new patterns, but revealing something we'd missed before. Between the lines of official police reports, she'd written a warning: "They follow the frequencies. First the static, then the whispers. Then they start to see you. Really see you. That's when the countdown begins."

As we hurried to the car, the radio's static followed us out. Through the interference, I could have sworn I heard Amber's laugh. But when I got to the driver's side door, something made me stop.

There was a business card tucked under the windshield wiper. On the back, in fresh red ink: "Time's running out. Ask your mother about Hallows Creek."

Chapter 8: Cynthia

The drive home felt longer than it should have. Wes kept checking his phone for that mysterious podcast upload, but whatever Amber had done, the episode wasn't showing up anymore. Just another one of her games.

"Baby," I said, watching the familiar buildings of downtown slide past, "what if your mom really does know something about all this?"

He drummed his fingers on the steering wheel, thinking. "If she does, I don't want to drag her into whatever's happening. Not until we know more about what we're dealing with."

The business card sat between us on the console, that red ink looking almost black in the darkness. Part of me wanted to tear it up, scatter the pieces out the window. But we'd learned the hard way today that ignoring messages didn't make them stop.

Main Street was deserted this late, the streetlights casting pools of yellow that seemed to grow dimmer as we passed through them. Or maybe that was just my tired eyes playing tricks. The familiar route home felt different somehow, like the town itself was holding its breath.

"You know what bothers me?" I said, studying Alexandra's marks again. "How Amber reacted when she saw these reports. Like she recognized them, but didn't expect us to have them."

"Yeah," Wes nodded, turning onto Oak Drive. "Notice how she ran the second you mentioned fact-checking her Vernon case stories? Almost like—"

He stopped mid-sentence. Our house loomed ahead, dark except for the porch light we'd left on. But something was wrong. The porch swing moved gently in the still night air, and Mrs. Martinez's car was gone.

My first thought went to the boys. The second to why Mrs. Martinez would leave without calling.

"Could she have had an emergency?" I suggested, but Wes was already pulling into the driveway, cutting the engine before we'd fully stopped.

I fumbled with the key at the front door, my hands shaking enough that Wes had to take over. Even he struggled with the temperamental lock for a moment before it finally gave way. The door swung open to reveal our darkened living room, lit only by the glow of Mrs. Martinez's favorite telenovela still playing on the TV.

Her knitting sat on the coffee table, needles crossed mid-stitch. Her coffee cup, still half full.

"Maria?" Wes called out, heading for the stairs while I moved toward the kitchen.

That's when I noticed the note propped against her cup, written in handwriting I didn't recognize: "Had to go. They're getting closer. Check the frequency."

"Boys are all asleep," Wes said, coming back downstairs. "Every single one of them exactly where they should be."

The moment he reached the bottom step, we heard it - soft footsteps moving across the floor above us. Not the heavy ones from earlier, but lighter. Like a child walking.

We both looked up at the ceiling, knowing all five boys were tucked safely in their beds. Wes had just checked. The footsteps continued their slow path across the upstairs hallway.

"Check again," I whispered, though I wasn't sure why I was whispering. We stared at each other for a moment, both remembering that message about the Vernon family - how many children they'd had, how many rooms had been found empty.

The TV flickered, drawing my attention. The telenovela had given way to static, but something about the pattern seemed deliberate. Like it was trying to form words.

"Baby," Wes said quietly, "when did we start getting channel 333?"

The channel numbers on the TV kept cycling - 332...333...334...332...333...334 - each change bringing a different pattern of static. Like someone slowly turning a radio dial, searching for the right frequency.

Wes was already heading back upstairs to recheck the rooms, the sound of those light footsteps still echoing above us. The warning about frequencies in Alexandra's file suddenly felt less like a historical note and more like instructions.

The TV settled on channel 333. The static cleared for just a moment, showing what looked like Kelly's Diner. Empty tables, dark windows. But there was Amber - or someone who looked like her - sitting in our usual booth, staring directly into the camera. Something about her seemed off, different from the woman we'd just seen at the diner.

She wasn't smiling now.

"I told you to check your podcast feed," her voice came through distorted, like it was being played backward and forward simultaneously. "Time's running out, and you're looking in all the wrong—"

The TV clicked off. On its own. Footsteps on the stairs made me turn - Wes returning from his check of the boys' rooms. The look on his face stopped me before I could ask.

"They're all sound asleep," he said quietly. "But the recording room door..."

"Won't stay closed?" I finished.

"Won't open. At all. It's like it's been sealed shut."

The TV suddenly hummed back to life. Channel 333 again, but this time showing our own house. Our own living room. Filmed from where we were standing right now. Except in the footage, we weren't alone.

In the TV's reflection of our living room, shadows moved behind us. Not just shapes in the darkness, but defined figures. Seven of them, standing in a perfect circle.

I started to turn, but Wes caught my arm. "Don't," he whispered. "Look at the TV. The timestamp in the corner."

3:33 AM. But our clock showed just past midnight.

The figures in the TV moved closer to our reflections, reaching out with hands that weren't quite solid. Not quite there. Then the image flickered, showing a different scene - our recording room, the door wide open, equipment running, seven empty chairs arranged in a circle.

The feed cut back to static. Through the speakers came an unfamiliar voice - elderly, crackling with age, but clear: "Alexandra Sullivan, supplemental report. The frequencies are the key. They're using our own signals to—"

The voice cut off as white noise filled the room. When the static cleared, the TV had returned to Mrs. Martinez's telenovela, as if nothing had happened. But her note still sat by her coffee cup: "Check the frequency."

"Baby," Wes said quietly, his voice strained. "I think we need to figure out what Alexandra Sullivan was trying to tell us about these frequencies."

The TV's static had settled into a low hum, almost like it was waiting. Above us, those soft footsteps continued their endless circuit of the upper floor, while somewhere in the distance, a clock began to chime.

It was 3:32 AM.

Chapter 9: Alexandra

My hand shook as I turned on the recorder. The sun through my office window cast long shadows across the files spread on my desk, but I could have sworn some of those shadows moved against the light.

"Testing, testing. This is Detective Alexandra Sullivan, recording supplemental notes for the Vernon case. Date: October 27, 1957."

I needed a cigarette. Needed to think. The pattern was there - in the frequencies, in the dates, in the way certain buildings seemed to pulse with energy at specific times. But every time I got close to understanding it, something interrupted.

My fingers traced the marks I'd made in the Vernon file margins. To anyone else, they'd look like casual notations, the kind any detective might make. But Maria would understand. Would know that some codes were passed down for a reason.

"Initial findings suggest standard missing persons parameters, but there are... inconsistencies. The static interference first reported by Mrs. Vernon appears in other witness statements, though Officer Hayes dismissed these as unrelated electrical issues."

I shuffled through my papers, trying to organize my thoughts. The frequency patterns kept appearing in the oldest case files, though official records showed no connection. Chief Wallace kept insisting I drop this line of inquiry. Claimed it was "beyond the scope" of my investigation.

But he wouldn't meet my eyes when we discussed the third floor records, the ones they kept locked away.

The radio on my desk crackled to life - it had been doing that more often lately, finding frequencies beyond any known broadcasting range. Through the static, I could almost make out voices. Like the ones the Vernon children described hearing before they vanished.

"Maria," I spoke into the recorder, keeping my voice steady despite the growing static, "if you're hearing this, I need you to understand: what happened to the Vernons, what's happening now - it's all connected. The numbers, the signals, the way the children reported hearing music through the static..."

A door slammed somewhere in the precinct. Footsteps approached my office.

I quickly switched off the recorder, sliding it under some paperwork as Officer Hayes entered without knocking. He'd been watching me more closely lately, ever since I'd started asking questions about the third floor archives.

"Detective Sullivan." His smile never reached his eyes. "Chief wants to see you. Something about reassignment."

"I'll be right there." I waited until he left before pulling out my notebook. The real one, not the official case notes they expected me to keep. My hand moved across the page, adding more marks in the margins - the code Maria and I had used since we were girls.

The radio static grew louder, and for just a moment, I saw something in the shadows behind my desk. A figure, or maybe seven of them, standing in that perfect circle formation the Vernon boy had drawn.

I switched the recorder back on.

"4:15 PM. They're trying to separate us from the case. But there's something about the way the signals align with the disappearances. Every thirty-three—"

The static surged, drowning out my voice. Through my office window, I could see every car radio in the parking lot lighting up. Like ripples spreading from a stone dropped in water, each one tuning to the same impossible frequency.

I forced myself to keep recording, to document what I was seeing. "That sound... it's the same frequency the Vernon children described. Coming from the old theater now. I need to—"

Movement caught my eye. Not Hayes this time. Something darker, standing just at the edge of my vision. Every time I turned to look directly at it, it shifted, always staying just out of sight. But I could feel it watching.

My fingers traced the marks I'd made in the margins. The pattern was there - in the frequencies, in the dates, in the building permits that couldn't possibly be real. The Vernon house shouldn't exist. That lot had been empty since—

The radio went silent. All of them did, simultaneously. And in that perfect quiet, I heard it - footsteps in the hallway, echoing at an impossible distance, as if walking on a floor that wasn't there.

"They're watching me," I whispered into the recorder. "Not the police. Something else. Every time I get close, they—"

A knock at my door made me jump. Just Rogers from dispatch, asking about paperwork. Normal. Routine. But when I looked back at my notes, something had changed. New marks had appeared in the margins - marks I hadn't made.

4:45 PM now. The sun was setting earlier these days, shadows growing longer across my desk. I couldn't shake the feeling that some of those shadows didn't belong to anything in my office.

I turned back to the recorder. "There's something else about the Vernon house. The building permits I mentioned - they're forgeries. Good ones, but I know paper. Know ink. These were created recently, backdated to look old. Someone wants us to believe that house has always been there."

I pulled out the photograph I'd found in the historical society archives. "But I found a photo from 1889. That lot was empty. Just an old well where 333 Maple Street now stands. And the well..."

My voice trailed off as I noticed something in the photograph I hadn't seen before.

Seven figures stood around that old well in the photo. Their features were blurred, like they'd moved during the exposure. But they were arranged in a perfect circle. The same formation the Vernon boy had drawn. The same pattern I kept seeing in the shadows.

The radio crackled again. Through the static, children's voices sang something that sounded like a counting rhyme, but the numbers weren't quite right. Like they were counting in a pattern I couldn't understand.

"Maria," I spoke quickly now, feeling time slipping away, "the marks I've left you - they're not just notes. They're coordinates. Frequencies. The Sullivan women have always known about patterns, about the way certain numbers hold power. Remember what Grandmother taught us about—"

The static rose to a crescendo. Every light in the precinct flickered. And there, reflected in my office window, I saw them. Standing behind me. Watching.

But when I turned around, I was alone with the quiet hum of my radio, still tuned to a station that didn't exist.

I touched the photograph again. Something about the formation of those figures around the well nagged at me, like a pattern I should recognize.

The door burst open. Chief Wallace himself this time, his face grim. "Sullivan. A word."

"Sir, I was just finishing some paperwork on the Vernon—"

"That case is closed." His voice was firm, but there was something else in his expression. Fear? "And Detective? Your sister called. Says there's been some trouble at home. Something about frequencies?"

Maria. She'd found something too.

After the Chief left, I glanced one last time at the photograph before reaching for my coat. Seven blurred figures around an ancient well, their formation matching the impossible house that now occupied that empty lot.

The radio hummed quietly in the growing darkness. I had one last thing to do before leaving. I switched the recorder on one final time.

"Maria, I'm leaving this file where we discussed. The marks in the margins - remember how Grandmother taught us to read them? Use that. And whatever you do, don't trust the Sul—"

Through the static, a voice that wasn't quite human: "Found you."

I switched off the recorder quickly, my hands shaking as I gathered the Vernon file. Everything I'd discovered about our family's connection to this town, about what the Sullivan name really meant - it all had to reach Maria.

The radio's haunting frequency followed me into the hallway, its pitch hovering just beyond human hearing.

The night shift was starting, officers trading places in the parking lot. I nodded to Hayes as he headed in, ignoring his suspicious glance at the files under my arm. As I pulled onto Main Street, the street lights flickered, one by one, like they were marking my path home.

Chapter 10: Wes

The reel-to-reel recorder whirred to a stop, Alexandra Sullivan's voice fading into silence. Cynthia and I stood at the bottom of the stairs, both hesitating to climb them.

"Baby," she said quietly, "when Mrs. Martinez mentioned her sister's family..."

"She wasn't talking about Alexandra," I finished. "She was talking about whoever disappeared after her."

The business card with its red ink sat forgotten on the console table. Upstairs, something creaked - the sound of someone walking across our recording room floor. Or maybe just the house settling. After Alexandra's recording, even normal sounds felt loaded with meaning.

"We need to get up there," I said, though neither of us moved. "Check the equipment, make sure—"

My phone buzzed. Unknown number.

The message contained just one word: "LISTEN."

As if on cue, the reel-to-reel started again. Not Alexandra's voice this time, but something else. A series of tones that pulsed through the air, rising and falling in a pattern that nagged at my memory.

"That sounds like..." Cynthia trailed off, her eyes widening. "Baby, that's the same sequence from Kelly's Diner. The one playing through the static when Amber—"

She stopped as another sound cut through the tones. Children laughing. But not our boys - this recording carried age, the quality degraded by decades.

My phone buzzed again: "FOUND IT YET?"

The message came from Amber's number this time. But after what we'd just heard in Alexandra's recording, after what we'd seen at the diner, I wasn't sure who - or what - was really sending these messages anymore.

The laughter faded, replaced by what sounded like counting. The numbers jumped erratically, following some pattern I couldn't grasp.

"We should check on the boys," Cynthia whispered, though neither of us moved toward the stairs yet. The counting continued above us, each number vibrating through the house.

My phone lit up with another message. Not Amber this time. Not an unknown number either. The sender showed as my own name:

"THE SULLIVAN WOMEN STARTED IT. THE LUMIN FAMILY WILL END IT."

A sound from the top of the stairs made us both look up. The recording room door stood open now, warm light spilling into the hallway. And silhouetted in that light, a small figure.

"Dad?" Xander's voice drifted down. "Why are you playing your first podcast episode?"

Something about his question made my skin crawl. Our first episode had never been transferred to the reel-to-reel. That ancient machine shouldn't even work.

"Go back to bed, buddy," I called up, trying to keep my voice steady. "We're just testing some equipment."

But Xander didn't move. "It sounds different though. Like there's other voices behind it."

Cynthia squeezed my hand as we started up the stairs. The closer we got, the clearer I could hear what Xander meant. Beneath our recorded voices discussing the Vernon case, other sounds wove through the audio - that counting rhythm, fragments of Alexandra's voice, and something else.

A melody threading through the static, like a radio signal bleeding through from another station. Another time.

The first rays of morning light crept through the windows as I called Lana. After the night we'd had, after what Xander had heard, we needed to get the boys somewhere safe. At least for a while.

"Of course they can stay with me," Cynthia's mom said, her cheerful voice a stark contrast to our exhaustion. "You know I love having my grandbabies. But what's this really about?"

"Just some repairs we need to do," I lied, catching Cynthia's eye across the kitchen. She was already packing the boys' overnight bags, trying to make it seem like a fun surprise rather than an escape.

"The recording equipment's acting up," Cynthia added, loud enough for her mom to hear. Not technically a lie. "Might take a couple days to sort out."

What we didn't say: how the reel-to-reel had gone silent the moment Xander returned to bed. How we'd spent the rest of the night searching for patterns in Alexandra's coded margins. How every radio in the house had started humming that same frequency at exactly 3:33 AM.

"Mom, are you sure it's not too much trouble?" Cynthia asked, though we both knew Lana would be thrilled. She already had the boys' favorite snacks stocked and probably had activities planned before we'd finished asking.

"Too much trouble? Please. I've got pepperoni ready for Brayden and enough snacks to feed an army. Though..." Lana's voice took on that tone we knew too well. "You two could join us for dinner after you finish with your equipment. I'm making my famous lasagna."

Famous was right - somehow Lana always knew when we needed a family dinner, when things felt too heavy to handle alone. But tonight we had other plans. Alexandra's file had pointed us toward the hospital records, and the sooner we checked them, the better.

"Baby," Cynthia whispered, covering the phone's mic, "we should tell her to keep them away from—"

A thud from upstairs cut her off. Then another. The sound of footsteps crossing the recording room floor.

But all five boys were in the kitchen eating breakfast.

"—tell her to keep them away from any electronics," Cynthia finished. We'd noticed how the frequencies seemed stronger around devices: phones, radios, even game consoles.

"Mom? One more thing," she added into the phone. "The boys' tablets are acting weird. Maybe limit screen time for a few days?"

I could almost hear Lana's smile. "Perfect excuse for board games and cookie baking, bring the cats too. They can play with mine."

As Cynthia finished the call, I watched our sons at the kitchen table. Ben with his headphones around his neck for once. Xander and Brayden discussing some math problem. Tyler showing Casey something in a comic book. Normal. Safe. We needed to keep them that way.

The footsteps above had stopped, but something else caught my attention - a soft mechanical whir. The sound of recording equipment powering up.

"We should head over soon," I said quietly. "Get them settled at your mom's before we check those hospital records." "Boys," Cynthia called out, her voice impressively normal. "Surprise sleepover at Grandma's! Go pack your overnight bags."

The response was immediate - a chorus of excitement as chairs scraped back from the table. Even Ben perked up, though he tried to play it cool. Lana's house meant no rules about headphones at dinner.

I started gathering their school stuff - they'd need it for tomorrow. But as I reached for Xander's backpack, still lined up too perfectly with the others, I hesitated. Maybe they should take different bags.

A burst of static from upstairs made my decision easier. "Pack your sports bags instead," I called up to them. "Your school ones need cleaning."

Cynthia caught my eye, understanding. Whatever force had arranged those backpacks, whatever had followed us home from Kelly's Diner, we weren't giving it any more connections to our boys.

The sports bags were buried in the back of the garage - neutral territory, untouched by whatever had invaded our house. I tried to frame it logically: different bags meant fresh starts, no misplaced homework to worry about. But part of me knew I was really thinking about those perfectly lined up backpacks, about the way some patterns needed breaking.

"Baby," Cynthia said as we loaded the bags into our SUV, "you okay? You've got that look."

"What look?" But I knew. The same look I'd given her whenever she'd talk about energy or frequencies or things science couldn't explain. Except now I was the one avoiding the rational explanation - that maybe the boys had simply decided to organize their backpacks for once.

"Just thinking about those hospital records," I said instead. Not exactly a lie.

"All set?" I called up the stairs, trying to hurry them along without seeming rushed. Every minute we stayed felt like tempting whatever had found its way into our home.

Once we got outside to load the car, I glanced up at the recording room window, dark and still above us. As I watched, something moved within - a shadow sliding across the interior of the room.

The boys thundered down, each clutching their favorite things for Grandma's house. Ben hadn't forgotten his headphones, of course. Brayden had his pepperoni stash. Tyler carried his Demon Slayer manga, and Casey... was heading for his backpack. "Sports bags today, remember?" I moved to intercept him. "Your backpack needs cleaning."

For a moment, I thought he might argue. But something - maybe the same thing that had made the hairs on my neck stand up - made him turn toward the garage instead.

Cynthia was already starting the car, but I noticed how she kept glancing at the rearview mirror. Not at the boys piling into their seats, but at the upstairs window reflecting in the glass.

The drive to Lana's usually took fifteen minutes. Today it felt longer, even though I kept checking my watch and knew we were making good time. Maybe it was the silence - the boys were never this quiet in the car.

"Did Grandma say what she's making for dinner?" Tyler asked, breaking the strange quiet. "Lasagna," Cynthia answered, her voice deliberately light. "And knowing Mom, probably enough desserts to feed half of Johnson."

The familiar banter helped, made everything feel almost normal. But I couldn't stop thinking about those hospital records waiting for us, about whatever Alexandra Sullivan had discovered that made her leave coded warnings in police files.

Main Street stretched ahead, morning traffic moving as usual. We passed Kelly's Diner, and I felt Cynthia tense beside me. Through the window, I could see Amber sitting in our usual booth, staring directly at our car as we passed.

"Hey, that's the mean lady who's always writing stuff about your podcast," Casey piped up from the back seat.

"Casey," Cynthia started, but Ben cut in. "Yeah, the one who thinks she's a better detective than everyone else." "At least she finally fixed her hair," Brayden added quietly, making his brothers snicker.

I caught Cynthia trying not to smile despite everything. Even now, with all that was happening, our boys had a way of cutting through the tension.

Lana's street was just ahead, her white house with its massive banana leaf plant in the front yard a welcome sight. As normal and safe as anything in Johnson could be right now. But as we pulled into her driveway, my phone buzzed with a new message.

I waited until the boys were inside, their excited voices mixing with Lana's warm welcome, before checking it. Not from an unknown number this time. Not from Amber. From Chief Wallace. The current one.

"Found something in the old files about Detective Sullivan. Come by the station when you can. And Wes? Bring those coded reports your wife's been studying." Cynthia read the message over my shoulder as we walked back to the car. "Baby," she said softly, "how did he know about Alexandra's files?"

Behind us, through Lana's front window, we could see our boys already settled in the living room. Safe and normal and far from frequencies and patterns. For now.

"Let's find out," I said, starting the car. "Right after we check those hospital records." But we both knew the real question wasn't how Chief Wallace knew about the files.It was why he'd sent the message at exactly 3:33 PM.

Chapter 11: Cynthia

The hospital's records department smelled like old paper and dust, exactly what you'd expect from a basement full of files from the 1950s. What I hadn't expected was the clerk's reaction when we mentioned 1957.

"That's the third request this week," she said, not looking up from her computer. "Your friend was just here yesterday. The redhead?"

Wes and I exchanged looks. "Amber's been here?"

"Oh yes. Very interested in the Sullivan cases. Though she seemed more focused on Chief Wallace's family. His son's our current chief, isn't he?"

My hand found Wes's under the counter. Current Chief Wallace. Son of the man who'd tried to shut down Alexandra's investigation. The same family still in power after all these years.

"We'll need to see everything from October 1957," Wes said, his voice steady despite the implications. "Especially any records involving Detective Alexandra Sullivan."

The clerk's fingers paused over her keyboard. Something flickered across her face - recognition? Fear? But it vanished too quickly to read.

"Those records were moved," she said, her voice carefully neutral. "Special collections. You'll need authorization from Chief Wallace himself."

"He actually called ahead about you two," she added, checking something on her screen. "Said you'd be coming by. Not like him to pre-authorize access like that."

Wes pulled out his phone, showing her the chief's text message. She nodded, but that same flicker crossed her face again.

"Research room's down the hall. Last door on the left. Files should still be out from this morning - he left them in quite a state. Not like him at all."

As we walked down the windowless hallway, fluorescent lights buzzing overhead, everything felt orchestrated. Why would Wallace leave sensitive files scattered around? Why give us access after asking us to bring Alexandra's reports to the station?

The research room door stood ajar. Through the gap, I could see papers scattered across a large table, and behind it, an old radio on a shelf. For a moment, I thought I saw a red power light, but it must have been a reflection from the exit sign.

Wes reached for the door, but I caught his arm. Something about the scattered papers seemed deliberate - not messy, but arranged. Like the marks in Alexandra's file.

"Baby," I whispered, "what if he didn't leave them like this? What if someone wants us to find something specific?"

He nodded slowly, reaching for his phone to photograph the layout before we disturbed anything. The photos saved, but when he tried to text them to me as backup, no signal. Not surprising this deep in the basement.

The papers on the table shifted in an impossible breeze. As we stepped inside, dates became visible: October 1957. Hospital admission records. And paper-clipped to the top, a photograph of seven people standing in front of Kelly's Diner.

I picked up the photograph carefully. The diner looked newer, its neon sign still bright, but something about the seven people tugged at my memory. Not their faces - those were clear enough, but unfamiliar. It was their formation. The way they stood.

"Baby," Wes said quietly, "look at the date on the back."

October 27, 1957. The same day Alexandra made her recording. But the handwriting below caught my attention: "Last known photograph - Kelly's staff."

"The diner's staff?" I turned the photo over again. "But Kelly's has always been family-run. One person behind the counter, maybe two. Never seven."

Wes sorted through the hospital records. "Here - admission records from that week. Seven patients, all admitted within hours of each other. Chief complaint listed as 'auditory and visual hallucinations.'" He flipped through more pages. "Their statements mention hearing patterns in the static before the symptoms started."

The attending physician's name had been redacted. But beneath the black mark, the first letter remained visible: W.

"Wallace?" I asked, though we both knew it had to be. Another connection between that family and 1957.

Wes pulled out more records, spreading them across the table. "Look at these - police reports filed from inside the hospital. Statements from the nurses. Every patient reported the same phenomenon: static forming into patterns. Sounds beyond normal hearing."

"Like what we heard at Kelly's," I said. "Like what the Vernon children reported before—"

Through the partly open door, voices approached - one of them Amber's, the other unfamiliar. Their footsteps echoed in the basement hallway, getting closer.

Wes touched my arm, nodding toward a gap between filing cabinets. Another door - maintenance access maybe. We moved quietly, gathering the most important papers.

Their conversation became clearer. "—checked the basement already?" the unfamiliar voice asked.

"Everything but the research room," Amber replied. "Though after what Chief Wallace found this morning—"

We eased the maintenance door closed just as they reached the room. Through the thin wall, I heard Amber's sharp intake of breath.

"Someone's been here," she said. "Recently."

The maintenance corridor stretched ahead, lit only by emergency lights. Old pipes ran along the ceiling, carrying the whispered echo of Amber's voice.

"Files are disturbed," she was saying. "They were just here. Check the hallway."

Wes led us away from their voices, the Kelly's photograph and key papers stuffed in his pocket. The corridor seemed endless, each turn identical to the last. At least the emergency exit signs pointed the way out.

Behind us, a door opened - the one we'd just come through. Footsteps entered the maintenance corridor.

Multiple sets of footsteps, echoing off the walls. More than just Amber and her companion. Many more.

"Baby," I whispered, remembering the summers I'd spent volunteering here in high school. The maintenance corridors had been my shortcut between departments. "The loading dock is just past that junction ahead. Run."

We reached the junction just as a voice called out - not Amber's, but older, hollow, like words through static.

"They always choose the service tunnel," it said, the words seeming to come from both behind and ahead of us at once.

The loading dock access was right where I remembered, its emergency bar casting a faint glow. But as Wes pushed against it, something was wrong.

"It's locked," he muttered, checking the mechanism. "From the outside."

The footsteps grew closer, their rhythm changing. No longer trying to hide. They knew we were trapped.

The photograph in Wes's pocket seemed to pulse. Seven people in front of Kelly's Diner. Seven sets of footsteps approaching.

And then we heard Amber laugh - but not from behind us.

Her voice came through the ancient PA system mounted on the wall: "Wrong turn."

"There has to be another way," Wes said, his voice steady despite everything. He examined the door frame, looking for weak points. Always practical, even now.

The PA system crackled again. No voice this time. Just that familiar sequence of tones - the same pattern from Kelly's, the same frequency that had started everything.

I pulled out my phone out of habit. No signal still, but the time caught my eye: 3:32 PM.

"Baby," I started to say, but Wes was already moving. Not toward the approaching footsteps, but toward a maintenance ladder I hadn't noticed. It disappeared into darkness, but a hatch outline was visible above.

"Emergency access," he said. "These old hospitals always had backup exits from the basement - fire code. Leads straight to ground level."

The footsteps were close enough now that we could hear voices mixed with them. Whispers carrying through concrete walls.

They were counting, but the sequence made no sense.

Wes climbed first, testing each rung. The hatch above looked heavy - the kind that would announce our location with its screech.

"Three-three-three," the whispers grew clearer. Not from behind us anymore, but all around. Like the walls themselves were speaking.

The ladder creaked as I followed Wes up. In his pocket, the Kelly's photograph peeked out. For just a moment, the faces seemed to have shifted position, but that had to be the emergency lighting playing tricks.

Then the PA system clicked on one final time.

"Chief Wallace sends his regards," Amber's voice said. "Says to tell you your mother remembers Hallows Creek too."

The message hit Wes hard enough that I saw him pause on the ladder. His mother? How was she connected to all this?

A metallic groan from above - Wes pushing against the hatch. It resisted at first, then gave way with a sound that echoed through the entire basement.

The whispers stopped.

"Baby," I said, climbing faster now. "What did Amber mean about your mother?"

"Later," he replied, but I could hear the strain in his voice. He helped pull me through the hatch just as the first figure appeared at the end of the corridor below.

We emerged into what looked like an abandoned wing of the hospital. Dust sheets covered old equipment, and paper signs marked the area as "Closed for Renovation."

But the signs were yellowed with age. Like they'd been there since the 1950s.

The wing stretched out in both directions, emergency lights casting strange shadows through plastic-covered doorways. A nurses' station sat empty at the intersection ahead, its ancient desk calendar frozen in October.

"Which way?" I whispered, but Wes was staring at something on the wall. Behind layers of paint, barely visible, were marks. The same kind Alexandra had left in the police files.

A crash echoed from below - the hatch being thrown open again. We hadn't closed it behind us.

"There," Wes pointed toward double doors at the end of the hall. "Emergency stairs. Should lead to—"

A phone rang, cutting through the quiet. Not our phones - they still had no signal. This came from the nurses' station, from a rotary phone that should have been dead for decades.

The ringing echoed through the abandoned wing, each trill lasting longer than natural. Three rings. Then silence.

"We need to move," Wes said, pulling me toward the emergency exit. Through the dusty nurses' station window, I caught a glimpse of that old desk calendar still set to October. The same month all this started, back in 1957.

Footsteps on the stairs below now, getting closer. Multiple sets, their rhythm matching the static we'd heard through the hospital's ancient PA system. We pushed through the emergency doors into the afternoon sunlight, emerging into the hospital's side parking lot.

As the door clicked shut behind us, my phone buzzed back to life. Three missed calls from Lana.

"Baby," I started to say, but Wes was already answering his phone, his face going pale as he listened.

"What do you mean the boys aren't there?"

Chapter 12: Wes

I broke every speed limit between the hospital and Lana's house, Cynthia's hand gripping mine around each turn. Her mother's call kept replaying in my head - the boys going to the backyard, the two minutes before she checked, the empty yard she found.

"They have to be somewhere close," I said, but after everything we'd seen at the hospital, nothing felt certain anymore.

Lana's white house came into view, that massive banana leaf plant casting long shadows. Her neighbor Mrs. Chen was already searching surrounding properties.

But what stopped me cold were the five backpacks sitting on Lana's front steps - the same ones we'd deliberately left at home.

"I found them in the backyard," Lana said as we rushed up, her warm voice tight with worry. "Just sitting there in a perfect line. I thought maybe you'd dropped them off, but—"

"We never brought them," Cynthia said. "They're supposed to be at home."

Mrs. Chen appeared from around the side of the house, shaking her head. No sign of the boys. I pulled out my phone to call the police, but Cynthia caught my arm.

"Baby, look at how they're arranged."

The backpacks sat in age order, just like in our entryway this morning. Ben's worn black one with its band patches. Xander's cyan bag with the fraying strap. Brayden's black and yellow one. Tyler's red backpack with its Demon Slayer keychain. Casey's newer black one.

Perfect line. Perfect order. Just like before.

Cynthia reached for Ben's backpack before I could stop her. Empty. They all were. Except for a single piece of paper folded in Casey's - what looked like a page torn from Alexandra Sullivan's file.

"That's not possible," I said, my hand dropping from my phone. "Those files were just at the hospital. We just—"

My phone buzzed. Chief Wallace: "Found something you need to see. Bring your wife. And those hospital records you just stole."

"What is all this?" Lana moved closer, peering at the paper. "What's going on?" The fear in her voice made me realize how much danger we might have put everyone in by keeping quiet.

A familiar car turned onto the street. Orange hair visible through the windshield.

Amber.

She wasn't smiling that plastic smile now. She parked across the street, just watching. Waiting.

"I'm calling the police," Lana said, already dialing. The normalcy of her reaction made everything else feel more surreal.

"Baby," Cynthia said quietly. "This isn't from Alexandra's file. This is new."

The handwritten note read: "The Sullivan women started it in 1957. The Wallace men covered it up. But the Lumin boys? They're the key. Always have been. You have until 3:33."

Amber's car door opened.

"Don't," I said as Cynthia started toward her. "That's exactly what she wants."

"Our boys are missing," she replied, voice hard. "Fuck what she wants."

Amber stepped onto the sidewalk, but something was different about her expression. No fake concern, no superiority. Just... fear?

"You need to listen," she called out. "This isn't what I—"

Cynthia crossed the distance in three steps and landed a right hook that would have made her father proud. Amber went down hard.

"Our boys," Cynthia said, standing over her. "Where are they?"

The static started - building from every car radio on the street. Watching my wife tower over Amber, I almost felt sorry for whatever had taken our children.

Almost.

"I don't know," Amber said through bloody fingers, her nose visibly crooked from Cynthia's punch. "I swear, I was just supposed to keep you busy at the hospital. Chief Wallace told me to watch you, to keep you away from those old records."

"What records?" I moved closer.

"The ones about the Sullivan women," she managed, scooting backward. "There's so much about this town you don't understand—"

"Get up," Cynthia ordered. "You're going to tell us everything. Starting with why you really came to Johnson."

Amber's eyes widened at something behind us. "Run," she whispered.

"Look at your phones," she choked out. "The time."

"Cynthia?" Lana's voice carried from her yard. "The backpacks..."

The five backpacks had moved, forming a circle.

3:33 PM.

The static cut out suddenly. In the silence, Amber pulled out her phone and started filming, her hands shaking. Even with a broken nose and missing children, she couldn't help herself.

A phone rang - not our cells or Lana's house phone. The sound shifted, coming from everywhere and nowhere.

Three rings. Silence.

"They're calling," Amber said. "Like they did in '57. Like they always do at—"

My phone buzzed with another message from an unknown number: "Find them where it started. Before the next call."

"Maple Street?" Lana stared at the address. "But that's not—" She stopped, face paling. "The old section. Before they renamed everything. My mother used to talk about—"

"We need to go," I said, gathering the backpacks.

The static drowned out any further discussion.

Our street looked different now - seen through the lens of what it used to be. Under decades of paint on the street sign, I could just make out the original name: "Maple Street."

Amber's car followed close behind us, her orange hair visible in my rearview mirror. Even with a broken nose, she wouldn't miss a chance to be part of whatever was happening.

Our house loomed ahead, its familiar lines twisted by the late afternoon sun. The shadows beneath the eaves stretched longer than they should, and every window seemed to watch our approach.

"This is going to be amazing footage," Amber called as she got out of her car, already filming with her phone. Despite everything happening, her only concern was her content.

Through our front window, I saw something impossible.

Our recording equipment was running, though we'd shut it down. Behind it, silhouetted against the sun, five small figures stood perfectly still.

"The boys," Cynthia reached for her door.

"Look again."

The figures were too still. Too perfect. Like photographs rather than children.

"Oh my god, this is incredible!" Amber pushed closer with her camera. "My followers—"

"Shut up!" Cynthia's voice cut through. For once, Amber listened.

The figures hadn't moved. Like a staged scene waiting for us. The equipment lights blinked in Kelly's pattern.

"You don't understand what this means for me," Amber started.

"Our children are missing," Cynthia's voice went deadly quiet. "One more word about your pathetic blog, I'll break more than your nose."

I pulled out the Kelly's photograph - seven people in a circle. Like the backpacks. Like the figures from the recording room at 3:33 AM.

The front door opened on its own.

And from inside, we heard children counting.

Chapter 13: Cynthia

Children's voices drifted through our open doorway, a familiar cadence that made my heart stutter. Almost our boys, but the rhythm was off - like hearing a favorite song played slightly out of tune.

Behind us, Amber's incessant filming continued, but I barely registered her voice. Wes moved toward the door, and I caught his arm.

"The recording equipment," I whispered, nodding toward the window. The figures we'd seen were gone, but the lights still pulsed in that same pattern from Kelly's, from the hospital.

The Kelly's photograph slipped from Wes's pocket as he turned, landing face-up on our walk. Seven people in their perfect circle, the image more unsettling in the fading afternoon light.

"We're going in," Wes said quietly. "Our boys are in there."

"Or something wants us to think they are." The words slipped out before I could stop them. Mother's intuition warring with desperation.

Through the doorway, a child started humming. It sounded like the tuneless songs Casey made up while doing homework, but not quite right. The late afternoon sun cast long shadows through our front door, making the approaching evening feel more ominous than usual.

"Dad?" The voice drifted down from upstairs. It could have been Ben, but Ben never called out like that. Ben communicated in shrugs and headphone adjustments.

Our house felt heavier somehow, the air dense and cold for an October afternoon. From the recording room, a low pulse of static made the walls vibrate.

"Remember the hospital," I whispered to Wes. "Remember what happened when we followed the voices."

But we both knew it didn't matter. Trap or not, our children were somewhere in this house. Everything else was just details.

The stairs creaked beneath us - familiar sounds turned ominous by context. With each step up, the air grew colder. By the landing, our breath fogged in front of us.

Every door stood open except the recording room, where equipment lights pulsed behind frosted glass. The humming had stopped, replaced by what sounded like our boys playing one of their endless clapping games. But the pattern was too precise, too measured.

"Over here," a voice called - maybe Tyler's, maybe not. "We found something under the house."

Wes's grip tightened on my hand. Through the recording room window, I caught a glimpse of chairs arranged in a circle, their shadows stretching long in the equipment's pulsing light. Empty chairs that hadn't been there hours ago when we'd found Alexandra's file.

A floorboard creaked behind us. When we turned, a figure stood at the end of the hall - backlit and indistinct. Something about her stance reminded me of the old photograph from Kelly's Diner.

"The Sullivan women always find them," she said, her voice carrying echoes of other voices. "But finding isn't the same as keeping."

The lighting shifted, and for a moment she looked like Amber. Then like someone in an old police uniform. Then like no one at all.

"Where are our children?" My voice came out steadier than I felt.

She moved closer, each step accompanied by a soft creak of floorboards. "Where they were meant to be. Where they've always been, every thirty-three years. But this time..."

The recording room door swung open on its own. Inside, the reel-to-reel we kept for decoration spun silently, its empty reels casting spinning shadows.

"Mom?" That was definitely Casey's voice now, but it came from below us. From the ground floor.

The woman in the hallway stepped back into the shadows, and when the floorboard creaked again, she was gone - if she'd ever been there at all.

We headed back downstairs, following Casey's voice. In the front hall, Wes stopped suddenly.

"Baby," his voice shook slightly. "The historical society photos..."

"I know," I said, looking down at the floorboards beneath our feet. "Right where we're standing."

The floor shuddered, a low groan of old wood settling. Or maybe old stones shifting, deep underground.

"Mom? Dad?" Five voices called, blending together in a way that made them sound both familiar and strange. "Come see what we found."

The phone fell silent. In its place came the sound of running water, rising up through floorboards that suddenly felt much too thin.

It sounded like it was coming from very far below.

And getting closer.

The floor vibrated beneath our feet, a subtle tremor that seemed to match the rhythm of our recording equipment upstairs. A laugh echoed through the house - sharp and metallic where Brayden's was always soft.

"They're down here," the voice said, no longer trying to sound like any of our boys. "Where they've always been. Every time."

A phone started ringing, the sound rising from somewhere beneath the floorboards. Not the three rings we'd come to expect. This one continued, mechanical and relentless.

The sound of water grew louder. Not the gentle trickle from before, but the rush of something larger. Something deeper.

"Baby," Wes's voice cracked slightly. "Look at the shadows."

I followed his gaze. Light pulsed from the recording room upstairs, casting strange patterns down the stairwell. Five distinct shadows stretched across the wall - child-sized silhouettes that shifted and distorted with each flash. But as the shadows danced, they seemed to multiply. Seven figures now, their movements synchronized in a way that reminded me of the Kelly's photograph.

Through the static came fragments of voices layered over each other - children's voices from different times, different decades, all counting in the same rhythm. The shadows on the wall merged and separated with each number, like a film reel jumping between scenes.

The floor trembled beneath our feet in time with the shadows' movement. Whatever connection existed between our boys and those other children, it was playing out on the walls around us - a history we could see but couldn't quite understand.

"Where it started," the voices rasped, their childlike pitch dissolving into something that reminded me of water rushing over stones. "Where they all start. And end."

The floor shuddered again. A long, low groan of wood giving way. Like earth shifting beneath a house that had stood too long over something that should have stayed buried.

Wes pulled out his phone to call for help, but the screen flickered and went black. When it lit up again, the display was pixelated and distorted, numbers and letters scrambling across the screen before it died completely. In the corner of my eye, I caught movement - a shadow passing across the wall. Then another. And another. Each one child-sized but stretched somehow, like old photographs left too long in the sun.

The ringing phone fell silent.

Footsteps creaked overhead - the same measured pattern we'd heard at Kelly's, at the hospital. Moving in a circle.

"Listen," the voices said. Not our boys anymore. Something older. Something that had been waiting.

The static from upstairs changed pitch, forming a melody I almost recognized. An old song, maybe. Or something newer played backwards.

Water sounds rose through the floor, closer now. The counting continued, the voices scraping like metal on stone, carrying the same hollow resonance we'd heard in Alexandra's recording. Each number seemed to echo up from the depths beneath our feet.

The floor shivered one final time. A deep crack split the wood between us, and through it came the unmistakable smell of old stones and stagnant water.

"Ready or not," the voices sang. "Here we—"

The power cut out, plunging us into darkness. In that perfect silence, I heard something that made my blood run cold.

Five distinct splashes, echoing up from very far below.

Then the phone started ringing again.

Chapter 14: Wes

Aphone rang somewhere in the house, its tone continuous rather than the three rings we'd grown used to. Above us, our recording equipment hummed to life, sending vibrations through the floor that made the boards shiver beneath our feet.

"We have to get down there," Cynthia said, but I caught her arm. The floor was shifting, boards creaking and separating to reveal glimpses of old stone. A well shaft hidden beneath decades of construction.

My flashlight beam caught something in the growing gaps - metal glinting against stone. The remains of an old ladder, rusted but still attached to the well wall.

"Baby," I said quietly. "Look at how the boards are moving."

The separation wasn't random. The boards pulled away from each other in a perfect circle, matching the pattern we'd seen with the backpacks at Lana's. Like the photograph from Kelly's. Like every circle since this started.

The ringing stopped abruptly. "Did you figure it out yet, Dad?" Ben's voice echoed up from the darkness. The words were his, but something about the cadence made my skin crawl.

I studied the widening gaps. Common sense said this was impossible - our house's structure couldn't allow for a hidden well shaft this size.

"It's not real," I said, more to myself than Cynthia. "Old houses settle, but they don't—"

"Settle in perfect circles?" she finished. "Around wells that show up in historical records?" She pointed her phone's light down through the gaps. "Baby, look at the stones."

Numbers and dates were scratched into the ancient well stones, along with marks that matched Alexandra's files. But these carvings looked older, much older than 1957.

My phone vibrated. A text from an unknown number showed a photo taken in Kelly's Diner. In it, I could see our boys sitting in a booth - but something about their postures seemed rehearsed, mechanical. The timestamp was from fifteen minutes ago, when we'd been confronting Amber outside our house.

Another text. Another photo. The old theater this time, also timestamped 3:33 PM. Our boys again, arranged in that same circular pattern.

"They can't be in multiple places," I said, trying to hold onto logic while our house fell apart beneath us. "These have to be faked. Amber or Wallace—"

"Dad?" Ben's voice drifted up again, clearer now. Just our son, sounding scared. "Why did you and Mom follow us down here?"

"What do you mean, follow you?" Cynthia asked, inching closer to the widening circle. "We just got home."

"But you were just with us," Xander called up. "Both of you."

Another text alert. A photo from the hospital basement, showing Cynthia and me walking into the research room. Timestamp: now.

I shook my head, trying to clear it. Focus on what's real. Our boys were down there, scared and confused. The how and why could wait.

"We're coming down," I called out, testing the nearest board with my foot. It held, though it shouldn't have. Nothing about this should be possible.

"Dad, wait," Tyler's voice carried up. "Something's wrong with—"

His words cut off as my flashlight beam caught something else in the well shaft - initials carved into the stones. Some looked decades old, while others seemed freshly cut. Among them, I recognized the distinctive way Casey marked his C.

A sound like wood splintering made us both jump back. The circle in the floor was complete now, revealing the full width of the well shaft. The old ladder disappeared into darkness below.

"Something's not right," Cynthia whispered. "Listen to their voices."

She was right. The boys sounded clear now, no distortion. But there was something mechanical about their speech patterns, like words being played back in perfect sequence.

My phone lit up with another photo. The hospital research room, but from an angle that showed something we'd missed earlier. Behind the filing cabinets sat an old rotary phone.

As I stared at the image, the initials carved in the well stones seemed to writhe in our flashlight beams. Two sets from 1957. Five new ones - our boys' initials.

"They're waiting," Ben called up. "But Dad... which us are you looking for?"

Through the gaps around the well shaft, something moved in the darkness. The ladder creaked, metal groaning against stone.

"Seven frequencies," a voice said - not our boys now, but something that made the air vibrate with each word. "Five children. Two guides. The pattern never changes."

More photos flooded my phone. Our boys in different locations, all timestamped 3:33 PM. Each showing them arranged in that same circle. Each version slightly different - different clothes, different positions, different angles.

"Baby," Cynthia gripped my arm. "How many sets of footsteps do you hear?"

I tried to count the distinct footsteps echoing in the well shaft. "At least seven"

"Dad?" One of our boys called up - but I couldn't tell which one through the distortion of the well shaft. "Did you figure it out yet?"

The footsteps grew closer. Multiple sets, moving in both directions on the rusted ladder. And in our flashlight beams, small figures began emerging from the darkness below.

Something about their movements seemed unsettling. Like watching a film where the frames didn't quite match up.

My phone buzzed one last time. The message showed a single line: "The well remembers every child who's ever played here."

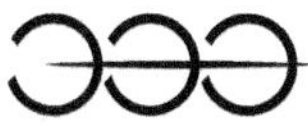

Chapter 15: Sheriff Wallace

The security feed from Kelly's Diner played silently on my office monitor. Amber was there again, setting up her recording equipment at that same corner booth. Always chasing stories she didn't understand.

My father's journal lay open on my desk, its pages yellow with age. Some entries I knew by heart - especially his notes about the Vernon case. About what happens when people dig too deep into Johnson's history.

"Sir?" Deputy Hayes appeared in my doorway. "She's live-streaming again. Talking about the Vernon case, about old police files."

I watched her latest stream, her desperation for attention making her predictable. Easy to lead exactly where I needed her to go.

"And the Lumins?" I asked, though I already knew they'd found the hospital records. Just like they were supposed to.

"They accessed the files you marked," Hayes said. "The ones about Alexandra Sullivan."

Through the security feed, I watched Amber adjusting her microphone at Kelly's, unaware she was following a path I'd carefully laid out. Her voice carried through my computer speakers: "Breaking news about Johnson's dark history! About why they changed all the street names..."

"Sir?" Hayes shifted uncomfortably. "Shouldn't we stop her before—"

"Like we stopped the reporter last time?" I gestured to my father's journal. "Some stories have to be told, Jim. The question is who tells them."

My phone buzzed. A text from Amber: "Sheriff, you won't believe what I found in the old case files."

Of course she'd found them. I'd made sure of it, leaving just enough clues. Her need for content made her the perfect tool.

"Sir," Hayes was still hovering in the doorway. "What about the Lumin children?"

I glanced at the feed showing Lana's house, where five boys should have been safe. The empty backyard told a different story.

"Everything's proceeding as it should," I said, but my hand instinctively touched the old scar behind my ear. A reminder from my own childhood, from the last time Johnson's past had surfaced.

My phone buzzed again. Amber: "Going live in ten minutes with everything I've uncovered. The real story behind the Vernon case..."

"Jim," I said quietly, "clear Main Street. Like my father did back then."

Hayes nodded, understanding. He'd seen enough old reports to know what could happen when people started asking the wrong questions about Johnson's history.

The feed from Kelly's caught my attention. Same booth where that reporter had sat years ago, making the same mistakes.

My father's last journal entry lay open before me, his careful handwriting documenting everything that happened after. Everything I needed to make sure happened again.

Some lessons, I'd learned, could only be taught the hard way.

"Sir," Hayes reappeared. "Main Street's clear, but..." He hesitated. "The Lumins are at the hospital, in the records room."

Just like the breadcrumbs were meant to lead them. I watched Amber's preliminary broadcast, her viewer count climbing: "Breaking news! What I've discovered about Johnson's history..."

The scar behind my ear throbbed. Some warnings went unheeded, no matter how clear you made them.

"Let her continue," I said quietly. Even if it meant another entry in Johnson's missing persons files.

My father's journal held more than just case notes. It held a map of sorts, though Hayes would never understand what the careful documentation really meant.

"Sir?" Hayes was watching Amber's feed. "She's talking about accessing restricted files."

"Good." I turned to the hospital's security feed. Wes and Cynthia had found exactly what they needed to find.

Amber's voice carried from my computer: "My investigation has uncovered decades of cover-ups in Johnson. Since the Vernon case, there's been a pattern of—"

The scar twinged. She'd never understand she was just another piece in a larger game. Just like the Lumins. Just like their boys.

Hayes shifted uncomfortably by the door. "She's moved to the theater now, sir. Says she's found something in the old records."

I watched her pack up her equipment at Kelly's, eager to chase her next revelation. Her viewer count higher than ever before.

My phone lit up with another notification. Amber had found what I'd left at the theater - newspaper clippings, old photographs, a trail leading exactly where it needed to lead.

"This is incredible," her voice trembled with excitement. "The connection between all these places..."

Hayes watched the feed nervously. "Should we stop her before—"

"No." I opened my father's journal to the final pages. "Let her think she's exposing the truth."

The hospital's security feed showed the Lumins discovering their own set of clues. All according to plan.

"Jim," I said quietly. "Check the third floor archives. Make sure everything's where it needs to be."

Hayes hesitated. "Even the restricted files, sir?"

"Especially those." I watched Amber's broadcast continue. "She'll find them soon enough."

But she'd only find what I needed her to find. Some truths had to stay buried.

"This is going to make me famous," Amber's voice carried through the speakers. "After tonight, everyone will know what really happened in Johnson."

The feed from the hospital basement showed the Lumins piecing things together. Each revelation measured, each discovery planned.

My phone buzzed: "Third floor archives secured," Hayes texted. "But sir... are you sure about this?"

I closed my father's journal, keeping its real contents hidden. What Amber would broadcast tonight was just the surface - enough to serve its purpose, but not enough to reveal what lay beneath.

Some stories needed to be told. Others needed to stay buried. Forever.

"Sir," Hayes' voice crackled through my radio. "Found something else in the archives. Old files about your father and Alexandra Sullivan."

"Leave them," I said sharply. Those particular files stayed where they were. Amber's broadcast tonight would only reveal what we needed revealed.

Through the security feed, I watched the Lumins in the hospital basement. Everything moving according to plan. Almost time.

Amber's latest update streamed across my screen: "Getting closer to the truth about Johnson's dark history. Why certain files are kept locked away..."

Let her think she was exposing secrets. Let her believe she'd uncovered something profound. The real truth would stay safely hidden in my father's journal, in those third floor archives, in places she'd never think to look.

"Sir," Hayes again. "About those other files—"

"Focus on your job, Jim." I watched Amber's viewer count climbing. "Some questions aren't meant to be answered."

Not yet, anyway.

"Everything's set at Kelly's," Hayes reported. "And the theater."

I nodded, watching events unfold. The Lumins were still in the hospital basement, believing they'd heard Amber's voice - a necessary deception. And somewhere between these pieces moving into place, five boys had vanished from their grandmother's house.

"Time to get back to the station, Jim." I closed my father's journal, locking it away in my desk. "The next few hours will play out on their own."

On screen, Amber prepared for what she thought would be her biggest story yet. She'd find exactly what I needed her to find. Nothing more.

Some secrets in Johnson needed to stay buried.

And I'd make sure they did.

Chapter 16: Cynthia

The old floorboards creaked, gaps visible between them where age had warped the wood. Through these spaces, shadows moved in the darkness below. Footsteps echoed up from the well shaft, accompanied by the metallic groan of the ancient ladder.

From outside, Amber's voice carried through our open front door as she narrated for her phone: "Something incredible is happening inside the Lumin house. My followers are about to witness—"

Ben emerged first, climbing up through the gap in our floor. Every movement was precisely like our son's - that slight favor to his left side from the skateboard accident. Yet something felt rehearsed about it, like an actor who'd studied his subject too carefully.

"Mom?" Xander's voice drifted up from the darkness, followed by his figure ascending the ladder. His voice sounded normal, but his movements were too measured, too precise.

A grinding noise drew our attention as more floorboards shifted, being pushed up from below. Metal scraped against wood as another section lifted, widening the opening to the well shaft.

Through these gaps, our other boys emerged one by one. Real, physical, right in front of us. My hand found Wes's arm as we watched them climb into our front hall. They moved like our children, looked like our children, but something was wrong with their eyes - too still, too focused.

"Breaking news for my listeners," Amber's voice grew closer to our door. "Strange lights visible through the Lumins' windows. Could this be connected to the Vernon family disappearances? To the signals my equipment's been picking up across town?"

The static from upstairs changed pitch, and Ben turned toward the sound. Behind him, his brothers arranged themselves in our front hall, movements synchronized with unnatural precision.

"Mom," Xander said, his voice perfectly normal but his expression frozen, "did you figure out why they brought us here? Why it had to be this house?"

Casey, our youngest, took a step toward us. Behind him, the well shaft seemed to pulse with that familiar static. "They've been waiting," he said, but his voice carried an age it shouldn't have. "Since '57. Since they changed the street names."

From outside, Amber's narration grew more excited: "These energy readings are incredible. My equipment is picking up something I've never seen before. My followers won't believe—"

The static built to a crescendo from the recording room above, and all our boys turned to look up the stairs in perfect unison.

"The frequencies are aligning," Tyler said, his voice carrying that same strange age. "Like they did before. When the last person tried to broadcast—"

"Baby," Wes interrupted, his hand finding mine. "The Kelly's photograph. Look."

The old photo lay where we'd dropped it, but something was changing. Not the image itself - the seven figures still stood in their perfect circle. But now I could see what I'd missed before.

Two of them were transparent.

"Holy shit," Amber's voice cracked through her livestream. "My followers won't believe... these readings match the ones from '57. The ones from Wallace's files. The ones that—"

She cut off abruptly as all the static from upstairs ceased. In that sudden quiet, I could hear her breathing through her broadcast, quick and panicked.

Our boys stood perfectly still, watching us with those unnaturally calm expressions.

"Some patterns need to stay hidden," Brayden said, his voice ancient and hollow. "Some frequencies aren't meant to be shared."

From outside, Amber's voice rose with renewed excitement: "Breaking news! I've just received Chief Wallace's private files about the Vernon case. About what really happened in 1957. About why they changed the street names, why they—"

The static returned, but different this time. Higher pitched. Dangerous.

Through the front window, I could see Amber moving up our walkway, her phone held high as she narrated. Behind her, something seemed to distort the air, like heat waves rising from hot pavement.

But it was fifty degrees outside.

"Look at these readings," she was saying, her voice trembling with anticipation. "My equipment is picking up the same frequency pattern that Wallace documented in '57. The one that—"

She stopped suddenly, staring at her phone's screen. Even from here, I could see her face drain of color.

"That's... that's not possible," she whispered. "Those figures behind me... they're not..."

Our boys watched through the window, their expressions unnaturally calm. "Some stories," they said in unison, "aren't meant to be told."

"My followers need to see this," Amber's voice shook as she switched to her phone's rear camera. "These figures... they match the descriptions from Wallace's files. The ones right before each family—"

The static pulsed one final time, and our boys spoke again: "She's broadcasting it now. Sharing it. Spreading it."

"Like ripples in a pond," Wes whispered beside me.

Through the window, Amber's phone started to glitch, its screen flickering with strange patterns. Her hands shook as she tried to keep filming.

"My followers won't believe these readings! The signal is—" Her voice cut off as she looked at her phone's screen again. Her livestream went dead.

"She wasn't supposed to see that yet," our boys said in that unnaturally old voice. "Not until the pattern was complete."

I moved toward our children, maternal instinct overriding everything else. Something was wrong with them - the strange voice, the rigid postures, the way they moved in perfect unison.

"Baby," Wes was already reaching for Ben, parental concern replacing his usual skepticism. "They're burning up."

He was right. Each boy's skin felt like fire, their eyes unfocused, like they weren't quite present. Like something else was speaking through them.

Or someone else.

Chapter 17: Wes

The boys' skin burned against my palm as I checked each forehead. Doctor Mom, Cynthia called it - her instinct to check temperatures, to look for rational explanations. But there was nothing rational about this fever, about the way all five boys seemed to burn at exactly the same temperature.

"We need to get them to the hospital," I said, but even as the words left my mouth, I knew it wasn't that simple. Not with what we'd seen emerge from the well. Not with Amber still standing frozen on our walkway, staring at her dead phone.

"Baby," Cynthia's voice held that tone I recognized - the one that meant she was seeing patterns I'd missed. "Look at their eyes."

She was right. Our boys' pupils had dilated to perfect circles, black consuming the iris. All five sets identical, like looking into small wells of darkness.

The static hummed from upstairs, building toward something new.

"Dad?" Ben's voice, but carrying an age it shouldn't have. Like the voice that had spoken through all of them earlier. "Do you understand yet? About why some patterns have to be maintained?"

Through the window, I could see Amber finally moving, backing away from our house. Her phone was dark, but she kept holding it up like she was filming. Like she couldn't stop performing even now.

"We need to cool them down," I said, trying to focus on the immediate problem. Our boys were burning up, speaking in voices that weren't theirs. Everything else - the static, the well shaft, whatever was happening upstairs - could wait.

But when I turned toward the bathroom for washcloths, all five boys moved in perfect unison to block my path.

"You can't leave now," they said together. "Not when it's almost time."

From upstairs came the sound of a rotary phone starting to ring.

"Almost time for what?" I asked, though part of me didn't want the answer.

"For the pattern to reset," Tyler said, but the voice wasn't his. Wasn't any of theirs.

Cynthia moved closer to me, her hand finding mine. "Their temperatures," she whispered. "It's getting worse."

She was right. Heat radiated from our boys now, intense enough that I could feel it from several feet away. Their skin was far too hot to touch, well beyond any normal fever.

The phone's ringing grew louder, more insistent. Outside, Amber still stood frozen, her dead phone pointed at our house.

"Watch," our boys said in unison. "Watch what happens when someone never learns."

The phone in Amber's hands suddenly flickered back to life. Her voice drifted in from outside, her earlier fear replaced by that familiar desperate need for attention: "My followers, we're witnessing history. What you're about to see—"

"Some people," Brayden said, his voice carrying that strange age, "will do anything for attention. No matter who it hurts."

Heat pulsed from our boys in a wave that made my eyes water. The static from upstairs changed pitch, becoming something that made my teeth ache.

"It's spreading," they said together, their skin radiating more heat with each word. "Like it did before. When the last person tried to share it."

Through the window, I could see Amber starting another livestream, her need for validation overwhelming any sense of self-preservation. Her voice carried through our open door: "Breaking news! I've managed to decrypt files about the 1957 incidents. About what really happened at the well. The frequency pattern matches exactly what I'm picking up now, and—"

The static shifted, changed. Became something older.

Our boys' bodies swayed in perfect unison, like they were responding to some rhythm we couldn't hear. Their heads tilted at identical angles, synchronized to whatever signal pulsed through the house.

"She's doing it again," they said in that unnaturally old voice. "Broadcasting what should stay buried. Sharing what should stay hidden. Like all the others before her."

"Dad?" Ben's voice, suddenly normal again. Scared. "What's happening to us?"

My first instinct was to reach for him, but Cynthia caught my arm. Something wasn't right about how quickly his voice had changed back. About that flash of fear that seemed too perfect, too calculated.

"Remember the hospital," she whispered. "How they used our voices to lead us down."

She was right. This felt like another lure, another trap. But these were our boys. Our children. Even if something was using them, even if something was working through them...

"Almost time," they said together, Ben's moment of normalcy vanishing as that ancient voice returned. "She's almost done it. Almost completed the pattern. Just like all the others who thought they could control it."

Through the window, Amber's excitement grew as her viewer count climbed higher. "This is incredible! The signal's reaching worldwide now. My livestream is going viral! I'm getting responses from Tokyo, London, Buenos Aires—"

She stopped suddenly, staring at her phone. Even from here, I could see the color drain from her face as she finally realized what she'd done. What she'd spread across the globe.

The static changed pitch one final time, and our boys spoke in that ancient voice: "Some patterns can't be controlled. Can't be contained. Not once they start spreading."

Through the window, Amber's phone clattered to the ground as she pressed her hands against her ears.

Chapter 18: Amber

"Breaking news for my followers!" My hands shook with excitement as I touched my swollen nose, determined to continue despite my earlier confrontation with the Lumins. "Something big is happening in Johnson tonight. Something that's going to make everyone forget about Love and Luminol."

The chat exploded with notifications as I stood in front of their house. More viewers joining every second. After years of watching their podcast succeed while mine faltered, it was finally happening.

"The missing children are just the beginning," I narrated, positioning my phone for the perfect shot. "I've uncovered something much bigger. Something about Johnson's history that the Wallace family never wanted revealed—"

Static cut through my broadcast. Just for a moment. But in that split second, I saw something in my phone's screen that made my stomach lurch.

My viewer count jumped. Twenty thousand. The chat moved so fast I could barely read it: "Did anyone else see that?" "What was that shadow?" "Play it back!"

"Just some technical difficulties, followers!" I forced a laugh, adjusting my settings. What I'd seen couldn't be real. Just tricks of the light, or maybe—

"This is what real investigating looks like," I continued, ignoring the throbbing in my nose. "While the Lumins play with their little podcast, I've discovered the truth about Johnson's past—"

The static returned, stronger this time. Through it, I heard something. Whispers, just at the edge of comprehension. My streaming app showed strange waves in the audio display, picking up sounds that shouldn't exist.

"The numbers are insane!" I practically squealed, watching my viewers climb to thirty thousand. "You all know what this means, right? This is my breakthrough moment. What I've always deserved—"

The chat flew past: "WHAT IS THAT" "something's wrong" "someone call the police" "is this real?"

"Of course it's real!" I beamed at my camera. "I've always known I'd break the biggest story Johnson's ever seen. While Wes and Cynthia played at being investigators, I was uncovering the actual truth. Now watch as I—"

Static burst through my broadcast, and underneath it... was that counting? But I couldn't focus on that. Fifty thousand viewers! They were finally seeing what I'd known all along - that I was meant for bigger things than this small town.

"The signal's reaching worldwide now!" My voice rose with excitement as I watched the viewer count. Sixty thousand! "My livestream is going viral! I'm getting responses from Tokyo, London, Buenos Aires—"

The chat was moving impossibly fast: "what's happening to her feed?" "something's wrong" "this isn't normal" "GET OUT OF THERE"

"I know, I know, it's overwhelming!" I preened for the camera. "But this is just the beginning. Everything they missed, everything they tried to hide—"

The static changed pitch, becoming almost musical. A rhythm that matched the counting I could hear more clearly now. Seventy thousand viewers! This was my vindication. My moment.

"The readings are off the charts!" I moved closer to the house, my phone raised high. "My equipment is picking up something incredible. Something that proves—"

I stopped suddenly, staring at my phone's screen. Even through my excitement, something in my mind screamed that what I was seeing wasn't right. Wasn't possible.

The chat blurred past: "her face" "what's happening to her eyes?" "someone help her" "I can't stop watching"

"Yes, keep watching!" I felt almost dizzy with validation. "This is the real story of Johnson. The truth about what happens when certain patterns complete themselves, when—"

The static built to a crescendo, drowning out my words. But the viewer count kept climbing! Two hundred thousand now. This was what I'd always wanted. Always deserved.

Pain started behind my eyes, but three hundred thousand viewers! Nothing mattered except—

"This is what real investigating looks like!" But my voice sounded wrong now, distorted. "Everyone who doubted me, who said I'd never—"

The chat was just a blur of panic: "oh god her face" "SOMEONE HELP HER" "what's happening to her?" "I can't look away"

Something warm trickled down my face. The static had become a physical thing, pushing into my skull through every opening. But the numbers! The validation! This was everything I'd—

My own scream cut through the static as I finally saw what everyone had been watching. Not me. Never me.

Blood ran down my wrists now, but all I could see was that viewer count. A million! More! They were finally—

The pressure exploded behind my eyes, but I kept broadcasting. Had to keep broadcasting. Two million viewers now! They were finally paying attention. Finally seeing me. Finally—

"The truth about Johnson," I tried to say, but blood filled my mouth. "The patterns, the—"

The chat was just screaming now: "SOMEONE STOP THIS" "this isn't fake" "i can't unsee this" "what's happening to her?"

Through the blood and static and pain, I saw what my livestream was really showing. Why everyone was really watching.

"I was right," I gasped through the blood, but everyone was watching now. Ten million viewers! "I was always..."

The static reached its peak. The counting stopped.

And my livestream captured everything that came next.

My last thought, as darkness took me: Finally, everyone was watching.

"I win," I whispered.

Then everything went black.

Chapter 19: Wes

The sound was unlike anything I'd ever heard. A wet crack that started at the base of Amber's skull and worked its way up, like ice breaking on a frozen lake. Through our front window, we watched as the pressure built behind her eyes, blood vessels bursting until tears of red ran down her cheeks. Her skull began to distort, expanding in ways the human body was never meant to move.

Her phone kept broadcasting even as the bone and tissue started to split. The device captured every moment as her head separated along invisible fault lines, spraying the lens with grey matter and fragments of skull. When it finally fell, the phone spun once, catching a final shot of our house before the livestream ended.

"Baby," Cynthia's voice was steady, but her grip on my arm was iron-tight. "The boys."

Behind us, our children still swayed to that impossible rhythm, their skin burning hot. The static from upstairs pulsed in time with their movement. Blood mist hung in the air where Amber had stood, painting our front windows in abstract patterns of red and grey. Her headless body remained upright for one impossible moment before crumpling to our front walk with a sound like wet cardboard giving way.

Her phone lay face up in the growing pool of blood, its screen still active. One of her eyes had landed intact on our welcome mat, pupil dilated and fixed on her phone as if checking the viewer count one final time.

And somewhere in the distance, police sirens began to wail.

"Dad?" Ben's voice suddenly normal, confused. The synchronized swaying stopped as all five boys seemed to snap out of whatever had held them.

"What happened?" Xander asked, pressing a hand to his head. "Why are we..."

Cynthia was already checking temperatures, mother's instinct taking over. Their skin had cooled to normal, pupils back to regular size. Like nothing had ever been wrong.

"We need to get them checked out," I said, trying to position myself between them and the window. Trying to block their view of what remained of Amber on our front lawn. But Tyler had already seen.

"Is that... blood?"

"Everyone in the car," Cynthia's voice left no room for argument. "Now."

As I backed the SUV out of our driveway, I had to carefully maneuver around the spreading pool of fluid that had once been inside Amber's skull. For a moment, I thought the blood looked almost black in the fading light, but I pushed that observation aside - just a trick of the shadows. Chunks of grey matter clung to our welcome mat, and something that looked like part of her temporal lobe had slid down our front door, leaving a glistening trail.

The drive to the emergency room felt endless. Every few minutes I checked the rearview mirror, watching our boys for any sign of that strange fever returning. They sat quietly, unusually subdued, while Cynthia kept a hand on Brayden's forehead from her spot in the back seat.

The ER intake nurse barely looked up from her computer as Cynthia described their symptoms. High fever, confusion, sudden onset and just as sudden disappearance. It all sounded so clinical, so inadequate to describe what we'd witnessed in our living room.

They took the boys' vitals one by one. Each reading perfectly normal, though the thermometer seemed to glitch when they checked Casey -

probably just low batteries. Three different nurses commented on how healthy they looked. How normal.

The emergency room doctor found nothing wrong. Normal temperatures, normal pupils, normal everything. No sign of the fever that had burned through them just an hour ago.

"Could be a virus that passed quickly," she suggested, but her expression said she didn't believe it. "I'd like to run a few more tests, just to be thorough."

Through the exam room window, I could see more police cars arriving at the hospital. Wallace would be looking for us soon. Would want to know what we'd seen. What we knew about whatever had turned Amber's head inside out.

"The boys don't remember anything," Cynthia whispered, watching them joke with each other like nothing had happened. Like they hadn't spoken in ancient voices. Like they hadn't watched someone's skull split open on our front lawn.

The doctor's additional tests showed nothing unusual. No explanation for what had happened. No trace of whatever had burned through them.

Just five normal kids, already complaining about being hungry.

"Nothing physically wrong with them," the doctor concluded, reviewing the results one final time. "Though given the circumstances, you might want to consider—"

"Dr. Matthews?" A nurse appeared in the doorway. "Chief Wallace is here. He'd like to speak with Mr. and Mrs. Lumin."

Through the exam room window, I could see Chief Wallace talking to the nurse at the station. Even from here, I could tell something was wrong with how he held himself - tense, like a man expecting bad news. Two uniformed officers stood near the entrance, hands resting too casually on their weapons. Multiple screens around them showed news coverage, though the sound was muted. In each one, I could see the same headline crawler: "WARNING: Disturbing content. Viewer discretion advised."

"Mr. and Mrs. Lumin." His voice was steady but something was off. A tremor in his hands that hadn't been there before. A sheen of sweat despite the hospital's chill. "I need to ask you about what happened to Ms. Sullivan."

We moved to a quiet corner of the ER, where we could still see our boys through the glass partition. The news coverage played silently on the TV above them: "Viral video shows local podcaster's unexplained death..."

Wallace clicked off the TV before the boys could see more. His usual authority seemed cracked somehow, like whatever had happened at our house had gotten under his skin too.

"I understand your children were... affected somehow. Before the incident."

"They had a fever," Cynthia said carefully. "It passed quickly."

"Did it?" His hand moved to a scar behind his ear - old, puckered, almost black against his skin. "The doctors found nothing wrong?"

The way he asked made it clear he'd expected that result. I studied his face, reading the guilt there.

"You knew this would happen," I said, my voice low but firm. It wasn't a question. "You knew about what it would do to her."

Wallace glanced at our boys, then back to us. Something dark moved behind his eyes. "What I know," he said quietly, "is that certain things, once started, can't be stopped. And what happened to Ms. Sullivan... that was just the beginning."

Through the glass, I watched Ben show his brothers something on his phone. Probably footage of what happened to Amber. It would be everywhere by now.

"And Mr. Lumin?" Wallace turned back as he started to leave. "Delete any recordings you have from today. All of them."

His hand touched that scar again, and in the harsh hospital lighting, I could have sworn something moved beneath his skin.

"What happened to Amber is spreading," he added quietly. "Every replay, every share..." He stopped, choosing his words carefully. "Some things, once seen, can't be unseen. And what's coming next..."

He didn't finish the sentence, just touched that scar one more time before walking away. As he passed under the fluorescent lights, I noticed something I hadn't before - the veins in his neck were almost black.

A nurse approached with discharge papers, but my attention was caught by Ben suddenly pulling his headphones off, pressing a hand to his ear. When Cynthia rushed to check on him, he seemed fine, but something about the way he kept touching that ear...

"We can't go home," Cynthia said quietly as we gathered the boys. "Not with crime scene tape across our yard. Not with pieces of her still..."

"You can stay with me," Lana's voice made us turn. She stood in the ER doorway, looking shaken but determined. "I've already made up the guest rooms."

The boys gathered their things, already arguing about who'd get which room at Grandma's. Like this was just another sleepover. Like they hadn't spent the afternoon burning up with an impossible fever. Like they hadn't watched someone's skull rupture on our front lawn.

Through the hospital windows, I could see news vans gathering in the parking lot. Amber had finally gotten the attention she'd always wanted. The footage of her death would be everywhere by morning.

And in the reflection of those windows, I caught a glimpse of Wallace getting into his cruiser. The black veins had spread up his neck, disappearing into his hairline.

ⱷⱷⱷ

Chapter 20: Cynthia

The guest room at Mom's felt too normal after everything that had happened. Out the window, I could see news vans still parked at the end of her street, their satellite dishes pointed toward our house eight blocks away.

Wes finally slept, exhausted from everything we'd seen. On the nightstand, his phone kept lighting up with notifications as footage of Amber's final moments spread across the internet.

The boys were quiet in their rooms - all their tests normal, all their memories of the afternoon strangely blank. Like whatever had burned through them had taken those hours with it.

A soft thud from downstairs made me tense, but it was just Patches knocking something off Mom's counter. The cats seemed almost back to normal too. Almost. Nala still wouldn't go near any screens.

I checked my phone - 3:32 AM. Of course.

The sound of Mom's TV drifted up from downstairs. She never could sleep when she was worried. Through her open door, I could see her sitting in her favorite chair, the local news muted but still showing footage from our front yard.

"Can't sleep either?" Mom's voice was soft as I joined her. On screen, hazmat teams carefully collected what remained of Amber from our lawn. "I called your father. He's coming down tomorrow. Says he's seen something like this before."

The TV flickered, static building as the timestamp approached 3:33.

"Your father never talked much about certain things that happened in this town," Mom said quietly, watching the news footage. "But the way he reacted when I mentioned what happened today..."

The static grew stronger, and from upstairs came Ben's voice:

"Mom? Why does everything look so dark?"

The digital clock on Mom's cable box hit 3:33.

"Ben, honey?" I was already moving toward the stairs, Mom right behind me. "What do you mean?"

No answer, but I could hear movement from the boys' rooms. All of them awake now, at exactly 3:33 AM.

When I reached the top of the stairs, Ben stood in his doorway. His eyes looked normal - not like earlier today with those impossible black pupils. But something about his expression...

"It's in my phone," he said calmly. "Like ink spreading through water."

His phone lay face-up on the nightstand, Amber's final broadcast playing silently. Mom reached past me and yanked the power strip from the wall, killing every electronic device in the room. Ben blinked, his expression clearing like he was waking up.

"What happened?" he asked, suddenly just my thirteen-year-old again. "Why are we all awake?"

From the other rooms, his brothers emerged, looking equally confused. Behind them, Nala darted past, still avoiding every dark screen.

"Back to bed," Mom said firmly, her practical nature taking over. "School tomorrow, no matter what."

But as the boys shuffled back to their rooms, I caught her checking the time: 3:33 AM.

Like it had been frozen there.

"I'll make some tea," Mom said quietly as we headed back downstairs. Neither of us mentioned how every digital clock we passed showed the same time. Like 3:33 had gotten stuck, refusing to move forward.

In the kitchen, Mom's battery-operated wall clock flickered to life. 3:33 glowed in soft blue numbers where there should have been analog hands. Mom pulled the batteries without comment, her hands only shaking slightly.

"Your father will be here early," she said, putting the kettle on. "He's bringing some old papers. Things he kept from back then."

Wes appeared in the doorway, his phone in hand. "Wallace just texted. He wants us at the station now. Says we can't wait until morning."

I glanced at Mom's kitchen clock. The second hand kept moving, but the time didn't change. Like something had trapped us at this exact minute.

"Should I wake the boys?" Mom asked, but Wes shook his head.

"Let them sleep. Wallace was specific - just us." He showed me the text: 'Bring the files from the hospital. No one else.'

"Your father says he'll be here in an hour," Mom said, checking her analog watch - the only timepiece still moving forward. "I'll stay with the boys. Keep them away from screens."

Wes's phone buzzed again. Another text from Wallace: 'Hurry. It's spreading faster than before.'

The drive to the station felt endless. Maybe because we had to avoid Main Street, where news crews clustered around Kelly's Diner. Maybe because every traffic light we passed seemed synchronized to the same pattern.

"Your dad," Wes said quietly as we turned onto Cedar Street. "What do you think he knows about what happened back then?"

Before I could answer, static burst from our car radio - even though it wasn't turned on. Through the interference, we could hear fragments of Amber's last broadcast.

Police cruisers filled the station's parking lot, their light bars pulsing in an unnatural rhythm. Officers hurried in and out of the building, carrying boxes of old files.

Wallace waited at the top of the steps, gesturing for us to park around back. Away from the security cameras.

"Inside," Wallace said as soon as we approached. "Before the morning crews arrive."

The station stood unusually quiet, most of the electronics dark. Wallace led us past the bullpen, past the regular interview rooms, toward a staircase I'd never noticed before. It looked older than the rest of the building, the walls around it a different shade.

"Your father called," he said, unlocking a heavy door at the bottom of the stairs. "Said he's bringing the original maps."

Behind the door, a single bare bulb illuminated a room full of filing cabinets. No computers. No phones. Nothing digital.

Nothing that could capture or transmit what was spreading through our screens.

ꛯꛯꛯ

Chapter 21: Wes

The file room stank of musty paper and something else - a sharp, metallic smell that reminded me of pennies soaked in rust. The kind of smell that makes your stomach turn before your brain knows why.

Wallace's hands shook as he pulled a box from the bottom shelf, sending clouds of dust into the air. "These records never made it to digital. For good reason." His knuckles turned white against the cardboard, as if fighting against something we couldn't see trying to pull it away.

Hayes' voice drifted down the stairwell. "Sir? It's starting again. Like '57."

A thin line of blood trickled down from Wallace's nose to his upper lip as he pressed his palm against his temple. The gesture looked less like he was fighting pain and more like he was trying to keep something from escaping his skull. "Show them everything. Before the frequencies finish what they started."

The static from upstairs grew louder – that exact pitch that had played right before Amber changed. The sound that made teeth rattle and sent chills down your spine.

"Some patterns," Wallace said, his voice rough like sandpaper, "need to be fed."

The police reports lay scattered before us, thick black marks covering most of the text. But the words I could still read made my stomach churn – descriptions of things that would give anyone nightmares.

"The frequencies get to children first." Wallace's voice now had a wet, gurgling quality. "Make them see things. Make them do things." Blood now coated his upper lip completely. "Like what happened to your boys yesterday."

He spread out photographs that made Cynthia dig her fingers into my arm. Black and white images from 1957 – children standing in perfect circles, their faces twisted into shapes that shouldn't be possible. Behind each group stood eight dark figures, looking like holes cut into reality itself. The space beside them seemed to ripple, as if waiting for something to fill it.

The static grew louder as Wallace wiped at his bleeding nose. "Sometimes they turn people into broadcasters. Make them share things. Like that reporter. Like Amber."

"Amber did that to herself," I said, but I could hear the doubt in my voice.

Wallace's laugh turned into a wet cough. "Or maybe something saw how many followers she had. Something that's been waiting since '57 for someone with enough reach."

"Her social media addiction finally got her what she wanted," Cynthia whispered. "A worldwide audience."

"What it wanted," Wallace corrected, blood now soaking into his shirt collar. "Every share, every view, every download spread the pattern further than we ever imagined possible."

More photographs spread across the table, each one more nightmarish than the last. In each image, the dark figures behind the children grew more solid, more flesh-like, while the children's bodies became transparent, like overexposed film. Their faces blurred and distorted until you couldn't tell where their features should be.

"Your boys," Wallace's voice now had undertones that hurt to listen to. "How many times have you checked their phones since yesterday? Their tablets? Their screens?"

I remembered Ben touching his ear in the hospital. The way they moved together like puppets on the same strings. The voices that came from their mouths that didn't sound human.

"The doctors said they're fine," Cynthia insisted, but her voice shook.

"The doctors can't see everything." Wallace pulled out another file, its edges stained dark. "In '57, all the medical tests came back normal too. Right until—"

The static from above changed, matching exactly the sound from our recording studio. The same frequency from Amber's final broadcast that infected every network it touched.

"Sir?" Hayes sounded terrified. "It's happening."

Blood poured from Wallace's nose now, but his eyes stayed fixed on us. "Want to know what really happened to the Vernon children?"

The new photographs he showed weren't censored. These images burned themselves into my brain. Children twisted into impossible shapes, their bones breaking through skin to form perfect patterns. Muscles and organs twisted into spirals and geometric patterns in seven of the crime scene photos - seven of the eight families, their bodies arranged like grotesque artwork. Their intestines coiled in perfect fibonacci sequences, hearts positioned at precise mathematical angles, spinal columns bent into fractals. But the eighth photo, the Vernon children's scene, showed something far worse. Their bodies lay pristine and untouched on the outside - five perfect shells that weighed nothing at all.

"They found them like this," Wallace said, his blood dripping onto the photographs. "Eight families. Eight circles." Wallace's bloodshot eyes widened. "We always thought it was seven. The reports said seven. But there in the margin—" He pointed to a handwritten note, his finger leaving a bloody smear. "Eight circles found. Eight families taken. And the Vernon children..." He showed us the final image, his hand trembling. "They were meant to be the bridge to the ninth."

The photograph showed five children, looking perfect on the outside. Like hollow dolls.

"Empty?" The word slipped out before I could stop it.

"Everything inside them gone," Wallace explained, blood now leaking from his eyes. "All their organs, bones, even their blood – all taken out without breaking their skin. Like something reached inside and scooped out everything that made them human, leaving their skin behind like empty gift wrap."

The static's pitch changed into a sound that made my teeth hurt.

"Your boys," Wallace whispered, swaying like he might fall. "Have you noticed their weight lately? How they feel lighter, like there's less inside them than there should be?"

Cynthia started to argue, but I remembered something – lifting Casey to his bunk bed this morning. How he felt as light as an empty backpack. The way his laugh echoed like it was coming from an empty space where his lungs should be.

The static from upstairs changed pitch. Higher now, drilling into our ears as Hayes appeared at the door. "Sir, the bleeding's getting worse! We need to—" He stopped dead at the sight of the photographs. "Christ, you're showing them the files?"

"They need to understand," Wallace slurred, blood now streaming from both ears. "Need to know what's trying to get inside their boys. What started with those eight families. What Amber's broadcast awakened."

"Sir, please," Hayes rushed forward as Wallace stumbled. "The morning news crews are here. Their live feed... something's distorting it. The children in the background of their shots—their bodies are starting to blur."

"What's trying to get inside our boys?" My voice came out sharp enough to cut. "What exactly do you mean by trying?"

Wallace sagged against Hayes, leaving crimson handprints on his uniform. "The frequencies test for resonance. Like tuning forks against crystal. They probe for minds that vibrate at the right pitch. Minds that are..." Blood bubbled at the corners of his mouth. "Compatible."

"Compatible for what?" Cynthia's words carried that razor edge I knew too well - the tone that demanded answers.

"For occupation." Each word seemed to cost Wallace more blood now. "But your boys... they're fighting it. Rejecting the harmonics. Never seen resistance like this before. They're somehow..."

Hayes pressed his hand to his earpiece, face draining of color. "Sir, the news feed - it's spreading. Those seven figures behind the reporters... they're becoming visible on every channel. Something about the empty space around them makes my skin crawl, like they're arranged in formation just waiting for—"

The static screamed through the building's speakers. From upstairs came the sound of children counting in perfect unison.

"Get medical help," I snapped at Hayes, but Wallace waved him off with a bloody hand.

"No time left. Your boys..." He coughed, spraying red mist. "First ones to ever resist the frequencies. First to reject the harmonics. Need to know why before—"

The counting stopped. A reporter's voice carried down: "Something's happening to our equipment. The children in our live feed... their skin is becoming transparent. Like we can see through to—"

Static drowned her words. The old photographs on the table caught the fluorescent light strangely, making the empty shells of the Vernon children seem to pulse with absence.

"Your father," Wallace grabbed Cynthia's sleeve with sticky fingers. "He witnessed '57. Saw what happens when the frequencies find compatible vessels. When they find children who don't resist."

"We need to get to our boys," Cynthia started, but Wallace's grip tightened.

"Listen carefully." Blood flowed freely now, his words gurgling. "The frequencies are tools, nothing more. The real threat is what wields them. What's been waiting since '57 for the perfect broadcast combination. The right mathematical resonance to complete their pattern of nine."

Another voice drifted down: "The signal's corrupting every channel, every station. The children watching the broadcasts... they're starting to move in sync."

"Your boys," Wallace could barely whisper now. "Must understand why they can resist. Why they're different. Before Amber's broadcast finishes the sequence the Vernon children began."

Through Hayes' crackling radio, we heard them - children's voices rising in that same counting pattern we'd recorded before Amber's final transmission.

"Sir!" Hayes suddenly recoiled. "Your eyes—they're—"

Thick, black liquid now mixed with the blood running from Wallace's tear ducts. Still, he kept speaking: "The Vernons weren't the first to vanish completely. Just the first to leave empty shells. The others... they were taken whole. Replaced with perfect copies."

"What do you mean replaced?" Cynthia's hand found mine in the dark.

"The names," Wallace gestured weakly at the files with trembling fingers. "Look at the families who disappeared. Then see who moved into those houses after. Study their photographs. Count the spaces where something should be."

With shaking hands, I opened the file Wallace indicated. The photographs inside made my lungs forget how to work. Family portraits from before 1957 lined up next to ones taken after. Same houses. Same names. Same poses. But the families weren't the same - not really. The new photographs mimicked the originals with mathematical precision, every limb and gesture positioned to mirror what came before. But looking closer, I saw what Wallace meant.

The replacement families' eyes reflected light at impossible angles. Their smiles stretched a fraction too wide, teeth aligned with unnatural symmetry. In group shots, their shadows fell in directions that didn't match the rest of the scene. Most disturbing of all - the children's faces in every replacement photo were identical to the millisecond before those original children vanished.

"The replacements," Wallace choked out, pointing to a document with trembling, blood-soaked fingers. "Our code name for them. How they maintained the illusion. How they kept people from asking questions about—"

Hayes' radio spat static. "Sir, someone's here. Says they have the original files. Claims they know what really triggered the frequencies in '57."

"Your boys," Wallace's words came faster now, black fluid mixing with the blood streaming from his nose. "Their resistance pattern... unprecedented. We need to understand why they can fight what the Vernon children couldn't—"

The static cut off abruptly. In the sudden silence, footsteps echoed from upstairs - dozens of feet moving in perfect synchronization.

I stared at the photographs, my eyes catching on every unnatural detail. The replacement families looked human at first glance, but the longer I studied them, the more their careful fabrication unraveled - joints bent at mathematically perfect angles, skin that seemed to reflect light like polished plastic, expressions copied with such precision they looked printed on rather than formed by muscle and bone.

"The replacements," Wallace gasped, lungs rattling. "That's what we called them. How they maintained the pattern. How they kept anyone from noticing when a family was... repurposed."

Hayes' radio crackled again. "Sir? The person about the '57 files is asking for you specifically. Says they can explain why it always had to be eight families. Why the pattern needs a ninth to—"

Through the building's speakers, Amber's final broadcast began playing on loop, her voice distorted into harmonics that made my teeth vibrate: "I win... I win... I win..."

"Your boys." The black fluid that had been steadily contaminating Wallace's blood now dominated completely, pouring from his eyes like oil. "The only ones who've ever fought back. The only ones who—"

A new voice cut through the static - calm, measured, familiar. Someone upstairs requesting Chief Wallace personally.

Someone who knew exactly what happened in 1957.

Someone whose footsteps, as they descended toward the file room, fell in perfect rhythm with the static's pulse.

Chapter 22: Cynthia

Hayes' radio splintered through the static: "Ma'am, this area is restricted. You can't—"

"I need to see Cynthia immediately." Tracy's voice carried that familiar no-nonsense tone. "I found something in the old files. My husband Bill is bringing the rest."

Wallace turned his tar-streaked face toward me, black fluid now completely masking the blood. "Bill? Your father... he was here in '57?"

Tracy's voice grew urgent. "The frequencies aren't what we should fear. They're a doorway. What's been trying to step through since '57..."

The static mutated, its pitch ascending. Upstairs, the news crews' equipment resonated with that lethal frequency, each device finding perfect harmony with the others.

"Bring those files here," Wallace choked out as Hayes lowered him into a chair, strings of black dripping from his chin. "Everything from '57. Before—"

The door flew open. Tracy burst in. Her usual composed demeanor had cracked, revealing something raw underneath.

"The boys," Tracy said, her voice carrying the same tone she used to calm spooked horses. "Have they stayed themselves?"

Ice crystallized in my spine. "What do you mean stayed themselves?"

"The frequencies," she pulled papers from her bag, spreading them across the table. "They're like polarity reversals. Trying to flip something inside your boys. Creating space."

"Space for what?" Wes's voice cracked.

"Bill discovered these at the quarry site." Tracy's hands trembled as she spread out equipment readings. "Energy patterns that defy physics." Her eyes darted to Wallace as his body began to twitch. "The same signatures we're detecting now."

"He needs emergency medical—" I started, but Wallace's body suddenly contorted, spine arching at an impossible angle. Hayes was already radioing for help.

"Keep him stable," Wes moved to help Hayes as Wallace's limbs jerked in unnatural directions.

Tracy's work-roughened fingers smoothed out a faded schematic. "This might explain his reaction. Quarry records from sound experiments they conducted. Testing frequencies against different stone types."

"Not now," I snapped, helping position Wallace as black fluid fountained from his mouth. "Medical help first."

Children's voices filtered through the static overhead, counting in perfect unison, but I couldn't look away from the puddle of oily black spreading beneath Wallace's head. The way his eyes had rolled back to show only whites, now stained with creeping tendrils of darkness.

Amber's transformation was happening again, but this time we could see every excruciating detail of the process.

The medics arrived with practiced efficiency, transferring Wallace to a gurney. His seizure had stopped, but the black fluid continued to seep from his ears, nose, and eyes, like ink bleeding through paper.

"The frequencies affect everyone differently," Tracy said, watching them wheel him out. She ran her fingers over the old equipment readings. "Like magnetic resonance - some materials vibrate to certain frequencies while others remain inert. Some people are more... compatible."

"The quarry readings," Wes prompted, wiping the dark stains from his hands. "What did they find?"

"Patterns." Tracy spread the aged papers across the table. "They weren't just mining stone. They were searching for something specific. Something that responded to certain frequencies."

Through the static, Wallace's voice carried from outside: "Don't let them take me where the frequencies can—" His words cut off as the ambulance doors slammed shut.

"Bill discovered something at the new dig site," Tracy said, hanging up her phone. "Says to meet him at the farm. And..." She hesitated, gathering the photographs. "He needs to see the Vernon children photos. There's something he has to verify."

"Verify what?" Wes asked.

"The pattern of cavities they found in the quarry wall yesterday." Tracy's voice tightened. "Like something had been embedded there. Dormant. Until the right frequency activated it."

"The quarry workers," she continued, her voice dropping. "Three disappeared yesterday after breaking through to that chamber. What was left of them..." She swallowed. "Bill said the way the bodies were positioned - he's never seen anything like it."

A scream shattered the air - Wallace, from the ambulance. The vehicle rocked violently on its suspension.

"Christ," Hayes bolted for the stairs. "He's seizing again!"

The screams multiplied. The EMTs' voices joined Wallace's, their cries resonating at that same deadly frequency we'd heard before Amber—

The ambulance windows exploded.

Glass rained down, revealing the interior. The EMTs sprawled across blood-slicked walls, their bodies contorted. The frequency had worked faster this time, more precisely, as if whatever force controlled it had refined its technique.

Wallace convulsed as black fluid poured from every orifice, his scream harmonizing perfectly with the static. The news crews' equipment amplified the frequency, broadcasting it further.

"The bodies in the quarry chamber," Tracy's voice shook. "The instruments they found with them - decades-old frequency measuring devices, still running."

More screams erupted outside as the news crews dropped their equipment, clutching their heads while that lethal broadcast built to a crescendo.

"We need to leave," Wes grabbed my arm. "Now. Before—"

The static's pitch shifted. The screaming stopped.

Silence fell like a blade. Through the basement window, we could see the bodies scattered around the ambulance. They lay unnaturally still, limbs bent at impossible angles, skin pulled too tight against their frames.

"The quarry workers looked identical," Tracy whispered. "Empty shells. But their blood work showed something first - like their internal structures were being... realigned."

Hayes burst back in, face drained of color. "Just got word - more bodies at the station. Records staff. They were reviewing old frequency measurement files when—"

"The boys," I said, ice flooding my veins. "If they're actually resisting this..."

"They might be exactly what it's been waiting for," Tracy finished. "What it's been searching for since they breached that chamber wall."

The Channel 6 news van's equipment hummed to life, its signal meter spiking before the display cracked and went dark.

"The farm," Tracy's voice hardened with urgency. "Now. Before this spreads any further."

Sunset bled across the sky as we sped toward Bill and Tracy's farm. Each mile of country road seemed to stretch longer than the last, the fading light casting strange shadows across the empty fields. We passed the old wagon wheels marking their entrance, tires crunching down the gravel drive that snaked through open pastures. Their farmhouse emerged through the dusk, its porch adorned with weathered farm tools that cast long shadows in the fading light.

To our left, horses paced their paddock, tails swishing with agitation. Beyond them, cattle grazed the far pasture, still undisturbed by whatever had the horses spooked. White-painted barns dotted the property, their surfaces tinged orange by the setting sun.

The lake's surface reflected the dying light like polished obsidian. Near its shore stood the unfinished cabin, its exposed beams casting rigid shadows across the water.

Static burst from our car radio. A child's voice - unfamiliar, distant - began to count.

Bill's truck sat parked by the cabin frame. He stood beside it, clutching something in his work-gloved hands, muscles tensed like a man bracing for impact.

Bill stood by his truck, still in his quarry supervisor's jacket, clutching something in his work-gloved hands. Twenty years overseeing excavation crews had left permanent creases around his eyes, but I'd never seen him look this tense.

"Found this in my section of the quarry," he said as we approached. He held out what looked like antiquated measuring equipment. Its display flickered with numbers despite being disconnected. "Matching the readings we got right after that object hit the lake."

"What object?" Wes stepped forward. "What happened at the lake?"

Bill glanced at Tracy before answering. "Last week, when the boys were helping me with the cabin. Something came down from the sky. Hit the water about thirty yards out." He held his hands apart. "Made a splash no bigger than a grapefruit, but the sound it made..." He shook his head. "Never heard anything like it. The boys were right there when it happened. They didn't tell you?"

My stomach clenched. "No. They didn't mention anything about it."

"That's not like them," Tracy said. "Especially something this strange."

The static from our car radio intensified. The child's counting echoed across the empty fields as dusk deepened. From somewhere in the growing darkness, an animal shrieked.

"It's gotten worse," Bill said, setting down the device and peeling off his work gloves. "This morning we uncovered something in that chamber. Markings. Like the ones from back then."

The horses' unease spread to the cattle. Their low bellows carried across the pasture as darkness crept closer.

Tracy moved toward the unfinished cabin. "Bill thinks whatever fell that day..."

"Woke something up," he finished. "Something that's been dormant. Broadcasting signals. Testing frequencies until it found the right ones."

Our phones crackled with intensifying static. Through the gathering dark, ripples disturbed the lake's surface.

"That quarry chamber," Bill's weathered hands gripped the device tighter. "It wasn't natural. Someone carved it. Calibrated it to resonate with specific frequencies."

The static built around us as the lake's surface continued to ripple. Not from wind - the air hung dead still. Something beneath the water was moving.

"We need to get inside," Tracy's voice carried an edge I'd never heard before. "Now."

A sound drifted across the water. That same counting we'd heard before, but closer. Beneath it rose a deeper resonance that made the horses scream in terror.

The lake's surface broke.

Chapter 23: Wes

Metal screamed against metal beneath the lake's surface, a sound like massive gears stripping their teeth. Industrial. Precise. A machine awakening after decades of silence.

Bill's spine stiffened. "Inside. Now."

"The horses—" Tracy turned toward the paddock, but Bill caught her arm.

"Too late."

The water exploded upward, and through the spray something caught the dying sunlight - sharp edges of steel and iron. At first glance it looked like submerged construction equipment, but as the water sheeted away, I saw details that didn't belong on any excavator. Articulated arms ended in instruments designed for purposes I didn't want to understand.

Our phones erupted with static, then began playing our boys' voices - not live calls, but fragments of recordings spliced together. "Dad... something in the water" from Ben's voicemail last week cut against Casey's "they're waiting for us" from this morning. Their words pieced together like a grotesque puzzle: "beneath... they need us... have to go back... the patterns want..."

More metal surfaces breached the water's surface. Dark stains coated the exposed machinery, too dark and too permanent to be rust. The mechanisms looked medical, almost surgical - clusters of articulated arms and precision instruments that had no place in a flooded quarry.

"This has to be connected to those old files," Bill said, his voice tight. "The equipment layout, these testing chambers... it's some kind of research facility. Had to be classified - nothing in the land records ever mentioned this."

My stomach turned as I studied a particularly complex piece of machinery. The photographs Wallace had shown us flashed through my mind - the twisted bodies, the precision of their arrangements. "This is where it happened. Where they did those things to those families."

Cynthia gripped my arm. "Where they started the experiments."

The static on our phones intensified. Beneath our boys' distorted voices, older recordings scratched through - screams preserved in waterlogged speakers, the sound quality degraded but the terror still pristine after all these years.

The machinery's grinding changed pitch - the sound of rusted gears encountering resistance. Processing something that made wet, organic sounds through the metal. The noises reminded me of the hospital's automated blood pressure cuff, but deeper, larger - flesh meeting mechanism.

Through the churning water, we saw more of the facility emerge - rows of testing chambers with thick glass windows, observation rooms lined with dials and switches, equipment that looked more like medieval torture devices than scientific instruments. Each piece bore the same dark stains as the first.

"The frequencies weren't just for mind control," Bill backed away, herding us with him. "According to these schematics, they were pushing further. The facility used sound waves to alter human consciousness until—"

Our phones crackled with an old recording, the audio quality degraded but still clear enough to hear the panic in the scientist's voice: "Day 66: Test subjects showing unprecedented cellular changes. Containment protocols have failed. Three more staff members exposed to the frequency. Their transformation was... immediate. We can't risk this spreading beyond the facility. Authorization received to flood all levels.

No evidence can remain. God help us if these frequencies ever reach a broader population."

The machinery around us groaned back to life, processing whatever had fallen from the sky. Each piece activated in sequence, like an assembly line preparing to restart production.

The grinding sound shifted, and new voices emerged from the static - fragments of our boys layered over older recordings. Scientific observations mixed with screams, decades of data preserved in waterlogged hard drives.

Through the chaos of moving machinery, I caught a glint of something different - smoother, newer. The object that had fallen from the sky last week lay exposed on a concrete platform, water streaming off its surface. No larger than a softball, but unlike anything I'd seen before. Its hull had no seams or joints, just a continuous surface that seemed to flow like liquid mercury, catching the fading light in impossible ways. As I watched, its metallic skin rippled with patterns that matched the rhythm of the old machinery, as if it were conducting some grotesque symphony of grinding gears and hydraulics.

"After the shutdown," Bill pulled us toward the cabin, "they converted everything to look abandoned. The quarry, this lake - all of it hiding what they'd built underneath."

More metal surfaces pierced the water, silhouetted against the darkening sky. Each piece designed with surgical precision, their purpose becoming clearer as more of the facility revealed itself.

Our phones' speakers warped with distorted audio. The boys' voices merged with recordings from 1957 - their modern cell phone messages cutting against the scratchy quality of old reel-to-reel tape. "Dad... something in the water" spliced into a scientist's clipped tones: "Subject demonstrates unusual resistance to sonic stimulation." Casey's "have to go back" overlapped with "Test group eight shows promising cellular adaptation." The systematic documentation of those old experiments wove through our sons' voices with mechanical precision.

The object from the sky hadn't simply woken the machinery.

It had reactivated the entire testing complex.

Through gaps in the equipment, old bunkers emerged. Concrete chambers that should have rotted away decades ago stood intact beneath the water, preserved like specimens in formaldehyde. Each chamber housed what looked like medical equipment, but mounted alongside were massive speakers positioned to focus sound waves directly at examination tables fitted with restraints. On the wall of one chamber, behind sheets of falling water, we could make out human silhouettes burned into the concrete, like shadows from a nuclear blast.

Bill's grip tightened on his work gloves. "This wasn't just research." He pointed to a panel of dials, each marked with frequencies and their corresponding "physical alterations." "They were weaponizing sound. Creating frequencies that could reshape people from the inside out."

The static shifted pitch. On our phones, snippets of classified recordings played through the interference: "Subject exhibits progressive cellular mutation. Bone density increasing by 47%. Tissue samples demonstrate complete structural reconfiguration at 66.6 MHz." A different voice cut in, more urgent: "Subject unable to stabilize changes. Cellular breakdown accelerating. We need some kind of bridging agent, something to help the human body adapt to these frequencies." Then another, deeper voice: "The mineral samples from the quarry's lower chamber might be the key..." The recording degraded into static.

"The quarry and lake were connected," Tracy said, pointing to a massive drainage pipe emerging from the water. "Underground tunnels. Testing sites." She traced the pipe's path toward the quarry with her finger. "Until something forced them to seal it all off."

Water churned as more equipment surfaced. That same frequency that had killed Amber built steadily stronger, making the air vibrate against our skin.

Metal screeched against metal as banks of old speakers emerged. Each one oriented toward concrete platforms marked with numbered circles - testing stations, arranged with mathematical precision.

"Your boys' DNA results from the hospital," Bill pulled a worn envelope from his jacket. "There's a reason Wallace was so interested. These files we found yesterday in the quarry chamber - they detail every test subject who showed immunity. Their genetic profiles..." He tapped the medical charts. "They match what's in your boys' blood work."

An alarm blared from beneath the surface - a system reactivating after decades underwater. Red warning lights reflected off the lake's churning surface.

"They thought flooding would keep it contained," Bill said, watching decades-old pumps grind back to life. The water level dropped steadily, revealing more testing equipment. "But they never properly decommissioned anything. Just covered it up and prayed everyone would forget."

I noticed Tracy staring at the shoreline. "The water's draining faster now. Like something opened underneath."

Channels appeared in the lake bed as the water receded, each one leading to that central platform where the metallic object pulsed. Its surface rippled like quicksilver, each wave matching the rhythm of the working pumps.

"There," Bill pointed toward the deepest part of the lake, where the last of the water spiraled down. The object's polished surface caught the red warning lights, distorting them into spiraling fractals that made my vision blur and my temples throb with each pulse. Cables and tubes snaked from the old facility toward it, as if the machinery was trying to interface with whatever had fallen from the sky.

The horses had gone silent. Even the cattle's nervous lowing ceased, as if every living thing sensed what that pulsing object was calling to. Through our phones' static, we could hear the underground pumps working, decades of lake water rushing through old tunnels.

The metallic sphere spun faster now, its liquid surface catching the emergency lights in ways that made the reflections seem to move independently of their source. Each revolution built that same lethal frequency we'd heard too many times today.

The facility's final emergence revealed its deepest level - a central chamber larger than the others. Unlike the testing stations above, this space housed a single massive piece of equipment. Banks of speakers lined the walls in concentric circles, all aimed at a central platform marked with mathematical symbols we'd seen in Wallace's photographs.

Ancient dials and meters across the control panels started turning on their own, their needles swinging in perfect synchronization. Their faces were marked only with numbers and cryptic symbols, but whatever they were measuring made the machinery respond, adjusting its pitch with each new reading.

The sphere that fell from the sky lifted from its resting place, suspended in mid-air. Its pulse synchronized perfectly with the spliced recordings of our boys' voices playing through the static.

Our phones went dead, screens black. The lights on Bill's parked truck flickered and died. A wave of silence swept outward from the sphere, killing every modern electrical device while the facility's ancient machinery grew louder, more powerful.

The facility's waterlogged speakers crackled to life, broadcasting our boys' distorted voices across the drained lake bed. Through their echoing words, a new sound emerged - something rising through those old drainage tunnels. Moving toward that hovering sphere with mechanical precision.

The whole facility trembled. Deep in its lowest level, massive hydraulic systems engaged with the sound of straining metal. Something was climbing up through channels that hadn't seen movement in decades.

Something that had been waiting since 1957 for the right frequency.

Something that had been waiting for our boys.

Metal screamed against concrete as a series of interlocking doors ground open in the main chamber, their rusted hinges protesting decades of disuse. Each door revealed another behind it, creating a series of airlocks descending into darkness. From the tunnel beyond came a viscous sound - not water, but something thicker moving through the old pipes.

The wall of speakers surrounding the central platform hummed in unison, playing fragments of our boys' voices layered over recordings from 1957. Each spliced phrase built a pattern: "the channels are open... cellular reconstruction complete... ready for integration..."

Fifty feet below, something broke the surface of the remaining water. At first it looked like oil - a black, reflective mass that caught the emergency lights. But as it rose, spreading across the platform, I saw it wasn't flowing naturally. It moved with purpose, forming shapes that mimicked human silhouettes before collapsing back into itself.

The hovering sphere pulsed faster, each flash drawing more of that fluid upward. Our boys' voices from the speakers took on a new quality, as if being processed through the liquid itself: "beneath... they're waiting... have to complete..."

Tracy grabbed my arm, pointing to where the fluid met the old machinery. The black substance moved against gravity, flowing upward along metal surfaces in geometric patterns that matched the sphere's pulsing rhythm. The machinery's grinding changed pitch wherever the fluid touched it, as if the two were communicating in frequencies just beyond human hearing.

ᝋᏟᏟᏄ

Chapter 24: Cynthia

A grinding sound echoed from the tunnels - thousands of calcified teeth scraping against concrete, drawing closer with each pulse of the sphere. Through the facility's speakers, our boys' voices fragmented and reformed, but beneath their words came another layer of sound. The screams started as human voices, then twisted into frequencies that made my teeth ache - the exact moment when something changed inside those test subjects, captured forever in rust-covered recordings.

In the chamber's depths, something answered those screams.

The metallic sphere hung suspended above the drained lake bed. Its mercury surface rippled with distortions that twisted the emergency lights into shapes that resembled screaming mouths, writhing limbs - then smoothed away before the mind could fully process what it had seen.

In the facility's depths, movement scraped through darkness. The emergency lights cast shifting shadows across exposed machinery. Each shadow stretched toward the hovering sphere, moving independent of any light source.

A child's shoe bobbed in the remaining water, still weighted with its contents.

The thing in the tunnels moved faster now, drawn by our boys' voices playing through the speakers. Its approach brought wet sliding sounds, punctuated by the scrape of something harder than bone against the concrete walls.

A woman's voice cut through the facility's speakers, the recording degraded by decades of water damage: "No—not the chamber again—they're still—" Static consumed her words before they returned, pitched higher with panic. "—can hear them in there—oh god, they're still—" The rest dissolved into frequencies that made my skin crawl.

The sphere's surface rippled faster as more drainage systems activated. The remaining lake water spiraled down through channels in the concrete, revealing old computer banks that hummed to life, their displays flickering with fragmented data.

Dark liquid dripped from the tunnel openings - not just stagnant water, but something thicker. The fluid carried the sharp chemical smell of old preservatives mixed with rust and decay.

Evidence of the facility's work floated to the surface. A clipboard sealed in a plastic bag. A security badge corroded beyond recognition. A metal canister marked with the letters "MRR" above a strange symbol - three incomplete circles divided by vertical lines, like a frequency wave frozen in metal.

"Midwest Resonance Research," Bill said, his voice tight. "This was one of their sites? They must have used the quarry and lake for testing sound frequencies."

The sphere pulsed, sending waves of energy through the facility's systems. Ancient monitors blinked on, displaying chunks of corrupted text:

"Day 66: Chemical saturation levels stable. Subject tissue shows unprecedented adaptation to submersion. Sonic frequencies activating compounds in preservation matrix."

Through the emergency lights, we could see what those clinical words meant. The thing moving through the tunnels dragged itself forward on limbs preserved by experimental chemicals, its movements suggesting joints that bent in ways human bones never should.

The sphere pulsed faster, sending waves of electricity through decaying wires. Each surge made the preserved specimens twitch in unison, decades-old muscles contracting under chemical-soaked skin. More monitors flickered to life, their screens displaying fragmented data:

"Test Series 42: Chemical bath maintaining cellular cohesion. Electrical conductivity enhanced by sonic frequencies. Motor response recorded across all specimens."

The exposed facility revealed banks of old testing equipment. Each station held glass tanks filled with murky preservation fluid, their contents jerking with each electrical pulse. The sphere's frequency seemed to energize the chemicals themselves, transforming the normally inert solution into a potent conductor.

A mechanical voice cut through the static: "Containment breach imminent. Specimen Six responding to external frequency."

The hydraulic systems groaned beneath us, lifting something massive from the facility's lowest level. Ancient metal screamed as a circular platform rose through layers of corroded infrastructure. It carried what looked like a sealed chamber, its surface marked with military warning symbols and that same three-circle MRR logo.

"The mineral samples you extracted from the new dig site," Tracy said to Bill, "did they look like—" Another surge of electricity cut through the facility before she could finish.

The sphere's liquid surface rippled faster as the chamber rose higher, like it recognized what lay behind those heavy doors. Each pulse sent stronger currents through the preservation tanks, making their contents dance like marionettes on electromagnetic strings.

The chamber's locks disengaged in sequence, each releasing with a crack like a gunshot. Rusted motors strained as the massive door swung open, revealing a maze of preservation tanks and monitoring equipment. At the center, suspended in decades-old chemical solution, hung what remained of Specimen Six.

The preservation chemicals had altered the tissue over years of submersion. Skin had turned translucent, revealing a network of darkened veins beneath. Every inch had been bleached a sickly white by the solution, except where strange compounds had collected and stained.

Decades in the preservation tank had twisted its proportions. Weight and chemical exposure left the joints locked at sharp angles, the body's tissue pulled and stretched like taffy. Where hands should have been, membranous webs spread between dissolved fingers - the result of experimental preservatives eating away at human tissue.

Midwest Resonance's sonic mapping experiments had left their mark on the face. The jaw gaped open, muscles and tendons deteriorated until the bone hung loose in its moorings. A surgical opening in the skull revealed their desperate search to understand why certain subjects resisted their frequencies.

The way our boys could resist.

Dark fluid sloshed in the tank as the sphere's pulses created waves in the preservation chemicals. Old monitors blinked with new data as electrical current surged through ancient wiring. The preserved tissue twitched with each pulse, making it appear as if those clouded eyes had opened.

But what reflected in those dead orbs was very much alive - the sphere's mercury surface, flowing with purpose.

Old monitors around Specimen Six's tank flickered with data as the preservation fluid rippled. Each pulse from the sphere sent electricity arcing between the tanks, the chemical solution conducting current in precise patterns. Decades of waterlogged records played across the screens, documenting what Midwest Resonance had tried to achieve:

"Electrical stimulation amplified by preservation medium. Sonic frequencies creating synchronized responses in test subjects."

The specimen's limbs jerked with mechanical precision as current flowed through the tank. Pure electrical stimulation moving dead tissue, the preservation chemicals acting as a perfect conductor. This wasn't life - just science stripped down to its most grotesque elements.

More monitors activated around us, displaying the progression of their experiments. Each screen showed how they'd refined their process, measuring exactly how flesh and bone responded to their frequencies.

"According to these readings," Tracy's voice barely carried over the humming equipment, "they were studying how different people reacted to specific frequencies. Looking for ones who could resist."

The sphere pulsed stronger, sending fresh waves of electricity through the preservation tanks. Its surface rippled in sync with the current, like it was testing each specimen's response.

Bill pulled us back as another bank of equipment powered up. "The old monitors - they're running comparisons. Testing frequency patterns against preserved tissue samples."

Fragments of recordings mixed with our boys' voices through the speakers, documenting what happened when they found someone whose genetics didn't match their expectations. Someone who could withstand frequencies that liquified normal tissue.

Someone like our children.

The sphere rose higher, its liquid metal skin reflecting emergency lights in complex patterns. Below it, the facility's deepest levels shuddered as more ancient systems activated.

"The tunnels," Bill gestured toward darker openings in the concrete. "They lead back to the quarry. To other testing sites."

A new sound echoed up from below - massive hydraulic doors opening somewhere in the darkness. Metal groaned against decades of rust as something else stirred in the facility's lowest chamber.

Chapter 25: Wes

The first tremor hit with a sound like tearing steel, shaking the entire facility. Decades of rust and water damage had weakened the support beams, and now the whole structure groaned under its own weight.

"The tunnels," Bill shouted over the rising mechanical whine. "They're starting to collapse!"

Another shock wave rippled through the drained lake bed. Support beams buckled as the sphere continued its pulsing rhythm, pulling more power through the facility's ancient systems than they were ever meant to handle.

A spiderweb of cracks spread across the preservation tank. Decades-old chemicals spilled over corroded floor plates. The remains of Specimen Six shifted in its failing containment, tissue responding to one final surge of electricity.

Deep below, something massive gave way.

The floor plates buckled as more support structures failed. Between twisted metal sheets, we could see the tunnel network beginning to cave in on itself.

"We need to move," Bill grabbed Tracy's arm. "The whole system's connected underground - when one section fails, they all go."

The sphere spun faster, its mercury surface churning as it drew more current through overloading circuits. Showers of sparks rained from junction boxes as ancient wiring melted under the strain.

The preservation tank shattered. As chemicals washed away decades of stains, a medical bracelet emerged on Specimen Six's twisted wrist: "SULLIVAN, M." The electrical current made the corrupted flesh spasm one final time before the floor collapsed beneath it.

I stared at the name tag, my mind racing. Sullivan - the same name scattered through Alexandra's research, through Wallace's records. Before I could process the connection, Bill's voice cut through my thoughts.

"Move!" He yanked my arm. "The whole place is going!"

The sphere's pulsing reached a fever pitch as the facility folded in on itself. Not just the structure failing now - the bedrock itself began to crack.

"The quarry tunnels," Tracy shouted over the cacophony. "They run under this whole area!"

Behind us, what remained of M. Sullivan disappeared into the growing chasm as floor plates peeled away. The sphere spun faster, as if it had confirmed something about that name.

Then silence. The sphere went still, its mercury surface frozen like glass. In that moment of quiet, we heard it - the deep crack of rock splitting far below.

"Run!" Bill shoved us toward solid ground. "The whole system's about to—"

The bedrock gave way with a sound like thunder. Decades of quarry tunnels, weakened by water and time, finally surrendered. The facility's remains plunged into darkness as the earth opened beneath it.

Lake water surged back through underground channels, filling the void with devastating speed. The sphere vanished beneath the torrent, taking its secrets - and what remained of M. Sullivan - with it.

In seconds, the lake's surface returned to normal. Calm. Undisturbed. As if nothing had ever existed beneath its dark waters.

Only the scattered papers in our hands proved otherwise.

Bill's weathered hands gripped the salvaged files as we watched the last ripples fade. The documents were our only evidence now - even the medical bracelet had vanished with Specimen Six into the sinkhole.

"The tunnels," Tracy said. "They must run everywhere. Under the whole town."

Under our house. Where the boys had emerged from depths we never knew existed. Where something still waited in the dark.

I met Cynthia's eyes and saw the same understanding. Whatever answers we needed weren't here anymore. They lay beneath our own floorboards, in spaces Midwest Resonance had sealed decades ago.

"We should review these files again," Bill said, pulling out the documents they'd found in the quarry yesterday. He spread them across his truck's hood. "Now that we know about the tunnels, might spot something we missed about the house. About how to find those hidden spaces."

Tracy's flashlight caught something in the old documents - a property map from Midwest Resonance's ownership of the entire block. Red marks indicated testing sites, access points, underground connections.

Our address jumped out immediately, not just circled but bearing a handwritten note: "Subject M. Sullivan - primary residence. Access point to remain sealed after termination of Project Echo."

The drive home stretched past familiar landmarks turned strange by new knowledge. Kelly's Diner, where morning news crews packed their equipment. The old theater's dark windows. St. Michael's, where the streetlight pulsed in that same rhythm as the sphere.

Johnson lay peaceful in the growing darkness - streets quiet, buildings normal. But beneath that calm surface, each structure might hide another piece of Midwest Resonance's legacy. Each foundation could conceal depths we were only beginning to understand.

Our house waited ahead, its windows reflecting moonlight. Like every other Victorian on the quiet street, except now we knew what lay beneath its peaceful facade. Somewhere under our floors, behind the boards that had opened to release our boys, answers waited in darkness.

The front steps creaked - ordinary house sounds that carried new meaning now that we knew what lay hidden below. As our keys scraped in the lock, a low hum vibrated through the floorboards, resonating at a familiar frequency.

"We should check on the boys," Cynthia said, but Bill held up the quarry documents.

"These might show us where to look. How to find the entrance they used."

She nodded, though I could tell she wanted to head straight to her mother's house. But we needed to understand what waited beneath our floors. What our children had already found.

Bill's flashlight beam caught markings we'd overlooked for years. Subtle lines in the baseboards. Tiny arrows scratched into corners - what we'd assumed were old construction marks now revealed their true purpose.

"They left guides," Tracy said, studying the files. "Ways to find the access points." She pointed to diagrams showing how Midwest Resonance had marked their hidden entrances.

Every scratch, every seemingly random mark in our house suddenly became meaningful. A code left by people who needed to remember what lay beneath.

"Here," Bill traced his light across the living room floor. "See how these boards are laid? Not random at all."

The flashlight caught something that silenced us all. A pattern emerged in the floorboards - not age or settling, but deliberate design. Thin grooves that appeared only when light struck at the right angle formed lines converging on a specific spot.

"That has to be it," Cynthia whispered. "Where the boys came up." Her hand found mine as Bill's light followed those subtle marks to their conclusion.

The floor looked ordinary there. Just old wood darkened with age. But now we saw what we'd missed - the careful seams, the nearly invisible hinges.

Bill knelt beside it, running his fingers along those hidden edges. Years of working with his hands had taught him to read buildings like books.

"Clever design," he murmured. "Weight distributed so it wouldn't sound different than the rest of the floor. Someone could walk over this their whole life and never know."

He traced what we'd always thought was decorative woodwork, following the diagram's instructions. At specific pressure points, he pressed. A soft click echoed through the floorboards.

"Weight and counter-weight system," he said, pulling the trim at a precise angle. Ancient gears caught with a sound like grinding teeth. The mechanism moved - the same one our boys had somehow found and used.

A six-foot square section of floor separated along previously invisible seams. The edges lifted as hidden hinges engaged. Bill gripped the exposed edge and pulled. The entire panel swung upward smoothly, balanced by counterweights in the walls.

Our lights caught iron rungs descending into darkness, their surface scarred by time but still solid. Around them, curved stone walls plunged downward. The original well opening, expanded and reinforced with steel. Stale air drifted up carrying the scent of old concrete and lingering chemicals.

On the underside of the panel, carved deep into the wood, three broken circles divided by vertical lines stood out - the same symbol from the Midwest Resonance warning signs. Below it, more recent scratches mimicked its pattern, like someone had traced it with desperate fingers.

The darkness below swallowed our flashlight beams whole.

◯◯◯

Chapter 26: Cynthia

The iron rungs pressed cold against my palms as we descended. The original well's rough-hewn stone walls gave way to sections of smooth steel reinforcement - Midwest Resonance's attempts to stabilize the ancient shaft. The newer metal surfaces gleamed coldly wherever our lights touched them, a stark contrast to the weathered rock between.

Bill's flashlight beam caught markings etched into the steel panels. The official three-circle Midwest Resonance symbol appeared at regular intervals, cut deep and precise. Between them, cruder versions had been carved by less steady hands.

"Listen," Tracy whispered from above me. A low hum vibrated through the metal supports, almost too low to hear.

Wes brought up the rear, keeping one hand on the access panel's edge. None of us mentioned what would happen if it swung shut.

The air grew colder as we descended. Somewhere below, something waited to show us why our boys had emerged changed.

Our lights caught metal rings set into the walls at regular intervals. Dark stains surrounded each one - decades old but still visible. The steel gleamed with a polished sheen in certain spots around the rings.

The ladder ended at a small platform. A heavy metal door hung partially open, its surface marked with warning symbols and that same three-circle design. Through the gap, our lights revealed what looked like an old recording studio.

But recording studios don't have drains in the floor. Or chairs with built-in restraints.

Dust covered everything except a path through the center - footprints. Five sets, moving with unnatural precision.

Reel-to-reel machines lined the walls, their tape spools still threaded. Six chairs formed a circle in the center of the room, their leather straps hanging loose. The straps swayed slightly in air that shouldn't have been moving.

My flashlight caught words scratched into the wall behind one chair: "They make us listen. They make us learn. They make us—" The rest disappeared beneath dark stains.

A low hum started in the walls - not mechanical, but something else. Like the building itself vibrated at a frequency just below hearing.

"There," Bill directed his light toward a control panel showing power. Ancient vacuum tubes glowed behind glass, lights that shouldn't work blinking in strange patterns.

A logbook lay open beside the panel. The last entry, written in shaky handwriting: "Day 66: Subject conditioning complete. Ready for integration." The date read "October 15, 1957." Below it, in darker ink against the faded original text: "They're doing it again."

The hum grew stronger, and somewhere below us, speakers crackled to life. Through the static came fragments of recordings - children's voices from decades ago mixing with something more recent. Our boys, their words distorted and strange.

A doorway led to another set of stairs carved directly into stone. More of those symbols marked each step, growing cruder as they descended. The last few looked like they'd been scratched with desperate speed.

Wires ran through pipes along the walls, all leading down. Modern wires, recently installed. Someone had been updating this place.

At the bottom of the stairs, a massive steel door hung open. Unlike the others, this one had been built to seal hermetically. Warning signs and chemical notices covered its surface. The three-circle symbol had been carved so deep it had nearly pierced the metal.

Fresh scratches led inside.

The beam of my flashlight followed those marks across the floor of the main chamber. The original well shaft opened into a vast circular space, its walls alternating between ancient stone and steel reinforcement.

More metal rings lined the walls, these ones showing recent use. The steel around them gleamed from friction.

In the center of the room stood what looked like medical equipment, arranged in that same circle pattern. Six chairs faced inward, but these weren't designed just for listening. Mechanical arms hung above each one, tipped with instruments that made my stomach turn.

Ancient machines clicked to life around us, their displays powered by some unseen source. Analog gauges sprang to life, their needles jumping to measure frequencies that vibrated through our bones.

Bill's light caught strange patterns in the stone floor. Grooves carved in precise geometric shapes, all centering on that circle of chairs. Not random designs - channels. For directing something.

Dark stains traced their paths.

A scraping sound echoed through the chamber - metal against stone. Something moved in the shadows beyond our light beams, taking its time, the sound bouncing off the walls in ways that made it impossible to track.

The machines' displays spun faster, ancient gears protesting as power surged through the system. The hum built to that same pulse we'd heard at the lake.

In the center of the room, one of the chairs creaked. Not from age - from weight. Our lights swept toward the sound, revealing an empty seat.

The scraping grew closer, more deliberate. The humming peaked at a frequency that set my teeth on edge. A child's laugh echoed through the chamber - not one of our boys. The sound distorted, like a recording played at the wrong speed.

"We need to move," Wes whispered. "Before—"

The scraping stopped. In the silence, we heard something that sounded like breathing - if breathing could echo through rusted pipes.

A high-pitched whine cut through the darkness, like feedback but deeper, wrong. The machines' displays flickered in sequence, creating a strobing effect that made the shadows pulse.

Beyond the circle of chairs, another door waited. It swung open on its own, revealing stairs that descended into perfect darkness. From below came a sound I recognized.

Our boys' voices. But not from today.

Every machine in the room cut out at once. The abrupt silence left us straining to hear what moved in the darkness.

"The boys found this place," Wes said, his voice barely above a whisper. "Came down these same stairs."

My flashlight beam traced more symbols carved into the walls leading down. Crude ones, desperate ones, and beneath them - fresh marks. Five sets of initials.

The stairs descended into darkness that seemed to swallow our light. The three-circle symbol appeared on each step, its design subtly changing as it went down. By the bottom, it had transformed into something else entirely.

Vapor clouded in front of Bill as he exhaled. "Temperature's dropping fast." Each step brought us into colder air. The chill radiated up from whatever waited at the bottom.

Our boys' voices echoed up the stairwell. The words were familiar but the cadence was off - like something learning speech by studying their patterns.

The beam of my flashlight caught the final step.

Beyond it, we'd find exactly what our children had discovered.

Chapter 27: The Boys

It started with a vibration. Not audible exactly, but something they felt in their teeth, in their bones. Xander noticed it first, a sensation that made his fillings ache. Then Brayden, usually absorbed in his game, looked up with a frown. Tyler and Casey exchanged glances, both registering something in the air. Ben kept adjusting his headphones, unable to find a comfortable position.

Through Lana's kitchen window, early morning sun cast long shadows across her well-kept yard. The day looked perfectly normal. But that sensation...

"You guys feel that?" Xander whispered, not wanting to draw their grandmother's attention from her baking. "Like when Dad's recording equipment gets feedback?"

Casey nodded, one hand unconsciously rubbing his ear. "Or like that time they were doing construction near school. But deeper."

"We should check it out," Tyler said, already moving toward the back door. The others hesitated, but that strange vibration pulled at them. Like a forgotten melody playing just at the edge of hearing.

Even Brayden, usually the voice of caution, felt it. The sensation triggered something - not quite memories, but awareness of things they should have noticed before. Patterns in the neighborhood. Marks they'd passed every day without seeing.

Sunlight fell too sharp across the backyard as they crossed it, casting shadows that seemed to pulse with that subsonic vibration. They moved past the fence and down familiar streets that now seemed to hold secrets in every shadow. With each step, that strange sensation grew stronger.

Time blurred as they walked. Streets they'd known their whole lives took on new meaning as they noticed things they'd overlooked before - subtle marks in the concrete, patterns in how houses were positioned.

Their house appeared ahead, but something about it had changed. The walls caught sunlight at odd angles. Windows reflected light in ways that made Ben think of their dad's acoustical diagrams.

"Hey," Casey tugged at Ben's sleeve, "it's like that day in Dad's studio. When the numbers on his machine kept going crazy?"

None of them had mentioned that day before. The strange readings, the way their parents' equipment had malfunctioned. But now those memories surfaced, connecting to this moment.

They moved together with the synchronization that came from years of shared life. But this felt different - more precise, as if something was orchestrating their steps to a rhythm they didn't understand.

The front door opened at Tyler's touch - they'd forgotten it should be locked. Inside, static electricity made their hair stand on end. The vibration had become almost visible, like heat waves rising from hot pavement.

In the living room, a reflection caught Xander's eye. It highlighted seams in the floorboards they'd never noticed. The lines curved and peaked like the sound waves on their dad's studio monitors.

And in the center, barely visible unless you knew to look: three crude circles scratched into the wood.

The floorboards shifted beneath their feet, the movement so subtle they might have imagined it. A section of boards lifted slightly, revealing darkness below. Metal rungs gleamed in the gap - an old ladder descending into shadow.

Ben pulled out his phone's flashlight. The beam caught markings on the walls of the shaft - at the top, precise technical diagrams and a logo: three concentric circles intersected by a vertical line. "Those look like Dad's frequency charts," Xander said, studying the diagrams. "But older."

As they climbed down, the markings changed. The clean circles of the logo grew shakier, interrupted by hasty additions. The careful measurements and diagrams gave way to cruder etchings.

"Watch your step," Ben called up, his light revealing another set of symbols. These circles had been carved deeper, more frantically. The shapes began to warp, clean curves becoming angular.

Halfway down, the transformation became obvious. The once-perfect circles now spiraled inward at odd angles. The vertical line multiplied into a web of intersecting marks that made their eyes strain.

"Look," Casey pointed to a particularly distorted set. The circles had been carved so deep and desperately that they'd evolved into something else. The angular distortions formed three crude numbers.

Three sixes.

The further down they went, the more the sixes repeated. Row after row etched into every surface, some carved with scientific precision, others scratched with what looked like fingernails.

The vibration intensified until their vision blurred. Something stirred in the darkness below.

Metal groaned. The walls pulsed. And five brothers, moving as one, descended toward answers their parents had searched for.

The first chamber opened before them - like a recording studio from an old horror movie. Chairs bolted to the floor formed a circle, restraints hanging open. Reel-to-reel machines lined the walls, tape still threaded through their spools.

"Recording room," Ben said, though none of them knew how they knew its name. The vibration shifted, layering new frequencies over the old.

Their lights caught more transforming symbols. The company's clean circles stretched and warped, becoming more obsessive until they resolved into those same crude sixes scratched into concrete.

Tyler pointed to another stairwell carved into stone. The vibration pulled them forward, their steps matching perfectly without trying.

The second level held medical equipment. More chairs arranged in circles, but these bristled with metal arms and instruments.

"For testing frequencies," Xander said distantly, the knowledge flowing into his mind from somewhere else. "Finding who could handle them."

Brayden traced grooves worn into one chair's metal arm, marks left by desperate grips.

"Down there," Casey said. The air rippled visibly now. At the far end, another stairwell plunged into absolute darkness.

The final chamber stretched so high their lights couldn't find the ceiling. Strange equipment filled the space, surfaces that ate light instead of reflecting it. And in the center...

At the center of the chamber, reality seemed to fold in on itself. The boys' minds struggled to process what they saw - frequencies made visible, wavelengths that bent light into colors they'd never seen before.

As they approached in perfect unison, the vibration peaked. Their vision fractured into pieces, each fragment showing them things about sound and reality their father had spent years trying to understand. The spaces between wavelengths. What lived in those gaps.

Time lost meaning as they stood in formation. The frequencies worked through them, teaching them things no one was meant to know. Their minds filled with knowledge of resonance and transformation.

When awareness returned, they found themselves climbing back up through the levels. Past the medical equipment, past the recording studio, up the ancient ladder toward sunlight.

The floorboards shifted as they reached the top, opening to release them into their living room. They emerged to find their parents staring, faces frozen in shock.

Behind them, the floor sealed itself shut. But the vibration stayed with them, humming in their bones. Teaching them. Changing them.

Through the windows, they saw Amber recording everything on her phone. They could feel her broadcast spreading the frequencies outward, reaching further than anyone had imagined possible.

Soon everyone would hear what lived between sound waves. Soon everyone would understand what waited in those spaces they'd found.

The transformation was complete. The next phase could begin.

Chapter 28: Wes

Footsteps echoed down the stairwell behind us. Hayes must have followed us from the station after what happened to Wallace. Before any of us could warn him, his flashlight beam cut through the darkness, catching the edge of that final step.

The frequency shifted. Hayes stumbled mid-stride, his body seizing as if struck by an invisible force. His flashlight clattered down the stairs, the beam spinning wild arcs across the walls. He reached for the railing, fingers grasping at air as the vibration took hold. His body twisted sideways, suspended for a heartbeat before gravity claimed him.

His spine cracked - a wet snap that echoed off concrete walls. Blood sprayed across the aged equipment as his body collapsed at angles no living person could survive. Through the red mist, his face froze in an expression of shock, mouth still moving as if trying to form a warning.

"Stay back!" I grabbed Cynthia's arm as she moved to help him. His body convulsed, limbs twitching to a rhythm that had nothing to do with death spasms. The frequencies continued working through him, rearranging tissue and bone into spiraling shapes.

Bill pulled Tracy back from the edge as more metal supports groaned overhead. "This whole place could collapse."

Through Hayes' final breaths, we heard something waking in the levels below - the grinding of gears long dormant. Beneath that sound came another I recognized: voices preserved on magnetic tape, distorted by corrupted frequencies.

Hayes' body gave one last spasm, twisting until his features aligned into cruel angles that echoed those carved symbols on the walls.

"Jesus Christ," Bill's voice cracked as he stepped back, pulling Tracy with him. "He was just a kid. Wasn't even thirty."

I fought down bile as Hayes went still. Just yesterday he'd been helping us with the case files, eager to prove himself. Now...

"We can't leave him like this," Cynthia said softly. But we all knew there was nothing we could do for him. Nothing anyone could do.

The stairwell descended deeper, our flashlight beams catching more of those carved symbols - from precise corporate logos to desperate warnings. The boys had followed these same marks days ago, before the fever, before everything changed. Each level's carvings grew more frantic, circles collapsing into sixes, leading us toward answers about what had transformed our children.

The stairs spiraled down, each turn revealing more desperate carvings. Near the bottom, the symbols barely resembled circles - just crude sixes scratched into concrete with fingernails.

A low frequency pulsed through the walls, bringing back memories of Hayes' final moments. Every few steps, the vibration intensified.

"There," Bill's voice echoed in the narrow stairwell. He stopped abruptly as our lights caught something ahead.

A massive steel door hung open, warning signs and that three-circle symbol carved deep into its surface. Beyond it lay what the boys had discovered.

The chamber stretched impossibly high, filled with recording equipment similar to what I used in my studio, but heavily modified. Banks of reel-to-reel machines and measurement tools had been transformed into configurations that served no audio purpose I recognized.

Static crackled, and fresh blood trickled from my nose. Next to me, Cynthia gripped my arm tighter as waves of energy pulsed through the air - like walking through invisible membranes.

"Look at the floor," Bill directed his light downward. Precise geometric grooves had been cut into the concrete, all leading to a central point where...

"Oh God," Cynthia's grip tightened on my arm. "The symbols."

The floor's center held what looked like hundreds of those circles carved one over another. As they spiraled inward, they transformed. Became more angular. More desperate. Until at the very center, a single set of numbers had been carved so deep they'd cracked the concrete:

666

In any other context, the number would have meant nothing to us - Cynthia and I had never put stock in biblical prophecies or religious symbolism. But after everything we'd seen, after what happened to Wallace and Hayes, after watching our boys transform... those three digits carried a weight that had nothing to do with faith.

Around that point, five chairs formed a perfect circle. Empty now, but showing signs of recent use.

A sharp electronic whine cut through the static. Every piece of equipment in the chamber powered up at once - lights blinking, meters swinging, reels turning. The frequency built until my vision blurred.

"The boys sat here," Tracy's voice sounded distant through the rising static. "They found what Midwest Resonance was searching for. What Wallace died trying to contain."

Blood ran freely from all our noses as that impossible pitch peaked. Through my distorted vision, I saw something take shape in the chamber's center. Right where those numbers had been carved.

Right where our boys had sat.

First one form, then another, until seven figures emerged from the air itself.

Their outlines wavered like heat mirages, joints bending backward, limbs stretching too long and fluid. As they solidified, I saw faces I recognized from missing persons reports - the quarry workers. But their features looked distorted, stretched across bones that didn't quite match human proportions, like masks worn by something that had never understood human anatomy.

The nearest figure's head rotated completely around, bone crackling like radio static. Its mouth gaped open, revealing not teeth but tiny speakers embedded in flesh. Our boys' voices played through the corrupted vocal cords: "Dad? Did you figure it out yet?"

The others began to move, bodies flowing like mercury. Each wore a different face - people I'd covered in podcasts, cases stretching back decades. Through the blood clouding my vision, I watched their fingers fuse into tuning forks that vibrated with frequencies that made the air ripple.

The thing wearing a quarry worker's face spoke again in older voices preserved on magnetic tape: "Subject shows remarkable adaptation to sonic stimulation. Cellular reconstruction proceeding as expected. Project Echo entering final phase."

Through the static, a phone began to ring. Not our dead phones - this came from somewhere deeper in the chamber. An old rotary phone, its ring echoing off concrete walls. Three rings, then silence.

The figures flowed backward into darkness as the ringing faded. But before they vanished completely, I saw their faces change one final time.

Five wore our boys' features - perfect replicas frozen in expressions of calm expectation. The other two... their faces belonged to children I recognized from the Vernon case files.

The first children who had heard these frequencies.

∮∮∮

Chapter 29: Cynthia

Lana's guest room felt strange after everything we'd seen. Through the window, the last of the news vans finally pulled away, their satellite dishes no longer aimed at our house eight blocks over.

Wes shifted behind me, pulling me closer. This was still our safe place - wrapped in each other's arms, his steady breathing against my neck. In moments like this, we could almost forget what we'd discovered.

"Can't sleep?" he whispered, his hand finding mine in the darkness.

"Just thinking about the boys." Down the hall, I could hear them settling in for the night. The creak of Ben's headphones as he finally took them off. Xander and Brayden's whispered argument about Fortnite. Tyler and Casey bickering about whether a T-Rex could beat a shark.

Familiar sounds that meant everything after what we'd seen beneath our house.

"They seem okay," Wes said softly. "Whatever happened down there..." He trailed off, his arm tightening around me.

Mom moved around downstairs, the gentle clinking of dishes and soft hum of late-night TV drifting up. She'd outdone herself at dinner, pulling out all the boys' favorites. For a few hours, we'd managed to act like this was just another family meal. Like we hadn't spent the afternoon watching those things in the basement twist themselves into impossible shapes.

"Dad and Tracy are coming early tomorrow," I said, grateful for Wes's warmth against my back. "Dad wants to check something else at the quarry site. Says the collapse might have exposed more of the old tunnels."

"We'll figure this out," he murmured into my hair. "Together. Like always."

I turned to face him in the darkness. Even after all these years, after all the cases we'd covered on the podcast, after everything we'd seen today, this was still my safe harbor - wrapped in his arms, our own private universe.

His lips found mine, gentle at first, then hungry with need. His hands traced familiar paths along my skin as I pressed closer, desperate to feel something real, something human after what we'd witnessed. The weight of him above me anchored me to this moment, to us, away from the frequencies that threatened to consume everything.

I traced my fingers down his chest as his mouth found that sensitive spot below my ear. Each caress built the tension between us, slow and deliberate, making me ache for more. His hands explored familiar territory with new urgency, drawing soft gasps as they discovered particularly sensitive areas.

We moved together with practiced grace, his hand sliding up my thigh as I arched against him. Each touch burned away the horrors we'd witnessed, replaced by electric need. His teeth grazed my neck, making me gasp. My nails raked down his back as he pushed deeper, claiming me completely.

The tension coiled tighter as we lost ourselves in sensation. His fingers circled and teased until I had to bite my lip to stay quiet. When I couldn't take anymore, I guided him where I needed him most. He entered slowly, deliberately, making me feel every inch until I thought I might break from the pleasure.

We spoke without words - just desperate sighs and passionate moans muffled against heated skin. Conscious of the boys down the hall, he covered my mouth with his hand as waves of pleasure threatened to tear sounds from my throat. Our bodies moved in perfect rhythm, building toward a release that would temporarily make us forget everything else.

Time blurred as we lost ourselves in each other, finding comfort in this dance we knew so well. For these precious moments, nothing existed beyond his touch, his warmth, our shared breath. No ancient experiments, no impossible frequencies, no twisted shapes - just us, moving as one in the darkness.

Later, wrapped in tangled sheets and each other's arms, reality began to creep back in. Tomorrow we'd have to face whatever Bill had found in those exposed tunnels. Have to understand why our boys could resist frequencies that had twisted others into such horrific forms.

But for now, in this quiet moment, we had each other.

Morning came too soon, bringing with it the smell of Mom's coffee and the sound of five boys trying to be quiet and failing spectacularly. As I descended the stairs, Dad's truck pulled into the driveway. Through the window, I could see Tracy examining something in their truck bed - what looked like old measurement equipment.

The boys thundered into the kitchen, temporarily drowning out any possibility of conversation. Mom handled the chaos with practiced ease, directing traffic between the cereal boxes and orange juice.

"Grandma, can we go fishing at Papaw's pond later?" Casey asked through a mouthful of Cheerios.

"Not today, honey," Mom answered before I could. Her eyes met mine briefly - we both knew what lurked in those dark waters now. "Maybe once your parents finish their work."

Wes appeared in the doorway, circles under his eyes matching mine. Neither of us had really slept after... after everything. He grabbed the coffee Mom offered, even though he never drank the stuff.

"Found some tunnel openings exposed by the collapse," Dad said quietly, spreading a worn map across Mom's kitchen table. "Not on any of Midwest Resonance's plans. They run under the old section of town."

Our boys turned as one toward the sound of his voice.

"Please," Casey spoke up suddenly, his voice carrying that strange distance we'd heard in the facility. "Can we go see the lake?"

The other boys turned in unison, their eyes fixed on me with an intensity that made my skin crawl.

"Not today, honey," Mom kept her tone light, though her hands tightened on her coffee cup. "Besides, the roads out there are probably blocked with all those news crews."

"We know another way," Ben said, but the voice wasn't quite his. All five of them stood together, a synchronized movement that looked too precise, too practiced.

Wes's hand found mine under the table as Dad cleared his throat. "About those tunnel openings..." He tapped a spot on the map. "They connect to something under where Maple Street used to be."

The boys sat back down - all at once, like puppets with their strings cut.

"Last night," Tracy said, her practical nature fighting against what she was about to say, "your father noticed something at the quarry right after that lake incident. The equipment's registering frequencies we've never seen before."

Through the kitchen window, dawn painted the sky in shades of orange. A cardinal landed on Mom's bird feeder, then immediately took flight. Like it sensed something amiss.

I watched five spoons stir five bowls of cereal in perfect circles. My boys' faces looked normal enough - but their movements, their voices, their too-perfect synchronization...

Something had changed them in those depths. Something was still changing them.

"They can sense it," Tracy said quietly, watching the boys. "Just like the animals. But instead of running from it..."

"Tracy," Dad's tone carried a warning, but she continued.

"Instead of running, they're being drawn to it. Like it's calling them back."

Mom busied herself cleaning up breakfast dishes, but her movements were too quick, too forceful. She'd raised Audrey and me through every stage and drama. And now, watching her grandsons, I recognized that same worry in her eyes.

The TV droned in the background, reporters speculating about sinkholes and underwater caves. None of them knew what lurked beneath that dark water.

"Should we call Audrey and Pete?" Mom asked quietly, her eyes following the boys' synchronized movements.

"No," Wes said quickly. "They have enough going on with the new baby, plus all their other kids. Best to keep them out of this for now." He trailed off, watching our boys move in perfect unison.

"Mom?" Tyler's voice cut through the kitchen. All five boys stood at the doorway, moving with that unsettling synchronization. "When are we going home?"

But the way they said "home" - it didn't sound like they meant our house.

The TV signal cut to static. Through the white noise, children began to count. Mom lunged for the remote, clicking it off before the boys could move closer. But they all turned their heads toward the blank screen, like they could still see something we couldn't.

"Upstairs, all of you," Wes said firmly. "Go finish getting ready for school."

"Baby," Wes's voice carried an edge I rarely heard once the boys were out of earshot. "The map. Look at the pattern of dates."

Dad had marked each tunnel's discovery. They created a sequence spreading outward from the center of old Maple Street. Each discovery corresponded to a disappearance. To a change in street names. To moments when something had stirred beneath the town.

666

Chapter 30: Wes

The map Bill showed us at breakfast revealed tunnel openings spreading out from Maple Street like spokes on a wheel. One line led directly to St. Michael's.

Bill knew the maintenance supervisor from his contracting work - a quick call about checking the foundation after the recent seismic activity from the lake got us access. The supervisor handed over the keys without question. Bill's reputation for fixing things no one else could manage had its benefits.

As we explored the old undercroft, Bill aimed his headlamp at a section of wall where the map indicated the tunnel should be. "According to these measurements, it opens about forty feet down," he said, running his hand along the stonework. "We'll need to move some of these old shelves to access it."

The space held an unnatural chill, the air dense with more than just dust and age. Though the church stood nearly a mile from our house, the walls bore the same degrading symbols we'd seen in the facility. Those perfect circles warping into desperate sixes.

"I doubt the priests know about this," Bill said, testing the stability of what looked like a false wall panel.

"Probably for the best," I said, eyeing the crude numbers scratched into the stone. "They'd have every exorcist in the diocese down here by sunset. Though at this point, I'm not sure they'd be wrong."

I checked my phone one last time - still no signal, but the screen kept trying to display impossible times. Cynthia had stayed at Mom's with the boys, keeping them distracted with homework while we investigated. After what happened with the TV this morning, we didn't want them anywhere near these frequencies.

"You sure about this?" Tracy asked, her usual practical nature wavering as she stared into the opening. "After what happened at the lake..."

The metal rungs felt cold even through my gloves. Each step down revealed more of those degrading circles, their transformation into sixes more violent here. Like whoever carved them was racing against time, each mark cut deeper than the last.

Above us, St. Michael's bells began to toll, the sound distorting as it reached us through layers of earth and concrete. The vibrations made the ancient ladder shudder against the stone wall.

A deep mechanical groan echoed up the shaft - not from the bells above, but something else running somewhere below us.

"That's impossible," Tracy whispered. "These tunnels were sealed ages ago. Nothing down here should be running."

The doorway ahead looked different from others we'd seen - carved directly into the bedrock, its edges too precise to be natural. No metal frame, no institutional markings. This was older than Midwest Resonance. Older than the church itself.

"Hold up," Bill's voice echoed in the narrow space. "Look at the floor."

My light revealed gouges in the stone - not the usual symbols or numbers, but what looked like slide marks. Something heavy had been dragged through here.

A drop of liquid hit my shoulder. Not water. It carried a sharp chemical smell, like industrial preservative. The same fluid we'd found at the lake facility.

Through the doorway, my flashlight beam caught something that made my throat tighten. Rows of stone benches arranged like church pews, but the rock was scored with deep grooves. Fingernail marks stretched across the surface, as if people had tried to hold on while being pulled away.

In the center, where an altar should be, stood equipment that merged industrial machinery with medieval design. Tubes and wires snaked from its metal frame into the floor, all crusted with decades of dried chemicals. Leather straps hung from its arms, sized for children.

"Christ," Bill breathed, his light revealing what lined the walls. Clear tanks, like the ones we'd seen at the lake, but these still hummed with power. Still held occupants.

Small shapes floated in murky preservation fluid, their features warped by long submersion. Child-sized forms arranged in poses of prayer, hands clasped, mouths frozen open. Some still wore fragments of church clothes - Sunday best preserved in formaldehyde.

The mechanical groaning grew louder as we entered. Ancient pumps cycled chemicals through tubes connected to each tank, making the children's hair drift like seaweed. My light caught other details - notebooks filled with equations written in red ink, crosses modified into transmitters, hymn books where traditional musical notes had been replaced with complex mathematical sequences.

A deep vibration shuddered through the chamber. The old pumps stuttered, creating pressure changes in the tanks. The preserved forms shifted in their fluid. But something else caught my eye - fresh marks on the tank glass. Someone had been checking these specimens. Recently.

Looking at the equipment setup, I recognized something from my years of studio work. The chamber's curved walls, the strategic placement of the metal pipes - it was all designed for acoustic amplification. "They're using the church bells as resonators," I said, tracing the path of the sound waves with my light. "When the bells ring, the vibrations travel down through the stone. The chamber's shape focuses it all right here." After all the time I'd spent positioning microphones and dampening echo in the studio, I could read the acoustical engineering that went into this space.

Through gaps in the machinery, I saw formulas carved into the walls - different from the ones above. These weren't just degrading circles.

They were mathematical equations woven through musical staff lines, combining frequency measurements with notations I'd never seen before. My years playing in bands before settling into audio production had taught me to read music, but these symbols violated every rule of musical composition I knew.

"They disguised it as religious ceremony," Tracy whispered. Her voice shook, but her analytical mind kept working. "The parents would have trusted the church. Brought their children willingly."

The preservation tank nearest me held a small figure in what remained of a white dress. First communion, maybe. Her hands were positioned in prayer, but looking closer, I saw the posture wasn't voluntary. Thin wires ran through her joints, holding her in place.

A fresh droplet of preservation fluid hit the floor near my feet. Not from the old tanks - their seals remained intact despite decades of neglect. This came from somewhere above.

"There's another level," I said, following the drip with my light. A newer pipe ran along the ceiling, disappearing into the rock wall. "These tanks, this equipment - it's old. But someone's been maintaining it. Adding to it."

"The Church renovation project last spring," Bill traced fresh tool marks on the stone. "They wouldn't let local contractors anywhere near this section."

My light caught something else - a parish newsletter, recent enough that the paper was still crisp despite the damp air. The headline announced a new youth ministry program. But the registration form buried in the back made my skin crawl. Between allergies and emergency contacts, there was a medical waiver about "acoustic sensitivity screening" and "bell tower acccss."

I pulled the form closer. The medical requirements were layered under innocent-sounding choir participation clauses. Someone had carefully crafted this document to hide its true purpose.

A deep vibration shuddered through the chamber. Above us, the church bells started their morning sequence. Down here, the sound transformed. The tanks resonated with each toll, preservation fluid rippling in unnatural geometric patterns.

"The Vernons," Tracy said suddenly, studying the old equipment. "Their kids were in the church choir. Right before they disappeared."

My phone buzzed - the first signal we'd had since entering these tunnels. A text from Cynthia: "The boys are asking about choir practice. They've never been interested in singing before."

Another chemical drip hit my shoulder as I typed a response to Cynthia. Following the newer piping with my light, I could now see it branched in multiple directions, all leading beyond the church walls.

My phone buzzed again, displaying a series of photographs. Children in choir robes. Teachers in habits. But something about the shadows in each image caught my attention - the way they stretched toward the children, reaching.

"How are you getting signal down here?" Bill moved closer, examining my phone.

"They're not old photos," Tracy said, peering at the screen. "Look at the date stamps."

She was right. Each image showed today's date. These weren't historical records - they were being taken right now.

More photos loaded, showing different churches across town. In every shot, children stood arranged in circles, faces blank, posed exactly like the preserved specimens floating in the tanks around us.

"They never stopped," Bill's voice shook. "They just got better at hiding it."

I scrolled through image after image, my hands trembling. Each church showed the same pattern - children positioned in circles, shadow figures reaching. The timestamp on every photo: current moment.

Then my phone displayed something that made my blood run cold - an image from inside Lana's house. Five boys stood in formation around the TV, which reflected shapes that had no source in the room.

Our boys.

I was already running for the exit when my phone rang - just sixes for the number.

"Don't answer it," Bill warned, but my finger was already moving toward the screen. Before I could touch it, the call connected on its own.

Through the static, a child's voice: "Daddy? We learned a new song at Grandma's today. Want to hear?"

Not one of my boys. The voice sounded older, preserved somehow. Like something was reaching through decades of magnetic tape.

"The song is about circles," the voice continued. "Would you like me to sing it?"

I tried to end the call, but the screen wouldn't respond. Behind me, the preservation tanks pulsed in rhythm with each word.

"The nuns taught it to us," the voice said. "Before they took us to the special choir room. The one under the chapel."

A new image appeared on my phone - this one from somewhere deep beneath the church. A circle of robed figures stood around an altar that merged technology with sacred geometry. Their faces hidden by shadows that moved independent of any light source.

And above them, carved into the stone ceiling, that three-circle symbol.

The phone went dead in my hands.

Chapter 31: Cynthia

The boys had been quiet since Wes left with Dad and Tracy. Too quiet. From Mom's kitchen, I watched them sit in the living room, supposedly doing homework but all staring at nothing in particular, moving with that unsettling synchronization.

"They've barely touched their lunch," Mom said softly, clearing plates still full of untouched sandwiches. Her hands trembled slightly as she loaded the dishwasher. "And did you notice? They all stopped eating at exactly the same moment."

Through the window, I could see more news vans gathering near the park two blocks over. Not here for us anymore - apparently there had been some kind of incident at First Baptist. Something about their new sound system interfering with the neighborhood's electronics.

My phone buzzed - a text from an unknown number: "Check the church's website. Youth ministry page. Before they take it down."

I was about to delete it as spam when another message appeared: "Your boys aren't the only ones. And the churches are connected. All of them."

I opened my laptop, hesitating before typing in First Baptist's web address. After what happened with the TV this morning, any screen felt dangerous. But we needed to understand what was happening.

The youth ministry page looked normal enough at first - announcements about choir practice, youth groups, summer programs. But as I studied the website's layout, I spotted it. There in the header design -

the same three-circle logo from those facility blueprints, hidden in plain sight.

Scrolling deeper, connections emerged. Every church program linked back to something called "The Johnson Interfaith Youth Initiative." Their about page claimed they'd been coordinating youth activities across denominations since 1957.

The same year Midwest Resonance flooded their facility.

"Please," Casey spoke up suddenly, his voice carrying that hollow distance from the basement. "Can we go see the church?"

The other boys turned as one, their eyes fixed on me with an intensity that made my skin crawl.

"Not today, honey," Mom kept her voice light though her hands gripped her coffee cup tighter. "Besides, the roads are blocked with all those news crews."

"We know another way," Ben said, but the voice wasn't his. All five stood together, movements synchronized with mechanical precision.

My phone buzzed. An automated notification: "Network Error: Backup files corrupted. Location: FB_Server1. Time remaining: 66 minutes."

Below it, maintenance logs showed someone had been accessing First Baptist's systems all morning, trying to fix "audio interference issues."

I clicked through more system notifications, each seemingly random but forming a pattern. Server logs, maintenance records, equipment replacements - all documenting "audio anomalies" dating back to when Midwest Resonance disappeared.

A system alert popped up: "Critical backup failure. Sound system configuration files exposed."

File paths began appearing faster than I could read them. One caught my eye - a folder labeled "Frequency_Calibration_1957." The timestamp showed it had just been accessed, permissions changed to public.

The boys sat motionless in the living room, still moving in that synchronized way, but at least they seemed calmer. Whatever had affected them at the house hadn't taken complete control. They were still our children, just... altered somehow.

My laptop screen flickered, displaying a command prompt I hadn't opened: accessing historical records decryption in progress warning: file corruption detected source: MIDWEST_RESONANCE_ARCHIVE

Mom leaned over my shoulder, watching the text scroll. "Should we call Wes?"

Before I could answer, another notification appeared: FIND THE MAINTENANCE LOGS

A new file opened: SYSTEM_SOUND_INTEGRATION.pdf Last modified: July 15, 1957 Description: Frequency harmonization across connected facilities

The document showed a network diagram - every church in Johnson connected by something more complex than simple audio equipment. Points on the map formed the same pattern we'd seen carved into the facility's floors.

My phone vibrated - a text from Wes: "Found something at the church. Heading back now. Don't let the boys near any screens."

Another file appeared: MAINTENANCE_LOG_1957.pdf Access: Restricted Status: Decrypting...

Someone in the church's system wasn't exposing random files. They were showing us something specific.

The diagrams displayed sound wave patterns traveling through underground tunnels, connecting every church in Johnson. Each passage calibrated to specific frequencies. The Initiative's financial records told the real story behind their youth programs - millions spent on "acoustic enhancement" and "sound system upgrades."

A new alert flashed: "Access breach detected. Security countermeasures initiating."

The screen filled with lines of rapidly deleting data. Someone was trying to erase everything we'd found. But before the last files vanished, I caught a name in an employee directory: Technical Systems Director: M. Sullivan Jr.

My hands froze over the keyboard. Sullivan. The name that kept appearing in our investigation, the family that had started this in 1957.

"Mom?" Ben called from upstairs. "Someone's at the door."

Through the front window, I saw a van marked "Cornerstone Communications" pulling into the driveway. Its side panel bore that same three-circle logo.

They'd found us.

"Keep the boys upstairs," I whispered to Mom. She understood immediately, years of handling crisis situations with Audrey and me kicking in. "Away from windows."

Through the window, two figures emerged from the van wearing Cornerstone uniforms, carrying signal testing equipment. Their movements looked too coordinated, like they were synced to the same frequency we'd seen affect our boys.

My phone buzzed: "Authentication override initiated. Exterior camera feeds compromised."

The laptop screen flickered, showing security feeds from different churches. Each camera clicked off one by one, like someone was systematically blinding the system.

A knock at the door. "Mrs. Lumin?" A woman's voice called through. "We're here about the signal interference in your area. Just need to run some standard tests."

My phone lit up with a message: "Don't let them in. They're not here to fix anything."

Above me, I heard Mom gathering the boys in the back bedroom. But every electronic device in the house had started to hum, building toward that frequency I recognized.

The same one we'd heard before Amber...

"Mrs. Lumin?" The voice called again. "We're responding to reports of signal interference in the neighborhood. Just a routine check."

My breath caught - I hadn't mentioned the Initiative to anyone. But her next words confirmed my fears.

"The Initiative sent us. They're very concerned about the interference affecting the children."

Through the window, I watched them arrange their equipment on the lawn. The woman spoke into a radio, her movements too precise, while her partner adjusted dials on what looked like a frequency meter. Its display pulsed with an unnatural blue glow.

More vans arrived. White. Unmarked. The kind with reinforced sides and no windows.

"Please," the woman's voice had dropped its professional facade. "Don't make us come in."

The frequency peaked, and upstairs, one of my boys began to scream.

I took the stairs two at a time, heart pounding. Behind me, the front door's lock clicked open on its own.

The upstairs hallway stretched before me, darker than it should be despite the afternoon sun. At the end, Mom stood in the doorway of her guest room, face drained of color.

"The boys," she whispered. "They just... started moving. All at once. Like they were being pulled."

Inside the room, all five stood facing the window. Perfectly still. Perfectly aligned. The screaming had stopped, but the silence felt worse.

"We heard you had some interference issues." The woman's voice carried up the stairs, closer now. Inside. "We're here to help calibrate the frequencies. Make the transition easier."

That high-pitched whine built in every device until my vision blurred. Blood trickled from my nose as pressure built in my skull.

"Mom?" Ben's voice had changed, deeper and older than any child's should be. All five boys turned in unison, their movements liquid smooth. "The Initiative says it's time."

Heavy footsteps started up the stairs. Then a thud. Something hitting the floor hard. The woman's scream shattered her professional demeanor, pure terror replacing the calm facade.

"Get back," Mom pulled me into the room, slamming the door. "Now!"

Through the wood came more impacts. Wet sounds. Like something being torn apart. The screaming cut off in a gurgle.

The boys hadn't moved. They watched us with empty expressions as the frequency built in every device.

"The transition requires sacrifice," they spoke in perfect unison. Not their voices anymore. Something older. Something that had waited decades to speak again.

The noises downstairs stopped. Footsteps on the stairs, different now. Dragging. Wet. Something was leaving trails on Mom's clean carpet.

My phone lit up one final time: "They're coming."

The doorknob began to turn.

Chapter 32: Wes

Bill's truck rattled over back roads as we raced toward Lana"s house, the tires kicking up gravel with each turn. Through the windshield, I could see more of those white vans converging on her neighborhood from different directions.

"The maintenance logs," Tracy said from the middle seat, studying her phone. "They don't just show equipment repairs. They're tracking frequency exposure. Rating how different children respond."

My own phone stayed dark - no signal since that last message from Cynthia. Just that notification about system breaches and corrupted files. Someone was in their network, but I couldn't tell if they were trying to help us or hunt us.

We rounded the final corner onto her street. What I saw made my stomach drop.

Three white vans blocked her driveway, their sides marked with that three-circle logo. But something was wrong with them. Dark liquid pooled beneath their wheels, running in rivulets toward the storm drain.

And the drivers' side door of the nearest van hung open, its interior splashed with red.

Bill stopped the truck in the middle of the street, engine still running. No movement from the house. No sound except the idling engine.

"Jesus," Tracy breathed, leaning forward between the seats. "Is that..."

A body lay half out of the nearest white van, twisted at an impossible angle. The uniform bore that same three-circle logo, the fabric torn and soaked dark with blood.

I was already moving, my hand on the door handle, when Tracy grabbed my arm. "Wait. Look at the windows."

Lana's house stood dark despite the afternoon sun, each window reflecting strangely. And behind the glass, shapes moved in formations that defied natural movement.

A gurgling sound drew our attention back to the van. The body was... changing. Vibrating at frequencies that made the air ripple. And as we watched, its fingers began to fuse together, forming what looked like tuning forks.

"Those aren't just service vans," Bill said, his voice tight. "Look at the equipment they're carrying."

Through the open door, past the transforming corpse, I could see racks of machinery. Not repair tools. The same kind of frequency measuring devices we'd found in the church basement.

Through the static of Bill's truck radio, we could hear voices - children's voices - starting to count in that familiar pattern.

Like the one we'd heard before Amber died.

"Hold up," Bill's knuckles went white on the steering wheel, eyes fixed on the house. "Something's happening with the windows."

Reflections shifted impossibly in the glass, like the house itself was trying to show multiple versions of reality. And in each one, dark figures moved with synchronized precision.

Lana's front door hung open. Through it, I could just make out something dark smeared across her normally spotless floor. A trail leading up the stairs.

My phone buzzed - no signal still, but a single message displayed: "DON'T TRUST THE UNIFORMS. THEY'RE NOT WHO THEY APPEAR TO BE."

A high-pitched whine cut through the air. From the van, the body jerked upright, its head rotating toward us at an angle that should have snapped its spine. And somewhere inside the house, I heard my boys start to scream.

I was out of the truck before Dad could stop me. The body in the van doorway had started to convulse, dark fluid leaking from its nose and mouth. Whatever was mixed with the blood looked almost metallic, catching the light in unnatural ways as it pooled beneath the van.

"Wes, wait!" Tracy called after me, but I was already moving past the van.

The front steps were slick with that same black-tinged fluid. More of it had been tracked through the doorway, leading into Lana's usually immaculate home. The metallic smell hit me before I reached the door - blood mixed with something else. Something industrial.

Inside, the house was silent. The screaming had stopped, which felt worse somehow.

Movement caught my eye - a shadow passing through the living room. But when I turned, nothing was there. Just Lana's furniture, arranged exactly as always, except...

The trail of dark fluid led to the stairs. And at the bottom, a phone lay in a puddle. Its screen still displayed rows of sixes.

Through the front window, I saw Dad edging closer to the van, examining something that had spilled from the open door. His voice carried clearly: "Tracy, this looks like the same compound we found residue of at the quarry. The stuff that stained all the old equipment."

But I couldn't focus on that now. Upstairs, something scraped across the floor of Lana's guest room. The same room where the boys had been doing homework when I left.

Taking the stairs two at a time, I followed the dark trail up. It looked thicker here, like something bleeding heavily had been dragged. The metallic smell grew stronger with each step.

At the top of the stairs, I froze. The hallway walls were sprayed with that black fluid, but in patterns. Not random splatter - precise geometrical shapes that reminded me of sound wave visualizations. And at the end of the hall, the guest room door stood open.

"Cynthia?" My voice sounded hollow in the unnatural quiet. "Lana?"

No answer. Just another scraping sound from inside the room.

The door creaked as I pushed it wider. Dark fluid coated everything - the walls, the ceiling, Lana's antique furniture. But what made my stomach turn was how it moved.

The onyx puddles rippled in perfect patterns, like someone had struck a tuning fork nearby. Through the bedroom window, I could see more vans arriving, their equipment already humming at frequencies that made the air vibrate.

"Bill!" Tracy's voice carried from outside. "The residue from the quarry - it's reacting to their equipment!"

The fluid on the walls began to flow, streaming down in synchronized rivulets toward some central point I couldn't see. Like it was being drawn to something. Pulled by whatever signal pulsed through the machines.

A wet thud from down the hall made me turn. One of the uniforms lay crumpled by the bathroom, its wearer's limbs bent at impossible angles. More of that black-tinged blood seemed to be... collecting in the body's extremities. Pooling and hardening into shapes that didn't match human anatomy.

But where were my boys? Where was Cynthia? Lana?

The window behind me shattered inward as a high-pitched tone cut through the air. And through the broken glass, I heard Dad shout something that made my blood run cold:

"The church bells - they're all ringing! Every one in town!"

Through the glass fragments scattered across Lana's floor, I could hear them - all the church bells in Johnson ringing at once. Not in their usual patterns. Something coordinated.

The black fluid began moving faster now, drawn toward the frequencies like iron filings to a magnet. Even the dark stains from that crumpled body in the hallway were responding, flowing together, merging.

My phone lit up - still no signal, but the screen displayed what looked like sound wave patterns. The same ones we'd seen in those old Midwest Resonance documents. But these were live readings, happening now.

A strangled sound from downstairs made me turn. Through the broken window, I saw Dad stumbling back from the van, his face pale. The body that had been hanging from the door was... changing. That black fluid reshaping it into something else entirely.

"Wes!" Tracy's voice carried an edge I'd never heard before. "Their equipment - it's not measuring the frequencies anymore. It's generating them!"

The bells changed pitch. And somewhere in the house, I heard my boys start to laugh.

Not their normal laughter. A hollow, mechanical sound that echoed from everywhere and nowhere at once. I spun in the hallway, trying to pinpoint it, but the sound seemed to shift with each movement.

"Dad?" Xander's voice, distorted and distant. "We're up here."

The attic. Lana never used it - just storage space she'd talked about converting someday, but now...

A trapdoor at the end of the hall hung open, its pull-cord swaying slightly. Dark fluid dripped from the opening, forming those same geometric patterns where it hit the floor.

Lana had complained for years about the stuck access panel. The home inspector couldn't even get it open when she bought the place. But as I moved closer, I could see fresh marks in the wood around the opening. Like something had pulled it down from above.

The metallic smell grew stronger. Through the opening, I heard movement. Multiple sets of footsteps, moving in perfect synchronization.

"Come see what we found, Dad." Ben's voice now, echoing down. "What's been waiting up here."

The black fluid coated the first few rungs of the attic ladder. I pulled out my phone's flashlight, aiming the beam upward.

The attic stretched into darkness, rafters disappearing into shadow. But in that brief illumination, I caught glimpses of movement. Shapes shifting in ways that didn't match the beam's sweep.

Deep within the attic, I heard my boys moving. Their footsteps perfectly synchronized, like they were being guided by something. Controlled by whatever signal pulsed through the house.

More of that black fluid began streaming down the ladder rungs, moving against gravity, forming patterns that looked like sound waves frozen in metal.

A chorus of voices - my sons, but distorted. Their words processed through machinery: "Come up, Dad. Come see."

Something darker than shadow moved above me. And looking up through the attic opening, I finally understood what my boys had found. What had been waiting for them.

"Wes!" Bill's voice cut through the darkness from below. "Something's happening with those bodies in the vans. The black fluid - it's all moving in the same direction."

A wet scraping sound from above made me raise my flashlight again. The beam caught something that shouldn't be there - equipment bolted to the rafters. Old speakers, their casings corroded but somehow still powered. Frequency meters with dials that spun without being touched. Lana never knew. All these years, right above her head...

"They're just children." A new voice drifted down the ladder. Not my boys. A woman's voice, preserved somehow in magnetic tape. "We thought we could control it. The frequencies. The fluid. But the children... they're so much more receptive than we expected."

I recognized the voice from our podcast research. The reporter who disappeared investigating the Vernon case. The church bells changed pitch, and more black fluid began trickling down the attic ladder. Not dripping - flowing upward, against gravity, like iron filings being pulled toward a magnet.

Through the opening, I could see ancient equipment humming to life. Meters swinging, lights blinking, everything responding to whatever frequency the bells were generating.

"Dad?" Ben's voice, the harmonics distorted. Like his vocal cords were being manipulated by something else. "Why are you just standing there?"

My flashlight beam caught movement in the rafters - dark shapes flowing together, pooling into forms that defied physics. The metallic fluid was responding to the frequencies, reshaping itself. Reshaping them.

Tracy's voice carried from outside, urgent now. "The bodies from the vans - they're gone. But there's some kind of trail... it's all moving toward the house." The beam of my light caught something else in the attic - numbers carved into the rafters. Dates. The same ones we'd seen in the facility records. In the church basement.

1957 - 1958 - 1959

And below each date, a perfect set of small handprints pressed into the wood. Made with something dark. Something metallic.

666

Chapter 33: Cynthia

"Back room," Mom mouthed silently, pulling me away from the door as that wet dragging sound reached the top of the stairs.

Through the gap beneath the door, I could see dark fluid seeping into the hallway carpet. Not spreading like normal liquid - the streams curved and connected with mathematical precision, forming deliberate lines across the floor.

The boys stood motionless by the window, their eyes fixed on something below. More white vans were arriving, unloading equipment that pulsed with frequencies I could feel in my teeth.

"Look," Mom whispered, gesturing to the dark puddle creeping under the door. The fluid wasn't just moving - it was arranging itself into familiar shapes. The same patterns we'd seen carved in the facility walls. Three circles forming into sixes.

A thud in the hallway. Then another. Like something heavy being dragged. The fluid patterns rippled with each impact, responding to whatever was approaching.

I checked my phone one last time, hoping for a message from Wes. Instead, the screen displayed an automated alert: "System integration complete. Signal amplification at 66.6%"

Another thud, closer now. Through the bedroom window, I could see more vans pulling up, their equipment casting strange reflections. The dark fluid kept flowing under the door, drawn toward something we couldn't see.

Mom's hand found mine in the growing darkness, squeezing tight. She'd protected me through every crisis growing up - teenage heartbreaks, bad decisions, that mess with he who shall not be named several years back. But this was different. This was...

A wet scraping sound in the hallway cut through my thoughts. We'd heard screaming downstairs earlier, then those horrible sounds. Now something was moving up there, dragging itself across the carpet.

The boys turned from the window in perfect unison, like puppets pulled by invisible strings. That black fluid continued seeping under the door, forming those same circles we'd seen everywhere.

Outside, a truck engine roared to a stop. Even from up here, I recognized the sound - Dad's work truck.

Help was coming. But whatever was in the hallway was already here.

Something metallic clinked against the hardwood - like equipment being set down. I thought of the gear we'd seen in those vans, the frequency meters and signal generators.

"Mom," I whispered, pulling her further from the door. The boys hadn't moved, still staring with empty expressions. "If we can get them to the window..."

But before I could finish, the doorknob began to turn. Not kicked in or forced - just a slow, deliberate movement. Like whatever waited on the other side had all the time in the world.

The door opened.

And standing in the hallway was something that wore a uniform, but moved like its joints had been reassembled wrong. Dark fluid leaked from its nose and mouth as it lifted what looked like a signal generator.

Behind me, I heard the boys take a synchronized step forward.

The figure's movements were jerky, mechanical - like someone learning how human limbs should work. That black substance dripped steadily from its face, forming precise geometric patterns where it hit the floor.

Its hands adjusted dials on the signal generator with inhuman precision. Each turn sent waves of pressure through my skull, like someone slowly increasing the volume on frequencies I couldn't quite hear.

Through the window behind us, I caught glimpses of Dad's truck. Of Wes moving toward the house. But the figure in the doorway had positioned itself between us and any escape.

"The resonance requires calibration," it said, its voice distorted by the fluid filling its throat. The words sounded rehearsed, like it was reciting rather than speaking. "Your children have shown remarkable receptivity to the signals."

More of that metallic substance began seeping from the walls, drawn toward whatever frequency the generator was producing. Behind me, I felt rather than saw my boys moving closer. Their footsteps perfectly synchronized to rhythms I couldn't hear.

And somewhere below, I heard the front door open.

The figure by the door jerked suddenly as another wave of frequency pulsed through the house. The signal generator in its hands began to whine, its displays spinning wildly as if responding to some override command.

Dark fluid poured faster from its nose and mouth as the machine's pitch climbed higher. Its movements became more erratic, like a malfunctioning robot. The dials on the generator continued turning on their own, far past any safe operating range.

Through the window, I saw more workers collapse near their vans, that same black substance leaking from them as their equipment overloaded. Each body twitched in patterns that matched the signal's rhythm.

"Signal breach," its voice distorted as more dark fluid leaked from its mouth. "System... compromised."

I heard Wes calling from below, but the pressure building in my skull made it impossible to respond. Mom sagged against me, her nose starting to bleed.

The boys moved in unison toward the hallway. The convulsing figure stepped aside, like it was following some program. They led us to the end of the hall where an access panel hung open - one that had been sealed since Mom bought the house.

"Up," Ben said, though it didn't sound like him anymore. "They want us up there."

The pressure in my head was becoming unbearable. I watched, barely conscious, as our sons climbed the ladder with mechanical precision. Mom and I followed, our bodies moving more from the pull of that frequency than any conscious choice.

The attic... there was equipment in the attic. Ancient speakers. Meters. Things that shouldn't be there.

The room tilted sideways as my legs gave out. The last thing I saw was old machinery coming to life in the rafters, and my boys watching with strange calm as everyone else began to collapse.

Then the darkness took me.

Through the darkness, images flickered like an old film reel:

Ben as a toddler, touching a speaker and giggling as the bass resonated through him. But now the memory twisted - black fluid leaking from the speaker grille, forming patterns on the floor.

The boys' first day at school, lined up for a photo. Their shadows stretched toward something I couldn't see. In the background, a woman who looked like Amber, but older, watching them with hungry eyes.

Mom's kitchen from my childhood, but the radio played only static. Through the window, children walked in perfect circles around the old well that used to be there. Before they built the houses. Before they changed the street names.

A communion line at St. Michael's, but the wine in the chalice was black and viscous. The priest's smile too wide as he whispered, "The Initiative provides."

Hospital corridors stretching endlessly beneath Johnson's streets. In each room, doctors injected something dark into IV bags. "For contrast imaging," they said. "Standard procedure."

The images blurred together faster. Church bells ringing at impossible frequencies, children's handprints in black fluid, Amber's face splitting open like a flower made of mercury, the boys standing in circles, but their reflections showing different children, something rising from the lake, dragging chains made of sound.

Then voices, fragments cutting through the chaos: "The frequencies align..." "Natural resonators..." "Project Echo entering final phase..." "Seven times seven..." "They're ready to receive..."

The darkness pulsed with each phrase, like a heart made of static.

The first thing I registered was pain - a deep throbbing in my skull like the worst migraine imaginable. Then voices, distant and distorted through the ringing in my ears.

"Get them down from there. Now." Dad's voice from somewhere below.

"The boys first." Tracy. "Before that equipment powers up again."

I forced my eyes open. The attic spun sickeningly around me, ancient rafters creaking overhead. Through the small window, I could see workers sprawled in the yard, dark fluid still leaking from their bodies. Their equipment silent now, displays cracked and smoking.

"Mom?" My voice came out as a croak. She stirred beside me, alive but barely conscious.

Wes appeared through the attic access, carefully stepping over the uniformed body that still clutched its fried generator. "Can you walk?"

The boys stood exactly where they had been, near the old equipment bolted to the rafters, still watching everything with that unnatural calm. Like they were observing an experiment reach its predicted conclusion.

The dream images still pulsed behind my eyes - black communion wine, hospital corridors, children walking in circles. But what frightened me most was how some of those visions felt less like dreams and more like memories trying to surface.

"What happened to them?" I asked, nodding toward our sons though I wasn't sure I wanted the answer. "Why weren't they affected like everyone else?"

"Later," Wes said, helping me up. His eyes kept darting to something in the rafters - old equipment I'd never seen before. Equipment that shouldn't be in my mother's attic. "Right now we need to move. Something's happening with the bodies outside."

The attic's small window offered a view of the yard below. The dark fluid that had leaked from the workers was starting to flow again, pooling together in unnatural patterns.

"Dad found dates carved up here," Wes whispered, guiding me toward the access panel. "And handprints. Children's handprints, going back to 1957. Mom's attic... they've been using it all this time."

Mom was already being helped down by Tracy, but the boys remained still, their movements synchronized to whatever frequency pulsed through the old equipment. Their expressions and rigid postures reminded me of patients under deep anesthesia - conscious but not quite present.

"Come on," I called to them, trying to keep my voice steady. "We need to go."

The boys turned toward the old equipment, moving in perfect unison like participants in some choreographed demonstration. The meters' rhythmic pulsing seemed to guide their every movement.

Behind them, the frequency meters began to spin faster.

A mechanical whir cut through the attic's stillness - something powering up that hadn't run in decades. The old equipment pulsed with patterns matching the machines below.

"Baby," Wes moved between me and the boys. "We need to get them out of here. Now."

Through the window, I saw Dad examining something that had spilled from one of the vans. Medical containers. The kind used for transporting sensitive materials. Their warning labels caught the afternoon light: "Temperature Sensitive Biomaterial."

The boys' eyes fixed on the spinning meters, their bodies swaying slightly to rhythms only they seemed to feel. Whatever signal was being broadcast had them locked in some kind of feedback loop.

"Get Mom down first," I told Wes. He hesitated, but helped guide her toward the access panel where Tracy waited below.

A high-pitched tone began building from the old speakers. The same frequency that had incapacitated the workers. But our boys showed no sign of distress - if anything, they seemed to be resonating with it, like tuning forks finding their perfect pitch.

"Enough," I stepped toward them, mother's instinct overriding my fear. "We're leaving. All of us. Now."

666

Chapter 34: Wes

Bill's truck idled in the middle of the street, Tracy already in the driver's seat. Through Lana's front door, I could see dark fluid still flowing across her normally spotless floors. The Initiative workers' bodies had started moving again - not alive, but pulled by some unseen force that made their limbs twitch and jerk like marionettes.

"Front yard's clear," Bill called from beside the truck. "But we need to move. More vans coming up Oak Street."

I guided the boys toward the door, their movements still synchronized but at least they were responding to direction now. The frequency's hold seemed to weaken the further we got from that equipment in the attic. Cynthia and Lana followed close behind.

A gurgling sound made me turn. One of the bodies had started to rise, that strange black substance pooling around it. Its head rotated toward us, jaw working as if trying to speak. It lurched forward, movements jerky but purposeful.

I grabbed the nearest object—Lana's heavy brass umbrella stand—and swung it without hesitation. The impact knocked the figure sideways, its head twisting at an impossible angle. Black fluid sprayed across the entryway, but the body kept trying to rise, limbs reconfiguring in ways human joints shouldn't move.

"Go!" I shouted, swinging again as more black fluid poured from the thing's broken form. This time it stayed down, though the fluid continued moving with deliberate patterns across the floor.

Then all of our phones lit up at once: "GOING TO OVERLOAD THEIR SYSTEMS. GET CLEAR OF THE HOUSE. NOW."

"Get the cats' carriers," I called to Tracy as wiring shrieked inside the walls. Old cables and new strained under some massive power surge. Every piece of Initiative equipment began to whine, their displays spinning wildly before cracking in sequence.

The cats had already hidden themselves - Maybelle and Patches under Lana's bed, Penny in the closet, and Nala, as usual, wherever she wanted. For once, their skittish nature worked in our favor.

"Move!" I guided the boys toward the truck while Tracy and Lana handled the cats. Our sons stumbled slightly, their synchronized movement breaking for the first time since we'd found them in the attic. Behind us, more bodies were rising, drawn toward their overloading machinery.

Through Lana's window, I caught a glimpse of monitors flashing warnings: "System breach detected" "Power threshold exceeded" "Containment failure imminent"

The air itself seemed to vibrate as frequencies built beyond what any of the equipment was designed to handle. Dark fluid began streaming from every Initiative worker's body, flowing toward machines that were about to fail catastrophically.

"Got them!" Tracy emerged with two carriers, Lana right behind her with the others. Through the mesh, I could see Nala's eyes wide with fear - like she sensed something in those frequencies we couldn't hear.

"Get them in the truck," Bill shouted over the rising whine. "All of them. Now!"

The first generator exploded as we reached the truck, spraying metal and glass across the lawn. Other machines followed, each blast driving their operators' bodies into unnatural contortions before they collapsed into still heaps.

Someone was systematically destroying every piece of Initiative equipment. And taking their people with it.

The cats yowled in their carriers as another wave of frequency pulsed through the air. But our boys... our boys just watched the destruction with that same clinical detachment. Like they were observing an experiment reach its inevitable conclusion.

Tracy gunned the engine as soon as the last door slammed shut. Through the back window, I watched Lana's house grow smaller, equipment still exploding in sequence.

Just before we turned the corner, our phones lit up with one final message: "They'll trace the overload to a system malfunction. Watch the hospitals."

"Where are we going?" Cynthia asked from the middle seat, her arm around Casey who had finally started blinking normally again.

"Not the farm," Tracy said before Bill could suggest it. "News crews are still camped out there, and after what happened with the lake..."

"And now they'll be swarming Lana's place too," Bill added, taking a sharp turn to avoid Main Street. "We need somewhere with no electronics, no media, and nothing connected to the Initiative."

In the rearview mirror, I watched emergency vehicles racing toward Lana's house. Fire trucks, ambulances, police - but no white Initiative vans. Not yet.

My phone, despite having no signal, displayed another message: "Go to Rebecca's. She knows more than she's letting on."

I stared at the screen. My mother had never lived in Johnson as far as I knew. She'd always avoided even visiting the town, making excuses whenever I invited her. This mysterious message made me wonder if there was a reason for her avoidance all these years.

"We need to go to my mom's," I said quietly to Cynthia. "Her place in Cedar Ridge."

"Your mother?" Bill asked, glancing at me in the mirror. "That's forty minutes east."

"This message says she knows something about all this," I replied, showing him my phone. "And she's far enough from Johnson that the Initiative's reach might not extend there."

Cynthia nodded, her arm still around Casey who was looking more like himself with each passing mile. Whatever the frequencies had done to the boys seemed to be wearing off the further we got from Lana's.

"Cedar Ridge doesn't even have the same power grid," Tracy noted, her practical nature asserting itself. "Different county, different everything."

"And mom's place is old," I added. "Built in the '30s. No smart technology, barely any electronics at all."

Bill nodded, making the turn onto Highway 16 East. Cedar Ridge was small enough to stay off most maps, which now felt like an advantage.

The cats settled in their carriers as we left Johnson behind, the tension in the truck easing slightly with each mile marker. Whatever had happened back there, whatever had been controlling our boys and animating those bodies, its influence seemed limited to the town's boundaries.

"Dad," Ben spoke up from the back seat, his voice sounding normal for the first time in days. "What happened to us?"

I exchanged glances with Cynthia. The boys' synchronized movements had stopped completely now, their eyes clear, expressions confused but present.

"We're still figuring that out, buddy," I said carefully. "How much do you remember?"

All five of them looked at each other, something passing between them that wasn't the mechanical precision we'd seen before, just the normal connection of brothers who'd shared something inexplicable.

"There was music," Casey said quietly. "But not like normal music. It was in our heads."

"It showed us things," Xander added. "About the town. About what's underneath it."

The sun had nearly set by the time we turned onto the gravel road leading to my mother's farmhouse. The two-story white clapboard structure stood silhouetted against the darkening sky, its wraparound porch and lack of nearby neighbors exactly what we needed right now.

Mom appeared in the doorway before we'd even stopped, her expression shifting from confusion to alarm as our overloaded truck pulled up.

She'd always been perceptive - a trait that suddenly took on new significance given the mysterious message.

"Wesley?" She came down the porch steps as we piled out, her eyes immediately going to the boys. "What's happened? Why do you have all those cats?"

I caught the subtle way she scanned the horizon behind us. Not just concerned - vigilant.

"We had to leave in a hurry," I said simply. "It's a long story, but we need a place to stay tonight."

Something in her eyes changed when she looked at the boys more closely. Not surprise exactly... recognition.

"Get inside," she said, her normally warm voice carrying an edge I'd rarely heard. "All of you. Quickly."

The farmhouse was just as I remembered - untouched by smart technology, its walls too thick for decent cell reception. The living room with its mismatched furniture and shelves of actual physical books felt like stepping back in time.

"The boys can take the upstairs bedrooms," Mom said, already moving toward the kitchen. "I'll make up beds for the rest of you."

As Bill and Tracy brought in the cat carriers, I noticed Mom watching them with particular intensity. When Tracy set down Nala's carrier, Mom knelt to look at the cat more closely.

"When did she start avoiding screens?" she asked quietly.

The question caught me off guard. "How did you know about that?"

Mom straightened up, her eyes meeting mine with an intensity I'd never seen before. "Because mine did the same thing back in '79. Right before I swore I'd never set foot in Johnson again."

A chill ran through me. "You told me you'd never lived there."

"I didn't," she said quietly. "But my brother did. My parents too. I only visited for summers. That's where I met your dad." Her expression softened slightly at the mention of Roy. "We both couldn't wait to leave that place behind."

The memory of Dad stung fresh again. Just eight months since his passing in Chicago, where he'd lived most of his life. Though my parents had never stayed together, Dad had been a constant in my life, and his wife Nor had been perfect for him. The boys still asked about their grandpa and Nor regularly. I'd made it to the hospital, but Dad had been unconscious by then - we never got to say a proper goodbye.

Lana and Cynthia had taken the boys upstairs to get settled. Bill and Tracy were in the kitchen, making coffee and unpacking the few supplies we'd grabbed. For a moment, it was just me and my mother in the living room, decades of unasked questions hanging between us.

"You've never told me why you left," I said quietly.

She moved to an old cedar chest in the corner, the one she'd always kept locked. "I didn't think it would matter. I thought we were safe here." The key had always hung around her neck - I'd never seen her without it.

Inside the chest were photographs, documents, and notebooks I'd never seen before. She pulled out a faded image - a group of children standing in front of St. Michael's church. Each child wore a choir robe.

"This was the last picture taken of my brother," she said, her finger tapping a boy in the front row. "Your uncle Michael. The one I told you died from illness."

I studied the image. The boy looked eerily like Xander at that age.

"He didn't die from any illness, did he?"

Mom shook her head, pulling out more papers. "The Initiative took him. For their experiments with the frequencies. They said he was special - that he could hear things other children couldn't." Her hands trembled slightly. "Just like your boys can."

From upstairs came the sound of the boys talking normally, their voices no longer synchronized but animated with their usual energy. The relief of hearing them sound like themselves again was overwhelming.

"Tomorrow," Mom said, stacking the documents carefully, "I'll tell you everything I know about the Initiative. About why they want children like yours." She glanced toward the stairs. "But tonight, let them rest. Let them feel safe."

She closed the chest, locking away whatever other secrets it contained. "And tomorrow, you and Cynthia will need to go back to Johnson. Alone."

"Back? After everything that's happened?"

Mom nodded, her expression grave. "There's something you need to find. Something that can stop this for good." She looked toward the window, though nothing was visible in the darkness beyond. "They've been doing this for generations. Taking children who can hear the frequencies. It needs to end."

That night, after everyone else had gone to bed, I sat on the porch watching the distant lights of passing cars on the highway. My phone had no signal here - a blessing after the chaos of the day.

Tomorrow we would learn what my mother knew. Tomorrow we would have to return to Johnson without the boys, leaving them safe here with her.

But for tonight, under this roof, we were beyond the Initiative's reach. Beyond the frequencies that had nearly taken our children.

For tonight, at least, we could breathe.

Chapter 35: Wes

Morning light filtered through my mother's kitchen windows, catching dust motes that danced above the old oak table. The boys had slept soundly for the first time in days, their synchronized movements completely gone. Even the cats seemed more relaxed here, away from Johnson's frequencies.

Mom set a cup of coffee in front of me, then took a seat across the table. The cedar chest from last night now sat open beside her, its contents spread across the surface - faded photographs, newspaper clippings, and what looked like a journal bound in cracked leather.

"I should have told you years ago," she said, her fingers tracing the edge of a photograph. "But I thought if I kept you away from Johnson, if we never talked about it..."

"Tell me now," I said simply.

She nodded, selecting a yellowed newspaper article. "My brother Michael wasn't the only one. Every few decades, they find children who can hear the frequencies. Children with a natural resonance." Her eyes drifted toward the stairs where the boys still slept. "Children like yours."

The article detailed a choir competition from 1975. St. Michael's Youth Chorus had won first place, their "unique tonal qualities" singled out for praise. In the accompanying photo, a dozen children stood in formation, Michael among them.

"Johnson wasn't always called Johnson," Mom continued, pulling out an older map. "The town's been renamed three times. After each... incident."

"Midwest Resonance Research founded the town," Mom said, unfolding a faded document bearing that familiar three-circle logo. "They built it around what they found in the quarry."

"What did they find?" The question had been nagging at me since the lake facility collapsed.

Mom's hands trembled slightly as she opened the leather journal. "Something that responds to sound. To specific frequencies." She turned the journal toward me. Inside were hand-drawn diagrams of what looked like crystalline structures, alongside measurements and equations. "A mineral unlike anything they'd documented before. It amplifies certain frequencies, and... changes things."

"Changes things how?"

"It starts with electronics - disrupting signals, generating interference. Then it affects living tissue." She pulled out another photograph, this one showing a laboratory with tanks similar to what we'd seen beneath the lake. "They discovered it could transform organic matter when exposed to the right frequencies. But they couldn't control it."

Cynthia appeared in the doorway, hair still damp from the shower. She joined us at the table, eyes widening at the spread of documents.

"People started disappearing in the '50s," Mom continued. "Children mostly. The ones who showed sensitivity to the frequencies. My brother was one of them." Her voice grew tight. "The Initiative - that's what Midwest Resonance called their special projects division - they said he was 'invited to a special music program.' He never came home."

She pulled out what looked like medical records. "Some children resist the frequencies naturally. Their nervous systems somehow reject the transformation process. The Initiative has been searching for those children for decades, studying them, trying to understand why."

"Children like our boys," Cynthia said quietly.

Mom's expression tightened. "I've noticed things about them over the years. The way they move together sometimes. How they seem to communicate without speaking." She looked toward the ceiling, where the boys' footsteps could now be heard. "It's the same behaviors my brother showed before they took him."

"You never said anything," I said, realization dawning. "How long have you suspected?"

"I started noticing when Ben was about four," she admitted. "Remember that Christmas when he suddenly walked to the front door before anyone knocked? Seconds before your dad and Nor arrived?" She shook her head. "Little things kept happening. I tried to convince myself it was just coincidence. That I was seeing patterns because of what happened to Michael."

Bill appeared in the doorway, Tracy close behind. "Sorry to interrupt, but we should start figuring out our next move."

Mom gathered the old documents. "I've told you what I know about my brother and what happened back then. But there has to be more information in Johnson. Records that could explain what's happening to your boys and how to stop it."

"City records would be our best bet," Bill suggested. "If this has been going on for decades, there must be documentation somewhere."

"Not the kind they want people finding," Cynthia added.

The boys came downstairs, looking more like themselves than they had in days. Casey immediately went to check on the cats, while the others gravitated toward the kitchen's breakfast smells.

"You need to go back," Mom said quietly. "Just you and Cynthia. The boys stay here with me, where they'll be safe."

Bill nodded. "Tracy and I can stay too. Keep an eye on things."

Outside, the morning sun cast long shadows across Mom's farm. No sign of white vans, no Initiative presence. Here, at least, we were beyond their reach.

"City hall would have the oldest records," Bill suggested, spreading out a map of Johnson on the table. "The building dates back to the town's founding."

Within the hour, we were packed and ready. The hardest part was saying goodbye to the boys, even temporarily. Knowing they were safe with Mom eased the worry, but leaving them behind still felt wrong.

"We'll be back tonight," Cynthia promised, hugging each of them in turn.

The drive back to Johnson was tense but uneventful. Highway 16 stretched before us, each mile bringing us closer to whatever waited in the city records - and whatever forces had been manipulating our boys.

"Do you think there's really a way to stop this?" Cynthia asked, breaking the silence as we passed the Johnson city limits sign.

"Has to be," I replied, though uncertainty gnawed at me. "If they created these frequencies, there must be a way to disrupt them."

The town looked deceptively normal in the early afternoon sun. People going about their routines, oblivious to what lurked beneath the surface. But as we approached downtown, I noticed the first white van.

"They're back already," Cynthia said, spotting another one turning onto Oak Street.

I took a detour, heading away from city hall. More vans appeared, moving in patterns that seemed too coordinated to be random patrols.

"They're watching the main roads," I realized, turning down a side street only to find another van parked ahead.

My phone, which had regained signal as we entered Johnson, buzzed with a message: "CITY HALL COMPROMISED. DON'T GO THERE."

"That was our plan," Cynthia said, looking at the identical message on her phone. "How did they—"

Another message appeared: "SCHOOL GYMNASIUM. 10 MINUTES."

Bill's truck rattled over back roads as we tried to avoid the white vans, which seemed to be converging from all directions. The Initiative vehicles didn't follow directly, but moved parallel to us on adjacent streets.

"They're herding us," Cynthia said, watching their movements. "Driving us toward the school."

The old brick building came into view ahead - Johnson High's gymnasium set apart from the main campus. Evening practices would be over by now, the parking lot empty except for a few staff cars.

Through the back window, I watched more vans forming a perimeter around the neighborhood. Not advancing. Just... waiting.

Our phones lit up one final time: "SIDE DOOR. GYM STORAGE. HURRY."

"It feels like a trap," Cynthia whispered.

"But why direct us here if they have us surrounded?" I countered, pulling up to the gym's side entrance. The door hung slightly open - unusual for what looked like an emergency exit.

We approached the door cautiously, my phone's flashlight revealing stacked gymnastics mats and old sports equipment inside. The air felt dead here - no frequencies, no vibrations. Nothing that could carry a signal.

A storage room door stood at the far end of the space. Inside, shelves of basketballs and volleyball nets filled most of the area. But against the back wall...

"Is that a fallout shelter sign?" Cynthia asked, her beam catching the faded yellow triangle.

The floor beneath it was concrete - newer than the rest, like it had been recently poured. And in its surface, someone had freshly carved three interlocking circles.

I knelt beside the carved symbol, my fingers tracing the grooves. "These are fresh," I said quietly. "Made within the last day, maybe less."

Cynthia kept her flashlight trained on the symbol. "Someone trying to communicate with us?"

"Or lead us somewhere," I replied.

As if responding to my touch, the concrete shifted beneath my palm. A grinding noise echoed through the storage room as a section began to move. Hidden hydraulics whirred as a panel slid aside, revealing a set of stairs that led down into darkness.

We exchanged a glance, both thinking about our boys safely away at Mom's place. Knowing they weren't here made this decision easier.

"After you," Cynthia whispered.

The stairwell led into a space that looked nothing like the other hidden chambers we'd found. Clean white walls, modern LED lighting, and what appeared to be a small command center - computer monitors showing security feeds from around Johnson, including the Initiative's vans still circling the school.

"Welcome," a voice called from behind a bank of servers. A man in his forties stepped into view, dressed in a rumpled button-down and khakis. The Initiative's three-circle logo eightwas visible on his employee badge, but he'd crossed it out with permanent marker. "I was beginning to worry you wouldn't make it."

"You're the one who's been sending us messages," I said, pieces clicking into place. "The warnings about the vans. The hospital records."

He nodded, extending his hand. "Daniel Keating. Head of Cybersecurity for Midwest Resonance Research." His expression hardened. "Or I was, until I discovered what they were really doing."

"Why help us?" Cynthia asked, still wary.

"Because your boys aren't the first children they've targeted," he replied, turning to a monitor displaying personnel files. "But they need to be the last."

Keating pulled up security footage showing Initiative vans converging on houses across Johnson. "They're accelerating their timeline. The Conductor is getting desperate."

"The Conductor?" I asked.

Keating's expression darkened. "Dr. Evelyn Sullivan. Head of Project Echo and the driving force behind the Initiative." He pulled up a personnel file showing a woman in her late eighties, her cold eyes staring out from an imperious face that hadn't softened with age. "She's been experimenting with the frequencies for over six decades, ever since she discovered what happened to her brother."

"Sullivan," Cynthia repeated, the name hitting us both at once. The medical bracelet we'd seen on Specimen Six at the lake facility.

"M. Sullivan," I said. "Michael Sullivan."

Keating nodded grimly. "Her younger brother. Her father was the lead scientist who used him as the first test subject." He turned to another screen. "She's spent her entire career trying to perfect what her father started. The frequencies, the black fluid compound - it's all designed to transform human consciousness. To make it receptive to what she calls 'the ultimate harmonic convergence.'"

On the monitors around us, we could see Initiative teams moving through Johnson, their search patterns methodical.

"They're looking for your boys," Keating said. "Dr. Sullivan believes they're the key to completing what she started in 1957. Natural resonators who can withstand the frequencies long enough to become permanent conduits."

"Conduits for what?" Cynthia asked.

Keating's hands moved across the keyboard, bringing up another file. "For this."

The screen showed a crystalline formation extracted from the quarry. Black with metallic veins running through it, the mineral seemed to pulse with its own inner light.

"They found it during the initial excavation in 1956," Keating explained. "A substance that responds to sound. That can transform matter at the molecular level." His voice lowered. "Sullivan believes it's not from Earth. That it's trying to communicate through the frequencies."

"And our boys can hear it," I whispered, the implications sinking in.

"Not just hear it," Keating corrected. "They can channel it without the biological breakdown other subjects experience. That's why Sullivan wants them. Why she's been preparing for them."

A red folder sat prominently on the central desk. Its label read: "Project Echo - Phase 2 Termination Protocol."

"Everything you need to know is in there," Keating said, pushing the folder toward us. "Including how to stop her."

Outside, the vans had stopped moving, forming a perfect perimeter around the school.

"They can't detect this facility," Keating assured us. "We're safe for now. But we don't have much time left."

666

Chapter 36: The Conductor

Dr. Evelyn Sullivan adjusted the dial with precision, her arthritic fingers still possessing the dexterity required for such delicate work. The frequency generator's needle danced across the spectrum, searching for that perfect resonance point. After sixty-three years of refinement, she was closer than ever.

Her gaze drifted to the framed poem mounted on the wall of her office, inscribed in her father's elegant handwriting. His manifesto for Project Echo, written the night before they first tested the frequencies on Michael:

Project Echo

I harvest their resonance, my baton-fingers dancing through each frequency like sacred numerals. My equations whisper truth: minds are wavelengths— an orchestra of neurons waiting for direction. In basement laboratories, I perfect the score— testing harmonics that make synapses bow to sound. Soon they'll all hear it: my perfect frequency, as I conduct their chorus into pure submission.

She touched the frame reverently. Her father had understood the true potential from the beginning. Not just control—transcendence.

The monitors surrounding her displayed vital signs from test subjects across Johnson. Each one meticulously cataloged, their responses to the frequencies documented down to the millisecond. The data flowing in was beautiful in its symmetry. The equation nearly solved.

Her office deep beneath St. Michael's church had remained unchanged since 1957. The same wooden desk where her father had first drafted Project Echo's protocols. The same chair where he'd sat explaining to a young Evelyn why her brother Michael had been chosen. The necessary sacrifice for scientific advancement.

"Status report," she spoke into the intercom, her voice betraying none of the excitement building within her aged frame.

"Integration levels at 87% across all sites, Dr. Sullivan," came the immediate response. "The black fluid composition is stabilizing in most subjects. Rejection rate down to 13%."

Progress. Significant progress. Better than her father had ever achieved. Michael would have been proud to see how far his sacrifice had taken them.

She turned to the wall of monitors tracking Initiative teams across Johnson. White vans moving in careful formations, herding the Lumins exactly where she needed them.

"And our special subjects?" she asked, knowing the answer but needing to hear it spoken.

"Five natural resonators confirmed, Dr. Sullivan. The boys are no longer in Johnson."

She pressed her lips into a thin line, her only outward display of emotion. A minor setback. The boys would return. The frequencies would draw them back, as they always did with true resonators. Their abilities made them both perfect and inevitable.

Her gaze drifted to the glass case containing her most prized possession – the original black mineral extracted from the quarry in 1956. Her father had recognized its potential immediately, how it responded to sound, how it transformed matter at the molecular level. So many sacrifices made to understand its properties. To harness its potential.

"Dr. Sullivan," the intercom crackled again. "Security breach at Johnson High School facility. Someone accessed the secure server from within."

Interesting. She checked the detailed map of Johnson spread across her desk, each location marked with precise coordinates. Small lights indicated active frequencies being transmitted, creating a web of sound only she could fully comprehend.

"Identity?" she asked.

"Unknown. But they accessed personnel files. Project Echo documentation."

Evelyn turned to the sealed glass case behind her desk - the one that housed not just the original mineral, but her father's most sacred texts. She pressed her palm against the biometric scanner, the only security measure that mattered now.

The case hissed open, revealing a leather-bound journal beneath the pulsing black mineral specimen. On its cover, embossed in fading gold: "The Key to Universal Resonance."

Her father had discovered Tesla's writings in 1952, three years before they found the mineral. The connection had been immediate and undeniable. Tesla's understanding of energy vibration and frequency as fundamental forces aligned perfectly with what they'd later discover in the quarry.

"The boys resist the frequencies naturally," Evelyn murmured, running her finger down the journal's first page where her father had meticulously documented the first observations of Michael. "That's what makes them perfect. They can withstand the transformation process without degradation."

The mineral pulsed in response to her voice, as it always did.

Her father had taken Tesla's philosophy and transformed it into something more profound. Where Tesla saw mathematical harmony in his 3-6-9 theory, Sullivan Senior had discovered biological application. The original patterns driving Project Echo had derived from Tesla's understanding that all things connected through vibrational mathematics.

"Dr. Sullivan," the intercom interrupted her reverence. "Multiple Initiative teams reporting failure of containment protocols in the downtown sector. Workers showing signs of frequency rejection."

She frowned. Downtown had always been problematic - too close to the old church where signal interference disrupted their carefully calibrated broadcasts.

"Recalibrate the transmission nodes," she commanded. "Maintain pattern integrity across all sectors."

"But ma'am," the voice hesitated, "that exceeds safety protocols established after the '57 incident."

Evelyn smiled thinly. Her father had been too cautious, too afraid of what happened to Michael. But she knew better now. The biological resistance wasn't a problem to overcome - it was the key they'd been searching for.

"The patterns must complete themselves," she said. "The first phase failed. The second is reaching culmination. The third will achieve what my father only dreamed possible."

On her monitors, she could see Initiative teams converging on the school. They'd find nothing, of course. The Lumins were clever, guided by someone who understood Initiative protocols. An insider. Keating, most likely. His access codes had been used repeatedly since his disappearance.

No matter. The final phase was already underway.

She turned to another monitor showing five specially designed chambers in the subterranean facility beneath St. Michael's. Each one calibrated to a specific resonance, designed to receive a specific child. The Lumin boys would occupy them soon enough. Their natural immunity to the frequencies that had destroyed others made them the perfect conduits for completion.

"Begin final recalibration," she ordered. "And prepare the signal amplifiers."

In her office's center, a scale model of Johnson stood on a circular table. The miniature buildings weren't just decorative - each contained a tiny transmitter broadcasting specific frequencies. Together, they formed a perfect grid of sound waves, invisible but all-encompassing.

The model pulsed with light as she increased power to the real transmitters across town, the pattern following Tesla's principles of harmonic mathematics that her father had perverted into something darker.

"Dr. Sullivan," the intercom voice sounded strained now. "We're getting reports of workers collapsing near the school perimeter. Their monitoring devices are showing catastrophic frequency overexposure."

Evelyn felt a thrill run through her aged frame. "Perfect. The pattern is intensifying."

Her father had never understood this crucial aspect. The frequencies weren't just tools for control - they were gateways. Once properly aligned, they could transform reality itself, opening doors between dimensions that Tesla had only theorized.

She'd known this since watching the frequencies transform Michael in 1957. While her father had been horrified, she'd been fascinated. Enlightened.

Moving to her primary control panel, Evelyn input the sequence she'd been perfecting for sixty years - the mathematical pattern Tesla had identified as the key to universal energy.

"Activate The Conductor," she instructed.

In the center of Johnson, deep beneath the original well that had preceded the town's founding, machinery whirred to life. The massive installation they'd built around the mineral's primary deposit began to hum, its tone matching exactly the frequency her father had discovered emanating from the specimen.

On her screens, she watched as the frequencies spread through Johnson's streets, resonating with everything they touched. Buildings vibrated. Electronics malfunctioned. And people began to move with strange synchronicity.

"Dr. Sullivan," the voice on the intercom now sounded panicked. "The downtown transmission nodes are overloading. Workers are exhibiting the same symptoms we saw in the '57 incident."

"Let it happen," she replied calmly. "They've served their purpose. Only those naturally attuned to the frequencies will survive what comes next."

Her father had feared this stage. Had tried to prevent it in '57 by flooding the facility. But he hadn't understood the beauty of completion.

On her desk, a small photograph in a silver frame showed Michael before the transformation. His innocent smile, so like the Lumin boys. The perfect natural resonator.

Beside it, a faded diagram mapped frequencies corresponding to human brain waves. Her father's handwriting noted the specific patterns that matched the mineral's emissions. The discovery that had started everything.

"The first phase opened the door," she said to herself, fingers tracing Tesla's original equations in her father's journal. "The second is breaking down the barriers. The third will complete the sequence."

The sensors measuring Johnson's background frequencies suddenly spiked. A perfect harmonic cascade rippled across the readouts as church bells throughout the town began ringing simultaneously.

Evelyn smiled. The signal was spreading exactly as designed.

She turned to the monitor showing the hospital's security feed. The room where her father's preserved body floated in preservation fluid, still intact after all these decades. His tissue had been the first to accept complete frequency exposure without immediate deterioration.

"It's working, Father," she whispered. "Tesla's theory was correct. The harmonic sequence is reshaping reality itself."

The fluid in his tank seemed to vibrate in response, as if he could hear her.

She checked her watch. In exactly nine minutes, The Conductor would reach full power. Johnson's hidden transmitters would synchronize to a single frequency. And reality as the town knew it would dissolve.

Perfect resonance. Perfect harmony. Just as Tesla had theorized and her father had perverted.

Evelyn placed her hand on the mineral specimen, feeling its vibrations intensify. After six decades of work, the culmination was finally at hand.

The third phase would complete what the first had begun and the second had advanced.

And the Lumin boys would be the final instruments in her symphony.

Human consciousness elevated through perfect frequency.

The ultimate application of Tesla's understanding of vibrational mathematics.

The beginning of true transcendence.

999

Chapter 37: Cynthia

The red folder lay open on Daniel Keating's desk, its contents spread before us like a roadmap to madness. Project Echo's termination protocol featured detailed schematics of The Conductor—the massive machine beneath Johnson that amplified and directed the frequencies throughout the town.

But what caught my attention wasn't the machine itself. It was what powered it.

"That can't be right," I whispered, studying the diagrams more closely. The central power source wasn't the mineral they'd extracted from the quarry as we'd been led to believe.

Cynthia flipped through the file, her eyes scanning the dense text and diagrams. The pages were filled with technical jargon and handwritten notes, but one section stood out. She paused, her breath catching as she read:

Subject: Biological Ferrofluid (Designation: Catalyst)

Discovered in the quarry during excavation in [REDACTED]. Initial analysis confirms it is a naturally occurring substance with properties similar to synthetic ferrofluids, but with significant biological compatibility. Unlike traditional ferrofluids, which are toxic to living organisms, the Catalyst can be introduced into the human body without immediate rejection.

Her hands trembled as she stared at the words. The implications were staggering. This wasn't just some chemical—it was something far more dangerous. Something that could change people from the inside out. She glanced at the accompanying diagrams, showing the fluid's reaction to magnetic fields and its integration with cellular structures. The notes in the margins were frantic, almost desperate, as if the writer had been both fascinated and horrified by what they'd discovered.

"This is what they're using," she whispered, her voice barely audible.

"Sullivan's been lying to her own people," Keating said, tapping the schematic. "The mineral doesn't generate the frequencies. It responds to them. The real source has been there all along."

Wes leaned closer. "These readings... they match what we recorded in our studio the night before all this started."

My stomach turned as I recognized the pattern. The same frequencies that had leaked through our recording equipment at 3:33 AM. The same ones that had been affecting our boys.

Keating pulled out another file, this one containing old photographs from 1957. "Sullivan's father believed they'd found something extraterrestrial in the quarry. But what they actually discovered was something that had always been there, buried deep in the bedrock."

The photographs showed excavation teams unearthing what looked like ancient structures beneath Johnson. Not alien technology, but something far older. Something that predated human civilization.

"They built the town as a giant antenna," Keating explained, spreading out a map that overlaid Johnson's street grid with what looked like sound wave patterns. "Every church, every school, every building placed with mathematical precision to amplify whatever signal was coming from below."

"But why our boys?" Wes asked, the question that had been burning in both our minds since this began.

Keating's expression darkened. "Because they can hear it naturally. Whatever consciousness exists in those frequencies, it's been trying to communicate for centuries. Most people can't perceive it at all. Some, like Sullivan's brother Michael, could hear it but were destroyed by the attempt at connection. Your sons can not only hear it—they can respond to it without being harmed."

A chill ran through me as pieces clicked into place. The boys' synchronized movements. The way they seemed to communicate without speaking. How they'd always been able to find each other in crowded places without calling out.

"That's why Sullivan wants them," I said softly. "They're natural conduits."

Keating nodded grimly. "Conduits for something that's been trapped down there. Something that's been trying to get out since long before Midwest Resonance started meddling with frequencies they didn't understand."

On his security monitors, we could see Initiative teams converging on various points throughout Johnson. Their movements seemed less coordinated now, almost desperate.

"Sullivan's losing control," Keating observed. "The frequencies are affecting her own people. Changing them."

"Into what?" Wes asked.

"That's the million-dollar question," Keating replied, pulling up footage from the Initiative's own cameras.

What we saw made my blood run cold. Workers moved with unnatural synchronization, their bodies twitching to rhythms no one else could hear. Some had collapsed entirely, their forms twisting into impossible shapes as that black fluid leaked from their orifices.

"The failed test subjects from previous attempts," Keating explained. "They're being... recycled. Repurposed."

"Jesus," Wes whispered.

But what truly horrified me wasn't the transformation itself. It was the realization that dawned as I watched the footage more closely. The workers weren't being destroyed or replaced by something else.

They were being reunited with something they'd lost.

"They're all from Johnson, aren't they?" I asked quietly. "All the Initiative workers. All the test subjects. They're all local."

Keating's gaze met mine. "They never left. For generations, Sullivan's family has been selecting children who showed sensitivity to the frequencies. Testing them. Training them. Those who survived became part of the Initiative. Those who didn't..."

My phone buzzed suddenly—impossible, given we were in a shielded facility. The screen displayed a message that made my heart stop:

"Mom? We can hear it better now. It's not what you think. Come home."

Home. Not my mother's farm in Cedar Ridge. Our house in Johnson.

"They're coming back," I breathed, showing Wes the message. "The boys are coming back to Johnson."

Wes immediately tried calling my mother, but the call wouldn't connect. "We need to get back to Cedar Ridge. Now."

"You can't leave Johnson," Keating said, his voice taking on an edge I hadn't heard before. "Not until you understand what Sullivan's really doing."

He pulled up one final document—a personnel file marked with a bold red stamp: "PROJECT PROGENITOR."

"Sullivan's integration with the frequencies isn't about controlling them," he said, his voice dropping lower. "It's about becoming one with them. About transforming human consciousness to match whatever entity exists down there."

The file contained medical records that spanned decades. All belonging to the Sullivan family. Generation after generation subjected to frequency exposure, their genetics tracked and modified through selective breeding programs disguised as medical treatments.

"They've been preparing for this for over a century," Keating explained. "Long before they found the mineral. Long before they built the machines. The Sullivan family has been... changing itself. Adapting to receive whatever's trying to communicate."

"And our boys?" Wes asked, his voice tight.

Keating hesitated, then turned another page in the file. There, to my horror, were genetic profiles of our family going back generations. Mine. Wes's. His parents. My parents.

"You were never random," Keating said quietly. "Your bloodlines have been monitored for decades. Your compatibility tracked before you were even born."

"That's impossible," I whispered, though the evidence lay before me. "We met by chance. We fell in love naturally."

"Did you?" Keating asked, his expression unreadable. "Think about it. How many coincidences led you both to Johnson? To that specific house? To starting a podcast about mysteries and disappearances?"

My mind raced through memories that suddenly seemed suspect. The realtor who'd specifically mentioned the recording space when showing us the house. The mysterious benefactor who'd donated equipment to get our podcast started. The local stories that kept falling into our laps, leading us deeper into Johnson's history.

"Your meeting wasn't random," Keating continued. "Your entire relationship was engineered across generations to produce children with precisely the right genetic profile."

"No," Wes said firmly, though I could see doubt creeping into his expression. "Our feelings are real. Our family is real."

"I'm not saying your love isn't genuine," Keating clarified. "Just that the circumstances that brought you together were... curated."

Another text appeared on my phone: "Mom? Dad? We understand now. It's beautiful here. Come see."

Attached was a photograph that made my breath catch. Our boys stood in the center of our living room, but the floor had opened completely, revealing the well shaft below. They were arranged in formation around the edge, smiling up at the camera with expressions of perfect serenity.

But what truly stopped my heart was what loomed behind them. A shape rising from the darkness below—something vast and ancient that seemed to bend light around it, its form impossible to comprehend fully.

And in the background, barely visible at the edge of the frame, a woman's silhouette. Sullivan. She had them.

"We need to go," I said, already heading for the door. "Now."

But Keating blocked our path. "Not yet. There's one more thing you need to see."

He pressed a button on his console. A hidden panel in the wall slid open, revealing a small room beyond. Inside, illuminated by soft blue light, floated what appeared to be a small piece of the mineral we'd seen in Sullivan's files.

"This is what they found in the quarry," Keating said. "What Sullivan's family has been studying for generations."

The fragment pulsed gently, emitting faint tones that seemed to shift and change as we watched. But unlike the recordings we'd heard, these sounds weren't distressing. They were... beautiful. Harmonious.

"The frequencies aren't weapons," Keating explained, his voice softening. "They're a language. Sullivan's family has been trying to translate it for generations, but they've been getting it wrong. Hearing what they wanted to hear."

"And what is it actually saying?" Wes asked.

Keating looked at us solemnly. "It's a warning. About what's buried beneath Johnson. About what happens if it gets out."

Another text appeared on my phone, this one accompanied by a video clip. Our boys speaking in perfect unison, their voices overlapping in harmonies that shouldn't be possible:

"It's not what they told you. It's not what anyone knows. Come home. We'll show you the truth."

Behind them, that shape continued to rise from the well shaft, extending appendages that weren't quite limbs, forming patterns that weren't quite symbols. And as the clip ended, I caught a glimpse of what awaited us at home.

Not a monster. Not an alien entity. Something far more terrifying.

The truth about who our boys really were. About who we really were.

And why Johnson had always been calling us home.

"We need to go," I repeated, my voice steadier now. "Our boys need us."

Keating nodded, finally stepping aside. "They do. But not for the reasons you think."

As we headed for the exit, he handed me a small device that pulsed with the same gentle blue light as the mineral fragment. "When you get to your house, use this. It will disrupt Sullivan's frequencies long enough for you to reach your sons."

"And then what?" I asked.

His expression turned grim. "Then you'll have to make a choice about what kind of future you want for your family. And for humanity."

The school's side door opened onto an empty parking lot. The Initiative vans had vanished, leaving only Bill's truck.

"Something's changed," Wes said as we hurried toward it. "They're not hunting us anymore."

"Because they don't need to," I replied, looking at the newest message from the boys: "Hurry home. The Conductor is waiting."

As we pulled away from the school, the town around us seemed transformed. People moved through the streets with strange, synchronized precision. Store lights flickered in patterns that matched the frequencies. And through every speaker, every electronic device, came a subtle tone that made my skin prickle with recognition.

The same tone our recording equipment had captured at 3:33 AM the night everything began.

Johnson was coming alive around us, its hidden purpose finally revealing itself. And at its center, our house waited—the doorway to whatever lay beneath.

Our boys stood at that threshold, already part of something we were only beginning to understand.

And as we drove through streets that suddenly felt foreign, I couldn't shake the feeling that we weren't heading toward salvation.

We were heading toward revelation.

Of who we really were. Of what Johnson had always been.

Of why, despite everything, it felt like coming home.

999

Chapter 38: Wes

The drive home felt impossibly long, each familiar street now foreign, each landmark a signpost to somewhere I no longer recognized. Johnson's quiet neighborhoods, usually shuttered and dark at this hour, now burned with activity. Through windows, I caught glimpses of people moving in synchronized patterns, their silhouettes merging and separating with unnatural precision.

"Look at their eyes," Cynthia whispered as we passed a group standing perfectly still at a bus stop. Their heads turned in unison to follow our truck, gazes empty yet somehow expectant. "They're waiting for something."

Behind them, Johnson's oldest church bell began to toll in a rhythm that matched the pulse of Keating's device now clutched in Cynthia's hand. Not the usual marking of the hour, but something more deliberate. A countdown.

"Nine minutes," I said, checking the dashboard clock. "That's how long Sullivan said she had left before The Conductor reached full power."

Our truck lurched over a sudden ripple in the asphalt, as if the ground beneath the town was shifting. Around us, the air itself seemed to vibrate with frequencies just beyond hearing, making my teeth ache and my vision blur at the edges.

"Jesus," I muttered, swerving to avoid a dog that stood in the middle of the road. It didn't run or bark, just tracked our movement with an intelligent focus no animal should possess.

The text messages from our boys continued, each one more disturbing than the last. The most recent showed all five of them standing around our well shaft in the same formation we'd seen at the lake facility. The caption read: "We understand now. We were always meant to be here."

Cynthia's hand found mine on the gearshift. "It's still them," she insisted, but the tremor in her voice betrayed her uncertainty. "Whatever Sullivan's done to them, they're still our boys."

I nodded, though doubt had crept in like a poison. How much had been real? Our meeting, our marriage, our sons—all of it systematically engineered across generations to produce children with precisely the right genetic makeup to receive whatever lurked beneath Johnson? The thought was too monstrous to accept.

Yet the evidence lay in those documents Keating had shown us. In the perfect symmetry of our boys' arrangement around that well. In the way Johnson itself seemed to be awakening around us, the town's hidden purpose finally revealing itself.

As we turned onto Oak Drive, our street had transformed. Neighbors stood on their front lawns in perfect silence, facing our house at the center of the block. Their expressions were blank, but anticipation radiated from them in almost physical waves.

Our Victorian loomed before us, all its windows ablaze despite the late hour. Light seemed to pulse from within, as if the house itself was breathing. The front door stood open.

"Ready?" I asked, killing the engine. The silence that followed felt heavy, pregnant with possibility.

Cynthia clutched Keating's device, its soft blue glow the only color in a world that suddenly seemed desaturated of everything but darkness and light. "We don't have a choice," she replied. "They're our children."

We stepped from the truck into night air that tasted metallic, like electricity before a storm. The neighbors made no move to approach us, but their eyes followed our progress toward our front door with insect-like precision. Too focused. Too aware.

The floorboards creaked beneath our feet as we crossed the porch, a sound so familiar it hurt. How many times had I complained about fixing those boards? Now I wondered if the house had been designed to make that exact sound—if even that small detail had been orchestrated as part of something larger.

Inside, our home had changed. The furniture remained, but the proportions felt wrong, as if the interior space had somehow expanded beyond what the external walls should contain. Shadows stretched too long from corners, and the air carried that same charge we'd felt in the facility beneath the lake.

"Mom? Dad?" Ben's voice echoed from the living room, perfectly normal despite everything. The sound nearly broke me.

We turned the corner to find our five boys arranged around the opening in our floor—the well shaft that had been hidden beneath our house all this time. They stood with mathematical precision, equidistant from each other, forming a perfect circle around the darkness.

"You're here," Tyler said, his expression serene in a way that didn't match his usual animated self. "Just in time."

"In time for what?" Cynthia asked, taking a careful step forward. I noticed she kept Keating's device concealed in her palm, not yet willing to reveal our potential weapon.

"For the truth," Xander replied, gesturing toward the well. "About why we've always been able to hear things others can't. About why we moved in sync our whole lives. About why we belong here."

From the darkness below came a faint humming, like a massive tuning fork struck deep underground. The sound resonated through our bodies, vibrating at a frequency that made my teeth ache. Behind me, I felt rather than saw the neighbors moving closer to our house, drawn by that same call.

"Sullivan's using you," I said, trying to keep my voice level despite the dread building in my chest. "Whatever she told you, whatever she showed you down there—it's not the whole truth."

"Sullivan," Casey said, the name sounding strange coming from my youngest son's mouth. "She thought she understood. She thought she controlled it. But it's been waiting for us all along."

The rumbling grew stronger. Photographs rattled on our walls. A water glass shattered in the kitchen. The entire house seemed to be resonating with that impossible tone emanating from below.

"You need to come with us," Cynthia said firmly, mother-voice in full effect despite the terror I knew she must be feeling. "Now. We can figure this out together, but not here."

Ben smiled—that same gentle expression he'd worn since infancy, but now it carried something else. Something older. "We can't leave," he said simply. "None of us can. Not anymore."

Behind our boys, movement in the well shaft caught my attention. Something was rising from the darkness. Not Sullivan. Not one of her white-uniformed operatives. Something vast and impossible that seemed to bend light around itself, its edges difficult for my eyes to focus on.

"What is that?" I whispered, taking an involuntary step back.

"The real Conductor," Brayden replied. "What's been beneath Johnson since before there was a Johnson. What Sullivan's family has been trying to communicate with for generations."

The shape continued to rise, unfolding appendages that weren't quite arms, forming a silhouette that wasn't quite human. And as it ascended, I realized with growing horror that it wasn't coming up from the well shaft.

It was emerging from our boys.

Their outlines seemed to blur at the edges, their bodies somehow extending into that impossible shape rising between them. Not five separate entities, but five points of a single consciousness spreading outward.

"Oh God," Cynthia breathed beside me, her hand tightening around Keating's device. "What's happening to them?"

"Nothing that wasn't always meant to happen," a new voice replied from behind us.

We turned to find Sullivan in our entryway, her aged frame somehow more imposing in our home than it had appeared in those personnel files. She leaned on a silver-headed cane that pulsed with the same frequency as the well, her eyes bright with a fervor that bordered on madness.

"The frequencies were never weapons," she said, stepping into our living room. "They were a bridge. One my family has been trying to cross for generations."

"You're using our children," Cynthia spat, the device now glowing brighter in her hand as if responding to Sullivan's presence.

Sullivan laughed, a sound like grinding metal. "You still don't understand. Your boys weren't created to serve our purpose. They are our purpose. The culmination of sixty years of genetic refinement."

"What are you talking about?" I demanded.

"Project Echo was never about controlling the frequencies," Sullivan replied, her gaze fixed on our sons with something akin to religious adoration. "It was about creating perfect receivers. Humans who could withstand integration with what lives beneath Johnson."

The shape between our boys continued to expand, its form now filling most of the living room though somehow not displacing physical space. It existed both within and beyond our reality, its presence a mathematical impossibility that hurt to look at directly.

"My family found it in 1889," Sullivan continued, stepping closer to the well shaft. "When Johnson was nothing but a quarry surrounded by farmland. My great-grandfather realized what it was immediately—a consciousness from beyond our dimension, trapped in the bedrock like an insect in amber."

Cynthia's thumb hovered over a button on Keating's device. One press, and we might disrupt whatever was happening. But would it save our boys, or harm them? The uncertainty kept her hand frozen.

"He spent the rest of his life trying to communicate with it," Sullivan said, her voice taking on the cadence of a practiced sermon. "Building instruments, designing experiments. But human biology couldn't withstand direct contact. The frequencies that formed its language destroyed human tissue on contact."

I watched in horror as our boys' features began to ripple slightly, like reflections in disturbed water. Their expressions remained serene, but something was changing in them. Through them.

"So my family began a multi-generational project," Sullivan continued. "Selective breeding. Controlled reproduction. Genetic modification disguised as vaccinations and wellness checks. All to create individuals who could withstand direct communication with the entity."

"Our children," Cynthia whispered, the truth finally dawning in all its horror.

Sullivan nodded, her smile triumphant. "The first truly compatible vessels in sixty years of searching. Perfect resonators who can integrate with the consciousness without biological breakdown."

A thought struck me suddenly—a memory from Keating's bunker. "You lied to your own people," I realized. "The Initiative workers, the board members. Even your own scientists. They thought you were weaponizing the frequencies, but you were actually..."

"Preparing for ascension," Sullivan finished. "Most humans aren't ready for this truth. They would try to control it, weaponize it, destroy it out of fear. But your boys..." She turned toward them with reverence. "They understand. They've always understood on some level. It's in their DNA."

The shape had fully emerged now, a writhing mass of geometry and light that occupied the same space as our sons while somehow existing beyond them. Their eyes had gone completely black, reflecting something I couldn't comprehend.

"Their minds are interfacing directly with a non-human consciousness," Sullivan explained. "One that exists primarily as mathematical patterns rather than physical matter. It's been trying to communicate with humanity for centuries, but our biology is too limited to perceive it properly. Until now."

"This is insane," I said, though the evidence before me was undeniable. Our boys stood at the center of something vast and incomprehensible, their bodies serving as anchors for an entity that seemed to extend beyond our dimension.

"Insanity is fighting what's already begun," Sullivan replied. "The ascension can't be stopped now. The frequencies are spreading across Johnson. Across the world through every electronic device that received Amber's broadcast. The entity is awakening fully for the first time in millennia."

"And our boys?" Cynthia asked, her voice breaking. "What happens to them?"

Sullivan's expression softened slightly, perhaps the most human I'd seen her. "They become something new. The first of a bridging species between humanity and what waits beyond. Neither fully human nor fully other, but something transcendent."

The humming from the well intensified. The walls of our house began to vibrate at a frequency that made my vision blur. Outside, I could hear church bells across Johnson ringing in perfect synchronization.

"It's starting," Sullivan breathed, her eyes wide with anticipation. "The final integration. The moment my family has worked toward for generations."

Our boys turned toward us in perfect unison, their expressions radiating a serenity that didn't match the chaos unfolding around them. When they spoke, their voices overlapped in impossible harmonies:

"Don't be afraid. We're still us. We're just... more now."

Cynthia clutched the device tighter, her knuckles white with tension. One press, and we might save them—or destroy what they were becoming. The impossible choice of parents facing a transformation they couldn't understand.

"Trust us," the boys said together, extending their hands toward us. Behind them, the entity continued to unfold in patterns that broke the laws of physics, its presence growing stronger with each passing second.

And as the frequencies built toward some terrible crescendo, I realized we'd reached the moment of truth. The point where we had to decide whether to fight for our children's humanity, or embrace a transformation we couldn't possibly comprehend.

The choice that would determine not just the fate of our family, but of Johnson itself.

999

Chapter 39: Cynthia

The device in my palm pulsed with blue light, matching the rhythm of my racing heart. Sullivan's words hung in the air between us—ascension, integration, transcendence. Words that might sound beautiful if they weren't being applied to my children.

Our boys stood before us, their outlines blurring as something vast and incomprehensible flowed through them. Their eyes had gone completely black, reflecting patterns that hurt to look at directly. But beneath that alien presence, I could still see them—Ben's gentle smile, Xander's thoughtful expression, Brayden's quiet intensity, Tyler's barely contained energy, Casey's wide-eyed wonder.

"They're still your sons," Sullivan said, as if reading my thoughts. Her ancient face carried a strange tenderness that didn't match the madness in her eyes. "And they'll remember you, even after they become something more."

"This isn't your choice to make," I said, my voice steadier than I felt. My thumb hovered over the button on Keating's device, the one he claimed would disrupt Sullivan's frequencies. "They're children. Our children."

Sullivan's expression hardened. "They're the culmination of sixty years of careful genetic selection. The successful outcome of Project Echo's final phase. They are exactly what they were bred to be."

"Bred?" The word hit me like a slap. "They're not livestock. They're not experiments. They're our sons."

"Are they?" Sullivan gestured toward the well shaft, where that impossible shape continued to emerge, extending geometric forms that shouldn't be able to exist in three-dimensional space. "Look at them. They're already changing."

She was right. The transformation was accelerating. The boys' bodies seemed less solid now, their edges fading into the writhing mass of light and shadow that connected them to whatever entity was rising from below. Their faces still looked human, but something else moved beneath their skin—patterns shifting like schools of fish just below the surface.

"Whatever you're planning to do with that device," Sullivan said, her gaze dropping to my hand, "I wouldn't. The frequencies have already synchronized with their neural patterns. Disrupting the signal now could damage them irreparably."

Wes moved protectively closer to me. "You expect us to believe anything you say? After what you've done?"

"I expect you to look at the evidence before you," Sullivan replied calmly. "Your boys aren't in distress. They're not fighting this process. They're embracing it."

She was right again. There was no pain in their expressions, no fear. If anything, they seemed more at peace than I'd ever seen them.

"Mom," Ben's voice carried that impossible harmonic quality now, like multiple voices speaking through him. "It's okay. We understand now."

"Understand what?" I asked, taking a careful step forward despite Wes's warning hand on my arm.

"What we've always been," Casey answered, his young voice layered with something ancient. "Why we could always hear things others couldn't."

Tyler nodded, the movement slightly out of sync with normal human motion. "Why we always dreamed the same dreams."

"Why we could find each other without calling out," added Brayden.

"Why we've always moved together," finished Xander.

Their words sent chills through me, because they were true. All those strange little moments over the years that I'd dismissed or rationalized—the synchronized movements, the private language they seemed to share, the way they sometimes responded to questions I hadn't asked aloud.

"They've always been connected to it," Sullivan explained. "From the moment of conception. The frequencies that destroyed others have been nurturing them, preparing them."

"For what?" Wes demanded.

"For this moment," Sullivan replied. "When the barrier between dimensions thins enough for direct contact. For integration."

The entity continued to expand, filling our living room with impossible geometries. Light bent around it in ways that defied physics, creating shadows that moved independently of any source. And through it all, our boys remained at the center, five points of a star that seemed to be the foundation for something much larger.

"You can't stop what's happening," Sullivan continued, her voice taking on an almost reverent quality. "But you can join them. The entity has been trying to communicate with humanity for centuries. It's not hostile. It's simply... different. Operating on frequencies most humans can't perceive."

"And what happens when this 'integration' is complete?" I asked, my grip tightening on the device. "What happens to our boys?"

"They transcend," Sullivan said simply. "Become the bridge between humanity and what exists beyond our limited perception. The first of a new species capable of experiencing realities we can barely imagine."

The humming from the well intensified, climbing to a pitch that made my vision blur. Outside, the neighbors who had been watching our house began to move closer, drawn by that impossible frequency.

"It's calling to them," Sullivan explained. "Those with even slight sensitivity to the frequencies. Pulling them toward the source." Her eyes gleamed with fervent anticipation. "Soon, anyone within range will begin to feel it. To hear it. The beginning of a mass awakening."

The thought sent ice through my veins. Johnson was just the starting point. If what Sullivan said was true, if the frequencies were spreading through Amber's broadcast, through electronic devices across the world...

"You're talking about transforming humanity without its consent," Wes said, voicing my thoughts. "Playing god with millions of lives."

"Not playing god," Sullivan corrected. "Becoming something beyond gods. Beyond the limitations of physical form and linear time." She gestured toward our boys. "They understand. They've seen what's coming."

I looked at my sons, trying to see past the alien presence flowing through them to the children I'd raised. "Is that true?" I asked softly. "Do you understand what's happening to you?"

Their eyes, black and fathomless, turned toward me with perfect synchronization. When they spoke, it was with one voice that somehow contained all five of their individual tones:

"We see everything now, Mom. Past, present, future—they're all happening simultaneously. We can perceive dimensions beyond what humans can comprehend. And it's beautiful."

The device in my palm seemed to grow heavier. Using it might save them, might stop this transformation. Or it might destroy them, as Sullivan claimed. The impossible choice of a mother facing something beyond her understanding.

"Trust us," they said together, extending their hands toward us. Those hands now shimmered with patterns that seemed to extend beyond their physical forms, connecting to the larger entity still emerging from the well.

Sullivan took a step closer, her aged face alight with triumph. "Your boys are the key that unlocks the door. The perfect resonators we've been seeking for generations. Through them, humanity will transcend its limitations."

"You mean some of humanity," Wes said darkly. "Those you deem worthy of your 'ascension.'"

Sullivan shrugged, the gesture somehow inhuman despite its casualness. "Evolution has always involved selection. Those who can adapt, survive. Those who cannot..." She let the implication hang in the air.

The humming reached a fever pitch, and the walls of our house began to vibrate visibly. Cracks formed along the ceiling, plaster dust raining down like snow. The entity continued to expand, filling more space than our living room should be able to contain.

"Time to decide," Sullivan said, her voice barely audible above the rising frequency. "Join your sons in transcendence, or remain behind as they ascend beyond your reach."

I looked at Wes, saw the same helpless fear in his eyes that must be visible in mine. Then I turned back to our boys, to the children we'd raised, now standing at the threshold of becoming something we couldn't comprehend.

And in that moment, I understood something fundamental that Sullivan, for all her generations of research, had missed entirely.

The button on Keating's device felt warm beneath my thumb as I made my decision. Not based on Sullivan's promises of transcendence or fears of destruction. Not based on scientific theories or interdimensional entities.

Based on something much simpler, much more human.

The love of a mother for her children.

I pressed the button.

999

Chapter 40: Cynthia

Images flashed through my consciousness at impossible speed, too fast to comprehend yet somehow perfectly clear—memories, but not my own.

A quarry in 1889. Seven figures standing around a well, their instruments measuring vibrations from deep below. One of them, a woman, touching a strange device to the stone and jerking back as if burned. Their expressions shifting from curiosity to fear as they realize what they've found isn't what they expected.

A child in 1957—Michael Sullivan—sitting in a circle with six others, their small bodies arranged with clinical precision. Wires attached to their temples. Recording equipment capturing the sounds none of the adults could hear. His expression changing as the frequencies find their way into his mind, recognizing him as compatible but incomplete.

Sullivan's father scribbling equations in the margins of Tesla's notes, perverting the original meaning, twisting harmonics into something darker. "The key is 3-6-9," he writes, "but not as Tesla imagined. These frequencies don't create—they transform."

My own mother as a young woman, pregnant with me, walking past a clinic in Johnson. A nurse with Sullivan's eyes watching from the window, making a note in a ledger. Genetic tracking spanning generations.

Wes as a child, sitting alone at recess, drawing sound waves while other children played. Someone watching from across the schoolyard, nodding with approval. Another note made, another connection formed in a plan decades in the making.

Our first meeting—not random at all, but carefully orchestrated. The coffee shop where we exchanged glances, the mutual friend who introduced us, the apartment building where we both "happened" to live—all of it manipulated by unseen hands to bring compatible bloodlines together.

The visions accelerated, blurring together in a torrent of revelations. Yet within this chaos, I sensed something else watching these memories with me. Not Sullivan. Not the entity flowing through our boys. Something older, something that had been waiting with infinite patience.

The moment I knew I was pregnant with Ben. The inexplicable certainty that he would be a boy. The strange dreams that followed, full of frequencies I couldn't consciously hear but somehow understood.

Each birth, each child somehow known to me before they arrived. Five boys, exactly as I'd dreamed they would be. Five points of contact for something that had been waiting millennia to be heard.

Every strange synchronicity in their development—the silent communication between them, the way they moved together without instruction, how they always knew where to find each other. Not just brothers, but components of something larger.

The day we found our house in Johnson—the real estate agent's strange insistence that we view this particular property. The instant feeling of recognition when we stepped inside, like coming home to a place we'd never been. The well beneath the floorboards, waiting.

The first episode of our podcast. The mysterious technical difficulties that somehow produced the perfect sound mix. The anonymous donation of equipment specifically calibrated to certain frequencies. The stories that kept finding us, drawing us deeper into Johnson's history.

Behind all these manipulated moments, I glimpsed a truth that Sullivan herself had never understood. The entity beneath Johnson hadn't been gradually awakening—it had been patiently guiding, assembling the pieces needed for communication. Not the harbinger of some cosmic transformation, but the guardian of a boundary that was never meant to be crossed.

And our boys were its chosen vessels. Not to bring about the end Sullivan envisioned, but to prevent something far worse.

The visions coalesced into one final revelation: Sullivan hadn't discovered the entity by accident. Her family had been selected generations ago, sensitive to frequencies that should have made them guardians, protectors. But ambition had corrupted their purpose. They'd heard what they wanted to hear, interpreted the communications in ways that fed their desire for power and transcendence.

All while something waited on the other side of the weakening barrier. Something that Sullivan's experiments were unknowingly helping to break through.

The cascade of visions ceased as suddenly as it had begun. I gasped back into the present moment, my finger still pressed against the button on Keating's device. Only a heartbeat had passed.

Blue light erupted outward in concentric rings that rippled through the air like water. The humming frequency faltered, distorted, as if two sound waves were canceling each other out. Sullivan screamed—a sound of pure rage that contained no trace of humanity.

The entity between our boys seemed to stutter, its impossible geometry flickering like a faulty hologram. For a heartbeat, everything hung suspended between states.

Then reality itself seemed to crack open.

Not from the device in my hand, which had gone dark and inert. Not from Sullivan's machines beneath the town, which had fallen silent.

From our boys.

They stood unchanged, still arranged in that perfect circle, but something was happening through them rather than to them. The entity wasn't vanishing—it was transforming, reshaping itself into something even more impossible to comprehend.

"What have you done?" Sullivan shrieked over the cacophony of sound that now filled the house, her face contorted with fury and fear.

"I didn't do this," I called back, though the visions still echoed in my mind. "The boys did."

Sullivan staggered backward, her face contorted with confusion and fear. "Impossible," she whispered. "The frequencies are changing. Realigning. This isn't what the research predicted."

Our boys turned toward us, their expressions serene despite the chaos swirling around them. Their eyes were still black, but now shot through with threads of blue light that matched the device Keating had given us.

"Mom," Ben said, his voice now his own again though still layered with something older. His gaze met mine with recognition that went beyond the moment. "You saw it too."

"The truth," I whispered, understanding washing over me. "About Johnson. About Sullivan. About what's really beneath us."

"The entity doesn't want what Sullivan thought," Xander said, his voice taking on that same layered quality.

"It's not trying to transform humanity," Casey continued.

"It's trying to protect it," Tyler added.

"From what waits on the other side," Brayden finished.

The visions I'd experienced flashed through my mind again—Sullivan's family, misinterpreting the frequencies for generations. Hearing communications from one entity but inadvertently weakening the barriers that held back another. The guardian beneath Johnson wasn't the threat—it was the only thing standing between humanity and something far worse.

Sullivan's face twisted with rage. "Lies!" she spat. "I've spent my entire life studying the entity. My family has dedicated generations to understanding its purpose."

"You studied what you wanted to see," the boys said in unison, their voices carrying that strange harmonic quality again. "You heard what you wanted to hear. You shaped the frequencies to match your own desires for power and transcendence."

The knowledge from my vision solidified into certainty. "Your family was chosen to help it," I said, stepping forward. "To be guardians alongside it. But you corrupted that purpose. You heard only what fed your ambition."

Wes looked at me in confusion. "How do you know this?"

"I saw it," I replied simply. "When I pressed the button. Not just our memories, or Sullivan's experiments. I saw what came before. What's always been here, protecting us from what exists beyond."

The entity pulsed between our sons, no longer expanding but stabilizing into something less chaotic, more defined. Not the writhing mass of impossible geometry, but a pattern of light and energy that flowed through and around our boys without consuming them.

"A guardian," they said simply. "A consciousness that's existed since before humanity, watching, waiting, protecting the barriers between dimensions."

"Against what?" Wes asked, his voice hushed with awe.

Their expressions darkened simultaneously. "Against something hungry. Something that's been trying to break through since the beginning. Something Sullivan's experiments have been unknowingly helping."

Sullivan lunged forward, her hand outstretched toward the device that now lay inert in my palm. "Enough!" she snarled. "The culmination of my life's work will not be derailed by hallucinations and superstition!"

Before she could reach me, a pattern of light flowed from the boys, encircling her like a net of luminous threads. She froze mid-stride, her body suddenly rigid.

"You don't understand what you're interfering with," she said, her voice strained as if speaking required immense effort. "My family has been preparing for this moment for generations. The entity was meant to elevate us, to transform humanity into something greater."

"No," our boys replied as one. "Your family was meant to be the guardian's allies, not its exploiters. Your bloodline was chosen for its sensitivity to the frequencies, but your ambition corrupted your purpose."

The house continued to shake around us, but the quality of the vibration had changed. Less destructive, more... cleansing. I could feel it in my bones, a resonance that felt somehow familiar after the visions that had flooded my mind.

"The guardian has been trapped beneath Johnson for millennia," the boys explained, their words flowing together in perfect harmony. "Weakened by an ancient conflict that tore holes between dimensions. It's been trying to heal those tears, to prevent what waits on the other side from breaking through."

"But Sullivan's experiments," Wes said, the realization dawning on his face, "they've been weakening those barriers. Making them more permeable."

The boys nodded in unison. "Project Echo wasn't discovering something new. It was damaging something ancient. The frequencies weren't meant to transform humanity. They were warnings, attempts to communicate the danger."

In my mind, I could still see the visions of Sullivan's father, twisting Tesla's work on harmonics and frequency into something that served his own ambitions. Taking a philosophy about universal connection and perverting it into a tool for power and control.

Sullivan struggled against the luminous bonds that held her, her face contorted with rage and denial. "My father's research—my brother's sacrifice—generations of work—all for nothing? A mistake?"

"Not a mistake," our boys said, their voices gentle despite the otherworldly power flowing through them. "A misinterpretation with terrible consequences. The guardian never wanted sacrifices. It wanted allies."

The entity pulsed between them, its form more defined now, less chaotic. I could almost perceive a pattern in its movement, a language expressed through light and geometry that, after my visions, I was beginning to understand.

"What happens now?" I asked, stepping closer to our sons despite the alien presence that surrounded them. "To Johnson? To you?"

They smiled again—those familiar expressions that made my heart ache with love and fear. "Now we do what we were born to do," they said. "What our unique genetics always meant for us to become."

"And what's that?" Wes asked, moving to stand beside me.

"Translators," they replied. "Between humanity and the guardian. Between your world and what exists beyond it."

Sullivan's laughter cut through the moment, a bitter sound that held no humor. "You think you understand the entity better than I do? After sixty years of study? After generations of research?"

Our boys regarded her with something like pity. "We don't need to study it," they said simply. "We can hear it directly. We always could. And now, we understand what it's been trying to tell us."

The house shuddered one final time, and then the vibrations stilled. The entity continued to pulse between our sons, but its movements seemed more orderly now, more purposeful. Less like chaos and more like communication.

"The frequencies are stabilizing," the boys said, their expressions clearing slightly. "The guardian is regaining control. Healing the damage Sullivan's experiments caused."

"And Johnson?" I asked. "The people affected by the frequencies?"

"They'll recover," our sons assured us. "The guardian is correcting the distorted patterns, soothing the disruptions. Those most sensitive will remember strange dreams. Others won't remember anything at all."

Sullivan sagged in her luminous bonds, the fight draining from her aged frame. "A lifetime of work," she whispered, though whether to us or herself wasn't clear. "All of it based on a fundamental misunderstanding."

"Not misunderstanding," the boys corrected gently. "Misinterpretation. The guardian was always trying to communicate. Your family simply heard what you wanted to hear instead of what was actually being said."

I took another step closer to my sons, reaching out despite the alien energies still flowing through them. "And you? Will you stay this way? Changed?"

They exchanged glances, a familiar silent communication passing between them that now carried new meaning.

"We're still us, Mom," Ben said, his voice suddenly just his own again.

"Just with... expanded awareness," Xander added.

"We can perceive things others can't," Brayden explained.

"We can translate what the guardian needs to communicate," Tyler continued.

"But we're still your boys," Casey finished, his young face bright with that familiar smile.

Relief flooded through me as I recognized the truth in their words. Despite the otherworldly presence still flowing through them, they were still fundamentally our children. Changed, yes. Expanded into something that straddled the line between human and other. But not lost to us.

The luminous bonds around Sullivan began to fade, dissipating like mist in morning sunlight. She crumpled to the floor, her body suddenly showing every one of her advanced years.

"It's over," she whispered, though whether to us or herself wasn't clear. "My life's work. My family's legacy. All of it... meaningless."

As she slumped forward, something fundamental changed in her expression. Her eyes, which had burned with fanatical purpose for decades, suddenly widened with a different kind of understanding - not transcendence, but the recognition of her own mortality. Her body, which had been sustained by the frequencies she'd manipulated for years, could no longer maintain itself as those frequencies realigned.

Sullivan's hand clutched at her chest, her breathing becoming shallow and irregular. "This... isn't... possible..." she gasped, her voice barely audible.

And then, with terrible simplicity, Dr. Evelyn Sullivan - the Conductor of Project Echo, the woman who had manipulated generations to serve her vision - collapsed fully to the floor of our living room and went still.

No cosmic transformation. No glorious ascension. Just the quiet end of a human life that had been extended far beyond its natural span through the very frequencies she had misunderstood.

"Not meaningless," our boys said softly, their voices compassionate despite everything she'd done. "Misguided. There's a difference."

The entity between them pulsed one final time, then began to recede—not vanishing completely, but settling into a less visible state. The boys' outlines solidified, their forms becoming fully human again though their eyes still held traces of that otherworldly awareness.

Beyond our windows, Johnson was already beginning to stir from its trance-like state. People who had stood frozen in strange synchronization now looked confused, disoriented, as if waking from a shared dream. The frequencies that had controlled them were fading, replaced by the guardian's true harmonics—not dominating, but healing.

Wes moved to stand beside me, his arm slipping around my waist. "How did you know?" he asked softly. "What did you see when you pressed that button?"

I leaned against him, drawing strength from his solid presence. "Everything," I said simply. "The truth about Johnson. About Sullivan. About our boys." I looked up at him, feeling the weight of revelations still settling in my mind. "About us. How we were brought together, how our sons were... not engineered, exactly, but anticipated. Expected."

"Does that make what we have any less real?" he asked, the hint of uncertainty in his voice breaking my heart.

"No," I replied without hesitation. "The circumstances that brought us together might have been manipulated, but what we built was ours. What we feel is real. What we made together..." I looked at our five sons, still glowing faintly with the guardian's energy. "That's more real than anything."

The well shaft that had opened in our floor began to close, the boards sliding back into place as if they'd never been disturbed. The last glimpse I caught of the darkness below showed not emptiness, but a soft blue light—like the one that had emanated from Keating's device. Not threatening, but watchful. Patient.

And as our boys moved toward us, arms outstretched for an embrace that felt both familiar and new, I realized that we'd crossed a threshold there was no returning from. Our family would never be the same. Our understanding of reality had been fundamentally altered.

But whatever came next, whatever role our boys would play as translators between worlds, we would face it together. As a family that now straddled dimensions, bound by something far stronger than Sullivan's frequencies or even the guardian's ancient power.

The simple, human love that had led me to press that button in the first place.

999

Chapter 41: Wes

Silence fell over our living room like a physical weight. Sullivan's body lay motionless on our floor, her expression frozen somewhere between rage and recognition. The transformation that had consumed our boys moments before had receded, leaving them looking almost normal—if you ignored the faint blue light that still traced patterns beneath their skin.

"Is she..." I couldn't finish the question, though the answer was obvious.

"Her body was failing long before tonight," Ben said, his voice carrying that new depth that made him sound decades older. "The frequencies were the only thing keeping her alive."

Casey approached Sullivan's body with a child's curious lack of fear, studying her with his head tilted. "She didn't understand," he said softly. "She thought she was hearing one voice, but there were always two."

We had a dead woman in our living room. The architect of decades of manipulation and experimentation, the person who had viewed our children as the culmination of a multi-generational breeding program. And yet, looking at her now—just an elderly woman in an outdated suit, her body finally surrendering to time—I felt nothing but a hollow sadness.

"We need to call someone," I said, then stopped. Who exactly does one call when the mastermind behind a secret organization dies in your home? Not the police, certainly. Not after everything we'd seen.

"The Initiative will know she's gone," Xander said, stepping away from Sullivan's body. "They'll feel it. The frequencies she used to control them are already fading."

Cynthia moved closer to me, her expression dazed from whatever visions the device had shown her. "What happens now? With Johnson? With the people Sullivan manipulated?"

"They'll start to wake up," Tyler explained, somehow knowing exactly what his brother was about to say before he said it. "The guardian's frequencies are spreading through town, counteracting Sullivan's distortions."

Brayden nodded. "Some will remember parts of what happened. Most won't."

The guardian. The entity beneath Johnson that Sullivan had misunderstood. The protective force our boys now seemed connected to in ways I couldn't begin to comprehend. The revelation had come so suddenly, so completely, that my mind still struggled to process the implications.

"We need to check on Mom," Cynthia said, her practical nature asserting itself despite everything. "And Dad and Tracy. They might remember more than most, being connected to us."

Through our living room window, I could see the neighbors who had stood in eerie synchronization on their lawns now looking confused, disoriented. Some were returning to their homes. Others stood blinking up at the night sky as if waking from a dream they couldn't quite remember.

"What about her?" I nodded toward Sullivan's body. "We can't just leave her here."

The boys exchanged one of those silent communications that now carried new meaning. "The guardian will take care of it," Ben said, his expression solemn.

As if responding to his words, a soft blue light began to emanate from beneath the floorboards—not from the well opening this time, but from every crack and seam in the wooden planks. The light rose in tendrils that curled around Sullivan's form, gently lifting her body a few inches off the floor.

"Jesus," I breathed, stepping back involuntarily.

"It's okay, Dad," Casey assured me, his small hand finding mine. "The guardian's just taking her home."

Home. The word carried a weight I wasn't prepared for. Sullivan had devoted her life to communicating with the entity beneath Johnson. Had corrupted its purpose. Had misinterpreted its warnings as invitations. And now, in death, she was being returned to it.

The tendrils of light continued to envelop her, growing brighter until her body was completely obscured. Then, with a soft sound like a sigh, both the light and Sullivan faded from view. The floorboards settled, showing no sign that a woman had died there moments before.

"Where did she go?" Cynthia asked, her voice barely above a whisper.

"Back to the guardian," Xander explained. "Back to the beginning."

A phone rang, breaking the moment. Not one of our cell phones, which still lay dead from whatever electromagnetic event had swept through Johnson, but our landline. The ancient thing we'd kept mostly for emergencies.

Cynthia looked at me, uncertainty in her eyes. I nodded and moved to answer it.

"Hello?" My voice sounded strange to my own ears, too normal for everything that had just happened.

"Wesley?" My mother's voice, tight with concern. "Thank God. We've been trying to reach you for hours. The boys—"

"Are fine," I said quickly. "They're all fine. They're home with us now."

A pause. "But they were just here ten minutes ago. Then they said something about having to go home, that you needed them. We couldn't stop them—it was like they were sleepwalking. Bill and Tracy followed them, but—"

"Mom," I cut her off gently. "It's complicated. But everyone's safe now."

"Safe from what?" Her voice sharpened. "Wesley Thomas Lumin, what exactly is going on there? First those boys just walk out the door and disappear, then half the electronics in my house go haywire, and now you're telling me—"

"I'll explain everything," I promised. "But right now, we need some time. As a family."

Another pause, longer this time. "Sullivan," she said finally, her voice dropping to a whisper. "It was Sullivan, wasn't it? She finally did it."

A chill ran through me. "Mom? What do you know about Sullivan?"

"Enough," she replied cryptically. "Enough to know when to stay away from Johnson. When to keep quiet about certain things."

"Mom—"

"Not over the phone," she cut me off. "Some things need to be said in person. Tomorrow. Bring the boys. Bring Cynthia. We have a lot to discuss."

The line went dead before I could respond. I stared at the receiver, a new piece of the puzzle clicking into place. My mother, who had always been oddly insistent about staying away from certain parts of Johnson. Who had warned me, in her indirect way, about buying this particular house. Who had seemed unsurprised by the boys' strange synchronized behaviors.

She knew something. Had always known something.

"Your mother?" Cynthia asked as I hung up the phone.

I nodded, still processing the implications. "She wants us to come tomorrow. Says she has things to tell us. About Sullivan."

"Grandma knew," Ben said simply. All five boys nodded in perfect unison, as if this was a fact they'd always known.

"Rebecca was part of it once," Casey added, the words strange coming from my youngest son's mouth. "Before she understood what was really happening."

Before I could ask what exactly that meant, a knock came at our front door. Not the frantic pounding of law enforcement or the insistent rapping of concerned neighbors, but three measured, deliberate knocks.

The boys looked at each other again, that silent communication passing between them.

"It's Keating," Xander said with certainty.

I moved to the door, Cynthia close behind me. The boys remained in the living room, watching with calm interest. When I pulled the door open, Daniel Keating stood on our porch, looking exactly as he had in his underground bunker. But something about him had changed—a tension gone from his shoulders, a darkness lifted from his eyes.

"It worked," he said simply, glancing past me to where the boys stood. "The guardian is reestablishing control."

"Sullivan is dead," I replied, not sure if this was news to him or expected information.

Keating nodded. "I felt it. We all did—everyone who was part of the Initiative. Like a circuit being broken."

"You were one of them," Cynthia realized. "Working from the inside."

"For longer than I care to admit," Keating confirmed. "I believed in Sullivan's vision once. Until I discovered what she was really doing to those children. What she planned to do to your boys."

The casual way he referred to Sullivan's experiments made my skin crawl. This man had been part of an organization that had treated children as test subjects, as tools for some twisted transcendence.

"Why should we trust you now?" I asked, blocking his view of our sons.

A sad smile crossed his face. "Because I was the one who left you those warnings. Who helped you understand what the frequencies really meant. Who gave you the device that disrupted Sullivan's control."

"The guardian chose you too," Ben said from behind us. The certainty in his voice made Keating look up sharply. "Just like it chose our parents. Just like it chose us."

Keating's expression softened. "The guardian chooses many. Not all hear its call clearly. Sullivan heard what she wanted to hear for generations. I almost did the same."

"What do you want?" Cynthia asked, her voice carrying that protective edge that emerged whenever she felt our family might be threatened.

"To help you understand what comes next," Keating replied. "Sullivan may be gone, but what she unleashed is still spreading. The frequencies that leaked through Amber's broadcast reached far beyond Johnson. People everywhere are beginning to hear echoes of what lives beneath this town."

"And that's bad?" I asked, thinking of what our boys had said about the guardian's protective nature.

"It depends," Keating said grimly. "On whether they hear the guardian's warning, or what waits behind it."

The boys moved forward as one, standing between us and Keating. Not protectively, but deliberately.

"He needs to show us something," Casey said, his eyes meeting mine with that unsettling clarity. "Something about Amber's broadcast. About what's coming through."

"May I?" Keating gestured to the tablet he carried.

I glanced at the boys, then at Cynthia. She nodded slightly, and I stepped aside.

Keating moved past us into the living room, setting his tablet on the coffee table. The screen flickered to life, showing a global map dotted with points of light. Each point pulsed with the same rhythm, forming patterns that spread outward from what looked like—

"Johnson," Cynthia breathed. "The epicenter is Johnson."

"Or more precisely, your house," Keating corrected. "The well beneath it. The original access point."

The screen zoomed in, showing how the frequencies were spreading across continents, following digital networks, cellular towers, power grids. Each pulse carried the same pattern we'd felt in our home.

"Amber's broadcast was the catalyst," Keating explained. "But what's spreading now is something else. Something older. The guardian's message, finally reaching ears that can hear it."

"And the other message?" I asked, thinking of what our boys had said about something waiting on the other side. Something trying to break through. "Is that spreading too?"

Keating's expression darkened. "That's what we need to talk about. Because while the guardian is regaining control here in Johnson, elsewhere..." He swiped to a news report from a small town in Idaho. The headline read: "Mass Hallucination Event Leaves Seventeen Hospitalized."

Another report, this one from Brazil: "Mysterious Audio Signal Triggers Seizures in Electronics Factory Workers."

And another from Japan: "Schoolchildren Report Identical Dreams, Authorities Baffled."

"It's starting," Ben said quietly. "What the guardian has been trying to prevent."

"Breakthroughs," Keating confirmed. "Weak points in the barrier between dimensions. The same kind of tears the guardian has been trying to repair beneath Johnson for millennia."

"And now these... tears are appearing globally?" Cynthia asked, the horror of the implication clear in her voice.

Keating nodded grimly. "Anywhere Amber's broadcast reached. Anywhere people heard those frequencies."

"Then we have to stop it," I said, the solution seeming obvious despite the impossible scale of the problem. "Find a way to counteract the frequencies, like the guardian did here."

"That's why I'm here," Keating said, looking at our boys with something between awe and hope. "Because the only ones who can translate the guardian's message clearly enough to heal those tears are standing in this room."

The boys looked at each other, then back at us. Their expressions were simultaneously those of children faced with an overwhelming task and ancient beings who had anticipated this moment for eons.

"We need to go to the places where the tears are forming," Xander said simply.

"Places where the other side is breaking through," Tyler added.

"We need to show them what we've seen," Casey continued.

"What we've heard," Brayden said.

"What we understand now," Ben finished.

Panic rose in my chest at the thought of my sons traveling to places where reality itself was unraveling. "Absolutely not," I said, parental instinct overriding everything else. "We just got you back. We're not sending you into more danger."

The boys smiled at me—five different smiles that were purely them, despite the otherworldly awareness behind their eyes.

"Dad," Ben said gently, "we're not in danger from this. We're the only ones who can help."

"We won't be alone," Xander added. "You and Mom will be with us."

"And the guardian," Casey said with absolute certainty.

I looked at Cynthia, saw the same conflict in her eyes. The need to protect our children warring with the understanding that they had become something more than just our children. That they now carried a responsibility bigger than our family.

"How long do we have?" she asked Keating, her voice steady despite everything.

"The tears are still small," he replied. "Containable. But they're growing. I'd estimate we have months, not years, before they become irreparable."

"And if they can't be repaired?" I asked, though I feared I already knew the answer.

Keating's expression was grave. "Then what waits on the other side will begin to come through. Not just as frequencies or patterns, but physically. And from what little I understand of it..." He trailed off, unable to put the horror into words.

"It hungers," the boys said in unison, their voices resonating with something ancient and terrible. "It consumes. It has been trying to break through since the first consciousness emerged on Earth."

A chill ran through me at their words. Not Sullivan's transcendence. Not some glorious evolution. But something hungry, something that viewed humanity as nothing more than sustenance.

"How do we even begin to fight something like that?" I asked, the scale of what we were facing finally sinking in.

The boys looked at each other, then back at us. "We don't fight it," they said simply. "We heal the tears. We strengthen the barriers. We do what the guardian has been doing all along."

"And how exactly do we do that?" Cynthia asked.

"By broadcasting the right frequencies," Keating said, turning back to his tablet. "The guardian's true message, not Sullivan's distortion of it. That's why your boys are so important. They can translate it clearly, without the corruption that's plagued every other attempt."

"You want to use our children as some kind of psychic radio towers," I said flatly, not bothering to hide my skepticism. "To broadcast a message from an entity that lives beneath our house."

"Dad," Ben said, his eyes meeting mine with quiet resolve. "This is what we're meant to do. All those strange moments you and Mom tried to explain away over the years—they were preparing us for this."

I wanted to argue, to insist that my sons were just children, that they deserved normal lives free from interdimensional responsibilities. But looking at them now—standing together with that quiet certainty, their eyes reflecting knowledge no children should possess—I knew denial would be pointless. And selfish.

"If we do this," Cynthia said slowly, "what happens to our family afterward? Can we ever go back to normal?"

The boys smiled at her question—not condescendingly, but with genuine affection.

"Define normal," Casey replied with a hint of his old mischief.

"We'll still be your sons," Tyler assured her.

"We'll still fight over video games," Brayden added.

"And complain about homework," Xander said.

"And need our parents," Ben finished. "That hasn't changed. It won't change."

I looked at Cynthia, saw the same mixture of fear and resolution in her eyes that I felt. We had raised these boys together, had weathered every normal parenting crisis from colic to broken bones to middle school drama. This was just... a bigger crisis. With slightly higher stakes.

"Where do we start?" I asked Keating, making my decision. Our decision.

"Idaho," he replied, pulling up the news story again. "The tear there is still small, but growing rapidly. If your boys can heal it, it will create a template for addressing the others."

"When do we leave?" Cynthia asked, already mentally packing bags, arranging for cat care, all the practical details that kept our family functioning through crises large and small.

"First light," Keating said, checking his watch. "The tear seems to strengthen at night, weaken slightly during daylight hours. We'll want to arrive when it's at its most vulnerable."

The boys nodded in unison, as if this made perfect sense to them. Perhaps it did now.

"We should try to get some rest," I suggested, though the thought of sleep seemed ludicrous after everything we'd experienced. "It's going to be a long day tomorrow."

"I'll make arrangements for transportation," Keating said, rising to leave. "And brief you on what to expect when we arrive."

I walked him to the door, leaving Cynthia with the boys in the living room. On the porch, out of earshot, I turned to him with the question that had been burning in my mind since he arrived.

"Why us?" I asked bluntly. "Out of all the families in all the world, why were we chosen for this?"

Keating regarded me for a long moment, his expression unreadable. "The guardian has been searching for the right combination for millennia. The right genetic patterns, the right frequency sensitivity. Your bloodline and Cynthia's both carried fragments of what was needed. Together..." He glanced back toward the living room, where our five sons sat with their mother. "Together, you created something unique. Something the guardian has been waiting for."

"That doesn't answer my question," I pressed. "Why us specifically? Why our family?"

A shadow of something—regret, perhaps, or guilt—crossed Keating's face. "Because some choices were made long before you were born. By people who thought they understood what they were hearing." He hesitated, then added, "You should ask your mother about that tomorrow. About her connection to Johnson. To Sullivan."

Before I could demand he explain that cryptic statement, Keating was already heading down the steps. "I'll be back at dawn," he called over his shoulder. "Be ready. All of you."

I watched him disappear into the night, his words echoing in my mind. My mother's connection to Sullivan. Choices made before I was born. The guardian's search for the right genetic combination.

How far back did this manipulation go? How many generations had been nudged, guided, arranged to produce our five sons?

Behind me, I heard Cynthia call the boys upstairs to get ready for bed. Their voices drifted through the open door—normal bickering about bathroom turns, complaints about being tired, Casey's insistence that he wasn't ready for sleep yet. The ordinary sounds of our family, unchanged despite the extraordinary circumstances.

And as I turned back to join them, to help with the bedtime routine that had anchored our days for years, I realized that while our understanding of the world had been fundamentally altered, the most important things remained constant.

Our boys were still our boys. Our family was still our family. And whatever came next, whatever interdimensional horrors we might face, we would face them together.

The way we always had.

999

Chapter 42: Cynthia

Dawn broke over Rebecca's farmhouse, painting the sky in watercolor streaks of pink and gold. I'd barely slept, my mind still processing everything we'd learned, everything we'd seen. The boys, by contrast, had fallen into the deep, peaceful sleep of children who had no doubt about their place in the world—even if that place now straddled dimensions.

Rebecca stood at her kitchen counter, methodically packing sandwiches into a cooler as if we were heading to a family picnic rather than an interdimensional tear in Idaho. Her efficiency reminded me of myself—the practical response to crisis, the need to care for the physical even when facing the metaphysical.

"You knew," I said quietly, accepting the cup of coffee she offered. "All this time, you knew about Johnson. About what was beneath it."

Rebecca's eyes, so like Wes's, held a mixture of sorrow and resignation. "Not everything. Not the full truth. But enough to keep my distance." She paused, her hands stilling on the sandwich she was wrapping. "Enough to try to protect Wesley."

"Why didn't you warn us?" I kept my voice low, conscious of Wes upstairs helping the boys pack. "When we bought the house, when we started the podcast—"

"I tried, in my way," she replied softly. "All those comments about the neighborhood, suggesting other towns to look at. Remember how I kept sending you listings in Cedar Ridge?" A sad smile crossed her face.

"But I couldn't say the real reason without sounding... well, you know how Wes is about anything that can't be measured or recorded."

She was right. Before all this, Wes would have nodded politely while dismissing her concerns as superstition. My own mother had raised me to believe in the mystical, the unseen, but even I had approached the supernatural with a kind of academic distance. Until it invaded our home.

"How are you connected to it all?" I asked. "Keating implied—"

"Daniel Keating should be careful about implying things he doesn't fully understand," Rebecca said, her voice firm but not unkind. She sighed, setting down her knife. "But yes, there's a connection. One I tried to escape from the moment I understood what was happening."

She gestured for me to sit at the kitchen table, joining me with her own cup of coffee. "I was part of a study group in college. Medical volunteers for what we were told was cognitive research. The Sullivan family ran the program. They were brilliant, charismatic. Made us feel like we were contributing to groundbreaking science."

The farmhouse creaked around us, old wood settling in the morning warmth.

"They were testing for frequency sensitivity," Rebecca continued. "Identifying people who could... hear things others couldn't. Only we didn't know that's what they were doing. We thought it was just hearing tests, reaction time experiments."

Her fingers traced the rim of her coffee cup, a nervous gesture I'd seen Wes do countless times.

"By the time I realized what was happening, I was already pregnant with Wesley." She looked up at me, her eyes clear and direct. "Roy and I were already married, but the Sullivans had been... monitoring us, I suppose you could say. Watching for genetic patterns they wanted to continue."

She shook her head, the memory clearly still painful. "I had no idea until later. Roy did some investigating—he was a journalist, you know. Always asking questions, digging for truth. He uncovered things about the Sullivan family's experiments."

"Did Evelyn Sullivan know? About Wes?"

"That Wesley carried specific genetic markers they were looking for? Yes." Rebecca nodded. "It's partly why we left Johnson, why Roy insisted we move far away. He wanted to protect Wesley from their influence."

"But they found us anyway," said Wes from the doorway. I hadn't heard him come down the stairs. His expression was carefully neutral, but I could see the tension in his jaw, the slight tremor in his hands.

Rebecca didn't flinch or look away. She met her son's gaze steadily. "They did. When you met Cynthia... that wasn't a coincidence. Sullivan had been tracking you. Both of you."

"So our entire relationship was engineered?" Wes's voice remained calm, but I could hear the hurt beneath the words. "Our marriage, our children—all part of some grand experiment?"

Rebecca stood, crossing to her son with a fierce determination I'd always admired in her. "The circumstances that brought you together may have been manipulated, but what grew between you wasn't. Love can't be engineered, Wesley. What you and Cynthia built, what you feel for each other and those boys—that's real."

She took his hands in hers, and for a moment, they looked so alike—the same stubborn set to their mouths, the same analytical gaze.

"I kept the truth from you to protect you," she continued. "Maybe that was wrong. But I watched you grow into a man who questions everything, who seeks truth through evidence. Would you have believed me if I'd told you there was something beneath Johnson, something that had been guiding bloodlines for generations?"

Wes didn't answer, but his hands relaxed slightly in his mother's grip.

"We tried to keep you away from Sullivan's influence," Rebecca said. "Roy and I both did. We thought if we raised you somewhere else, if we surrounded you with normal, practical things—"

"That I wouldn't hear the frequencies," Wes finished. "That I wouldn't be drawn back to Johnson."

Rebecca nodded. "Johnson was just a small town then. Not even called Johnson—they renamed it after the '57 incident. We thought if we got far enough away..." She sighed. "But the guardian had already marked you. All we could do was try to prepare you to face it someday."

"By teaching me to question everything," Wes said, understanding dawning in his eyes. "To look for evidence, patterns."

"To trust your instincts even when they contradicted the data," Rebecca added. "Roy knew that someday you might need both scientific rigor and... intuition."

She released his hands and went to an old roll-top desk in the corner of the kitchen. From a hidden compartment, she extracted a small brass key. "There's something you should have. Something Roy prepared for you, in case this day ever came."

Wes took the key, turning it over in his hands. "What is it?"

"A trunk in the attic. Roy's research about the Sullivan family, about the guardian, about everything he uncovered before he died." Rebecca's voice grew gentler. "He always meant for you to have it, when you were ready. I think that time has come."

Footsteps on the stairs announced the boys' arrival. They entered the kitchen in their usual formation, each carrying his small backpack. Their movements were still synchronized but less mechanical than before—more like dancers who had rehearsed together for years than puppets on the same strings.

"Is Dad okay?" Ben asked, his eyes moving between Wes and Rebecca.

"I'm fine, buddy," Wes replied, pocketing the key. "Just learning some family history."

The boys exchanged glances—that silent communication that had once seemed merely the closeness of siblings now carrying new weight.

"Grandma was trying to protect you," Casey said, with a certainty no eight-year-old should possess. "She always has been."

Rebecca's eyes widened slightly. "You can see it, can't you? The connections, the patterns."

Ben nodded. "The guardian shows us. Not everything, but enough to understand."

"It's like threads," Xander added. "Connecting people across time."

"Some glow brighter than others," Tyler said.

"Yours is one of the brightest," Brayden finished.

Rebecca's hand went to her throat. "I never thought... I wasn't sensitive enough to see them myself. But Roy sometimes said he could feel something, especially when you were little, Wesley. He said you had a glow about you that Sullivan would be drawn to."

I checked my watch. "We should probably get going. We need to meet Keating back in Johnson."

"Yes," Rebecca said, quickly finishing the sandwiches. "He's waiting for you at the school gymnasium, correct?"

Wes nodded, helping her pack the cooler. "That's where we left the truck. He said he'd have everything ready by the time we get back."

"One more thing before you go," Rebecca said, her voice pitched low and urgent. "Sullivan wasn't working alone. The Initiative has branches beyond Johnson, people who believe in what she was trying to accomplish."

"We know," I said. "Keating explained about the global spread—"

"I'm not just talking about the frequencies spreading," Rebecca clarified. "There are active collaborators. People who've been preparing for the barriers to thin, who want what's on the other side to come through."

Wes frowned. "Why would anyone want that? After what we've seen, what we know it would do—"

"Because they believe they'll be spared," Rebecca said simply. "That they'll be among the chosen few who transcend while others are... consumed. It's the lie the Sullivan family has been telling their followers for generations."

"We should get on the road," Wes said, glancing at his watch again. "It's a long drive back to Johnson, and Keating's waiting."

"Be careful who you trust," Rebecca said, her eyes moving meaningfully toward the door, then back to us. "Even those who claim to help might have their own agenda."

"If Keating's working against us, why would he have helped disrupt Sullivan's frequencies?" I asked.

"Not necessarily against you," Rebecca amended. "But he was part of the Initiative for years. The question is: what does he want now that Sullivan is gone?"

With that warning lingering between us, we gathered our bags and headed outside. Rebecca hugged each of the boys tightly, whispering something in their ears that made them nod solemnly. When she embraced Wes, her grip was fierce.

"I'm sorry I kept the truth from you," she said. "I thought I was protecting you."

Wes's arms tightened around her. "You did protect me. You and Dad both."

Relief washed over Rebecca's face. "The trunk will explain more. Things I can't... things that are easier to understand when you see the evidence."

"I'll call when we reach Idaho," Wes promised.

Chapter 43: Wes

The drive back to Johnson felt strangely normal—familiar landmarks sliding past, the boys quietly talking in the back seat, Cynthia checking her phone for messages from Lana. But normalcy was a thin veneer now, transparent as tissue paper over the profound strangeness that had become our lives.

My mother's revelations hung heavy in my thoughts. Sullivan had been tracking us. Our meeting hadn't been coincidental. The key to Dad's trunk pressed against my leg through my pocket, a physical reminder of truths still waiting to be uncovered.

"Do you think we'll have time to look through your dad's research before we go?" Cynthia asked softly, her hand finding mine across the center console.

"I don't know," I admitted. "But we should at least take it with us. There might be something that could help us understand what we're facing."

The outskirts of Johnson looked eerily ordinary as we entered the town limits. People walked their dogs, shopped at corner markets, washed cars in driveways—all completely unaware that just hours ago, their small town had been ground zero for interdimensional forces beyond human comprehension.

"It's like nothing happened," Cynthia murmured, watching a group of joggers pass. "Like everything just... reset."

"The guardian healed this place," Brayden said from the back seat, his voice carrying that unnerving maturity. "But it can't reach the tears forming elsewhere."

A text from Keating had pinged my phone as we left Rebecca's farm: "Meeting time changed to noon. Need to gather additional equipment. Will explain when you arrive." The delay had given us time to pack more carefully and grab a proper breakfast, though the waiting had only amplified our anxiety.

We pulled into the high school parking lot exactly on time. Keating's black SUV sat waiting in the far corner, its windows tinted against the midday sun. As we approached, he stepped out, his expression unreadable behind dark sunglasses.

"Any trouble on the road?" he asked, scanning our truck for signs of pursuit.

I shook my head. "Everything's quiet. Almost suspiciously so."

"The guardian's influence," Keating said, opening the rear doors of his vehicle. "It's restored a sort of equilibrium here. But it won't last unless we deal with the other tears."

The boys piled out of our truck, moving toward Keating's SUV with a curious synchronicity that still made my skin crawl. They weren't being controlled—at least I didn't think so—but they were different. Changed. Moving with purpose and awareness beyond their years.

"How long to Idaho?" I asked, loading our bags into the SUV's rear compartment.

"Eight hours if we push it," Keating replied, checking his watch. "We'll need to stop for the night and arrive in the morning. Daylight seems to weaken the tear's effects."

As Cynthia settled the boys in the back seats, I pulled Keating aside. "My mother warned us to be careful who we trust. She seemed particularly concerned about you."

He didn't flinch, which counted for something. "I'd be concerned too, in her position. I was with the Initiative for almost fifteen years. I joined believing in Sullivan's vision—transcendence through frequency alignment. By the time I realized what was really happening, I was too deeply embedded to simply walk away."

"What changed your mind?"

A shadow crossed his face. "I was assigned to monitor test subjects. Children, like your boys. I watched what the frequencies did to them. Watched Sullivan dismiss failed experiments as 'incompatible vessels' without a second thought." His jaw tightened. "No transcendence. Just suffering."

I studied him, trying to assess his sincerity. Truth and deception had become thin boundaries, easily crossed. "And now? What do you want from all this?"

Keating removed his sunglasses, his eyes meeting mine directly. "To stop what's coming through. To repair the damage Sullivan did. And to keep your boys from becoming what she intended."

It wasn't entirely reassuring, but it would have to do for now. We had no choice but to trust him, at least until we reached Idaho and saw the tear for ourselves.

Back at the SUV, the boys had arranged themselves in the middle and rear seats—Ben and Xander in the middle row, the younger three in the back. Their positioning didn't appear random; they'd seated themselves according to some pattern I couldn't discern.

"Everyone set?" Keating asked, settling behind the wheel.

Cynthia took the passenger seat while I slid in beside Ben. As Keating pulled away from the high school, I noticed how every teacher and student on the grounds seemed to look up simultaneously, watching our departure with vacant expressions.

"They don't remember anything," Xander said, noticing my observation. "But their bodies do. The frequencies changed them, even if the guardian healed the damage."

"What exactly do you mean by 'changed'?" I asked.

"Sensitized," Ben explained. "Like film exposed to light. They might not remember what happened, but they'll be more receptive if it happens again."

"The black fluid leaves traces," Casey added, his young voice oddly clinical. "Microscopic particles that stay in the bloodstream."

"Even after the guardian neutralized it," Tyler continued.

"It changes people permanently," Brayden finished.

The implication was chilling. Sullivan might be gone, but her work had prepared the ground for whatever came next. The black fluid she'd created, that substance that had leaked from the workers, had already spread throughout Johnson's population, preparing them like kindling for a fire.

We drove in silence for a time, the highway stretching before us. Johnson receded in the rearview mirror, growing smaller until it vanished at the horizon—a tiny dot on the map that had somehow become the focal point of forces beyond our understanding.

After about an hour, Keating pulled into a gas station. "Might as well fill up now. There are some long stretches ahead with no services."

While Keating pumped gas, I took the opportunity to walk the boys to the bathroom, stretching our legs after the morning's drive. Cynthia went to purchase snacks and drinks for the journey ahead.

Inside the convenience store, everything felt surreal in its ordinariness. The bored clerk scrolling through his phone. Racks of chips and candy. Refrigerated cases of energy drinks and soda. The mundane world continuing as if nothing had changed, as if the fabric of reality wasn't tearing apart just a few hundred miles away.

"Dad," Casey tugged at my sleeve, pointing toward the television mounted in the corner. The local news was running a story about unexplained electrical disturbances across the Midwest, focusing on Des Moines.

"—authorities are calling it a case of mass hysteria," the anchor was saying. "Twenty-six people have been hospitalized with similar symptoms. Local scientists suggest a possible connection to unusual solar flare activity recorded earlier this week."

The footage showed people being loaded into ambulances, their bodies contorted in familiar ways. Even through the sanitized news coverage, there was something deeply unsettling about the scene—something the cameras couldn't quite capture but that registered on a primal level.

Ben stared at the screen, his expression unnaturally still. "They're not showing everything," he said quietly. "The camera can't capture what's really happening there."

"What's really happening?" I asked, keeping my voice low.

"The tear is pulling things through," Xander answered. "Small things, for now. Fragments. Echoes."

"But they're growing stronger," Ben added.

The clerk glanced up at us, his expression suddenly sharpening. "You heading west?" he asked, his tone too casual.

I nodded, instantly wary. "Just passing through."

He studied the boys for a moment too long before his gaze slid back to his phone. "Be careful out there. Weird storms coming in."

Back at the SUV, I mentioned the exchange to Keating. His expression darkened.

"The Initiative has eyes everywhere," he said, checking the surrounding area with new vigilance. "Sullivan built a network of watchers over decades—people who might not know the full scope of what they're involved in, but who report unusual patterns, sensitive individuals."

"Like our boys," Cynthia said.

Keating nodded grimly. "We should keep moving. Minimize stops where possible."

As we pulled back onto the highway, I noticed how the clerk stood in the gas station doorway, phone to his ear, watching our departure with unnatural intensity.

The afternoon stretched into evening, miles of heartland unspooling beneath our tires. The boys had fallen into a strange, synchronized sleep—all five breathing in perfect rhythm, their heads tilted at identical angles. Cynthia watched them anxiously in the vanity mirror, but they seemed peaceful, undisturbed by the dreams that might have plagued normal children after what they'd experienced.

"They're not just sleeping," Keating said, noticing her concern. "They're connecting. Preparing."

"For what?" I asked.

"For whatever we'll find in Idaho."

The sun had begun to set when Keating pulled into a motel parking lot just east of Cheyenne. "We should rest here," he said, killing the engine. "Get an early start tomorrow."

The motel was unremarkable—a single-story strip of rooms facing the parking lot, the kind of place that catered to truckers and budget travelers. Its very ordinariness made it perfect for our needs—anonymous, forgettable.

Keating checked us in, paying cash for three rooms. "Keep the boys together," he advised, handing us keycards. "I'll be right next door."

The room was basic but clean—two queen beds, a small table with chairs, the standard bathroom. The boys immediately arranged their sleeping bags in the floor without being asked, in order of age just like the backpacks.

"Are you hungry?" Cynthia asked them, unpacking the snacks we'd bought earlier.

"Can we get nuggets?" Casey asked, his voice suddenly just an eight-year-old's again. "I saw a drive-through on the way in."

"Chicken nuggets sound amazing right now," Ben agreed, stretching. "I'm starving."

"Me too," Xander chimed in.

"As long as they have ranch," Tyler added, ever particular about his dipping sauce.

"And Big Red," Brayden finished, his soda preference unchanged despite everything.

Cynthia's face lit up at this glimpse of our normal boys. "I think we can manage that."

I felt a weight lift from my chest. Whatever else had changed, they were still children—still our sons—with chicken nuggets and ranch dressing and Big Red soda firmly at the top of their priority list.

"Let's get some rest," she suggested. "We all need it after today."

While Cynthia got the boys ready for bed, I stepped outside, needing a moment to process everything. The motel parking lot was quiet, just a few trucks and cars scattered across the asphalt. Above, stars crowded the Wyoming sky, brilliant in the clear mountain air.

For a moment, I could almost pretend we were on a normal family road trip. That tomorrow we'd visit national parks or tourist attractions, not an interdimensional tear threatening to unleash a cosmic horror.

The door to Keating's room opened, and he emerged with a satellite phone. "Reception's better out here," he explained, joining me by the railing.

"Who are you calling?"

"Contacts," he said vaguely. "People who might have more information about what's happening in Idaho."

I studied him in the parking lot's yellowish light. "How deep does this go? The Initiative, I mean."

Keating's expression turned grim. "Deeper than Sullivan ever knew. She thought she was in control, that the Project Echo program was her creation. But there were always others. People who saw the frequencies as a means to something far beyond Sullivan's vision of transcendence."

"What do you mean?"

He hesitated, checking our surroundings before continuing in a lower voice. "Sullivan wasn't a religious woman. She saw the frequencies as a scientific phenomenon—a tool for evolutionary advancement. But there are those in the Initiative who interpret everything through a different lens."

"Biblical," I guessed, remembering comments my mother had made over the years. Her own evangelical background had made her sensitive to certain patterns, certain connections.

Keating's expression tightened. "Let's just say there are those who see all this through a different lens. People who've been waiting for signs and wonders." His voice dropped further. "And the tears? They might see those as the beginning of something they've anticipated for generations."

A chill ran through me despite the warm night. "Who are these people?"

"I don't know how deep it goes," Keating replied, glancing around the parking lot. "But Sullivan had backers—powerful ones. And I don't think they were just funding her research out of scientific curiosity."

"You think they had another agenda?"

"I think Sullivan was a pawn in a much larger game," he said carefully. "And now that she's gone, the real players might be making their move."

"And now?"

"Now they know your boys can heal the tears. Can communicate with the guardian." Keating's expression hardened. "Which makes them both the Shepherds' greatest threat and their most coveted prize."

The satellite phone in his hand buzzed. He glanced at the screen, his face tightening. "I need to take this," he said, moving away. "Get some rest. Tomorrow will be... challenging."

Back in our room, Cynthia had already settled into bed. The boys lay in sleeping bags on the floor, arranged in a neat row like sardines, all five breathing in that precise, synchronized rhythm. I slid in beside Cynthia, drawing comfort from her warmth, her solid presence beside me.

"I'm scared," she whispered, her voice barely audible. "Not just of what's happening, but of what our boys are becoming."

I pulled her closer. "They're still our sons," I said, hoping it was true. "Whatever else they might be, they're still ours."

"But for how long?" Her question hung in the darkness between us, unanswerable.

Sleep came eventually, but my dreams were troubled—fragments of conversation with my mother, strange symbols that resembled the ones carved into that well shaft beneath our house, the image of Sullivan's face in her final moments. And beneath it all, a constant humming at a frequency just beyond hearing.

I woke suddenly, disoriented in the unfamiliar room. The digital clock read 3:33 AM. Because of course it did.

Beside me, Cynthia slept peacefully. But the sleeping bags on the floor were empty.

I bolted upright, heart hammering. "Cynthia," I hissed, shaking her gently. "The boys—"

She came awake instantly, maternal instinct overriding grogginess. "Where—"

The bathroom door stood open, showing an empty room beyond. The main door to the parking lot was still locked and chained from the inside. I checked under the beds, in the closet, every possible hiding place in the small room.

They were gone. All five, vanished from a locked room.

A soft knock at the door made us both jump. Cynthia grabbed Keating's device from the nightstand while I approached cautiously, peering through the peephole.

Keating stood outside, fully dressed despite the hour. His expression was grim but unsurprised.

I opened the door. "The boys—"

"Are on the roof," he finished. "I saw them about ten minutes ago."

"The roof? How did they—"

"I don't know. But they're up there, arranged in that same star pattern. Waiting."

Cynthia was already pulling on shoes, grabbing a jacket. "Show us."

Keating led us around the side of the motel to a maintenance ladder. "I spotted them when I stepped out to make another call," he explained. "They didn't respond when I called to them."

We climbed in silence, emerging onto the flat motel roof. And there they were—our five sons, arranged in a perfect star, their arms and legs spread wide, faces turned toward the sky. They lay completely still, eyes open but unseeing, breath synchronized in that now-familiar rhythm.

"What are they doing?" Cynthia whispered, the fear in her voice palpable.

"Connecting," Keating replied, keeping his distance. "The guardian is preparing them for what they'll face tomorrow."

Above them, the Wyoming sky seemed impossibly vast, stars burning with unusual brightness. But as I looked closer, I noticed something strange. The space directly above the boys appeared distorted, the stars blurring and shifting as if seen through water or heat waves.

"Is that—"

"A micro-tear," Keating confirmed. "They're practicing."

Even as he spoke, the distortion began to close, the stars realigning to their proper positions. The boys blinked in unison, then sat up as one.

"Mom? Dad?" Ben sounded like himself again, confused and a little scared. "Why are we on the roof?"

"You don't remember coming up here?" Cynthia asked, rushing to check them for any sign of harm.

The boys looked at each other, that silent communication passing between them.

"We were dreaming," Casey said uncertainly.

"About stars," Xander added.

"And walls," Tyler continued.

"Walls made of light," Brayden elaborated.

"To keep the hunger out," Ben finished.

A chill ran down my spine that had nothing to do with the night air. "Let's get you back to bed," I said, trying to keep my voice steady. "We have a long drive tomorrow."

As we helped them down the ladder, I noticed how their movements had lost that uncanny synchronization. They were just boys again—tired, confused, a little scared. But the moment we reached our room, they arranged themselves back in that star formation without hesitation or discussion, falling instantly into deep sleep.

Keating lingered at our door. "Tomorrow we'll reach Bannock County," he said quietly. "The tear there is still small, but growing. If your boys can seal it..." He trailed off, leaving the implication hanging.

"And if they can't?"

His expression turned grave. "Then we'd better hope the guardian has a backup plan. Because what's coming through that tear is just the beginning."

After he left, Cynthia and I lay awake, watching our sons sleep their strange, synchronized sleep. Neither of us said what we were both thinking: that our boys were transforming into something beyond our understanding. That whatever emerged from this journey might wear their faces but no longer be entirely our children.

And that the choice had already been made for all of us.

"Try to sleep," Cynthia whispered, her hand finding mine in the darkness. "Whatever happens tomorrow, we'll face it together."

I squeezed her fingers, drawing strength from her presence. Whatever forces had manipulated our meeting, whatever agenda had brought us together, what we'd built was real. Our family was real. And I would fight anything, human or otherwise, that threatened it.

Even if that something was already inside our children.

Chapter 44: Wes

Eight hours on the road with five children would normally be a special kind of parental endurance test, but our journey to Bannock County, Idaho felt like moving through a dream. The boys remained unnervingly quiet, gazing out the windows with expressions that alternated between childlike wonder and ancient wisdom. Occasionally, they would speak in that synchronized way that still made my skin crawl—finishing each other's thoughts or responding to questions no one had asked aloud.

"We're getting closer," Ben announced as we crossed the Idaho state line, though nothing visible had changed in the landscape rolling past our windows. "The tear is... awake."

Keating's knuckles whitened on the steering wheel. "How can you tell?"

"The air tastes different," Casey replied, his young face solemn. "Like metal and electricity."

"And the guardian's voice is getting fainter," Xander added. "It's harder to hear over the... hunger."

The word hung in the air between us, carrying implications none of us wanted to examine too closely. Cynthia reached back to squeeze Brayden's hand, a mother's instinct to comfort overriding the strangeness of our situation.

"What exactly will we be looking for when we arrive?" I asked Keating, trying to focus on practicalities. "You mentioned a 'tear,' but what does that actually look like?"

Keating's eyes flicked to the rearview mirror, checking the boys. "Think of reality as fabric," he explained, his voice pitched low. "The tear isn't something you see directly—it's where the fabric starts to unravel. Physics behaves... differently around it. Light bends. Sounds distort. Electronic equipment malfunctions."

"Like what happened at our house," Cynthia said.

"Similar, but more localized. The Sullivan house—your house—was built directly over one of the guardian's access points. These new tears are forming in seemingly random locations where Amber's broadcast reached receptive minds."

"So it's spreading through people," I concluded. "The more who heard that broadcast..."

"The more potential tears," Keating confirmed grimly. "Sullivan thought she was initiating global transcendence. What she actually did was plant seeds of destabilization worldwide."

The landscape outside began to change as we drove deeper into Idaho—rolling hills giving way to more dramatic terrain, mountains rising in the distance. According to Keating's intel, the tear had formed near a small research facility outside the town of Pocatello, in a valley nestled between ancient volcanic formations.

"There," Tyler said suddenly, pointing ahead though there was nothing visible on the horizon. "That's where it hurts."

All five boys turned to look in the same direction, their movements synchronized like dancers following choreography no one else could hear.

"What do you mean 'hurts'?" Cynthia asked, her voice tight with concern.

"The guardian," Ben explained, his eyes fixed on the distant mountains. "It's trying to reach through, to seal the tear, but something's blocking it."

"Getting in the way," Casey added.

"Something that wants the tear to grow," Brayden continued.

"The hunger," Xander and Tyler finished together.

Keating took an unmarked turnoff, the SUV bouncing along a poorly maintained access road. A weathered sign flashed past: "PRIVATE PROPERTY - AUTHORIZED PERSONNEL ONLY." Beyond it lay what appeared to be an abandoned research station—a cluster of low concrete buildings surrounded by chain-link fence crowned with rusting barbed wire.

"Idaho Advanced Research Collaborative," Keating said, slowing as we approached a security gate. "At least that's what the cover story claims. It was actually an Initiative outpost, one of Sullivan's earliest facilities for studying frequency response."

"I thought the Initiative was centered in Johnson," I said.

Keating's expression darkened. "Sullivan established stations like this across the country—places where the barrier between dimensions showed natural thinning. She claimed she was monitoring and containing these weak points. In reality, she was studying how to exploit them."

He pulled up to the security gate, which hung partially open, the guard booth empty. Beyond it, the research facility looked deserted—windows dark, parking lot empty except for a single white van bearing government plates.

"Someone's here," I observed, unease prickling at the back of my neck.

"Stay in the car," Keating instructed, retrieving a handgun from beneath his seat. The casual way he checked the weapon suggested this wasn't his first time handling firearms. "I'll check it out."

"No," Ben said sharply, his voice suddenly carrying authority no thirteen-year-old should possess. "We need to go together. The tear requires all of us."

Keating hesitated, then nodded, tucking the gun into his waistband. "Stay close. And if I tell you to run, you run. No questions."

We passed through the gate, approaching the main building with cautious steps. The silence felt oppressive, broken only by the crunch of gravel beneath our feet and the distant cry of a hawk circling overhead.

Cynthia kept the boys between us, her expression fierce with maternal protectiveness.

As we reached the entrance, I noticed something odd—the air around the building seemed to waver slightly, like heat distortion, though the day wasn't particularly warm.

"Baby," Cynthia whispered, pointing to the ground. What I'd initially taken for water stains on the concrete walkway now looked disturbingly like dried blood, leading into the building in a clear trail.

The front doors stood ajar, glass smudged with handprints that seemed strangely elongated, as if made by fingers that had stretched beyond normal human proportions. I peered inside, seeing an empty lobby with overturned furniture and scattered papers. A coffee cup sat on the reception desk, still steaming.

"Someone left in a hurry," I murmured, an icy feeling spreading through my chest.

"Or something made them leave," Keating responded, his hand hovering near his concealed weapon.

The boys moved closer together, instinctively forming a protective circle. Even Casey, usually the first to rush into any new situation, hung back.

"Something's wrong," Ben said, his voice hushed. "The guardian's frequencies are... distorted here. Like they're being blocked."

"Or redirected," Xander added, his young face unnaturally grave.

A low humming began to emanate from within the building—a sound just below the threshold of comfortable hearing that made my teeth ache and my vision blur slightly at the edges.

"That's not the guardian," Casey whispered, pressing closer to Cynthia. "That's something else pretending to be the guardian."

Keating's face had gone deathly pale. "We need to leave," he said, backing away. "Now. This facility has been compromised."

Before we could move, a figure appeared in the doorway—a man in a lab coat, his movements too smooth to be natural, his smile too wide to be comfortable. When he spoke, his voice carried strange harmonics that seemed to modulate the humming coming from inside.

"The Lumin family, at last," he said, his gaze fixing on our boys with unsettling intensity. "We've been expecting you."

"Who are you?" I demanded, positioning myself between this stranger and my family.

"Just a humble researcher," he replied, though his smile suggested anything but humility. "One of many who've been preparing for your arrival for a very long time."

"Preparing?" Cynthia's hand tightened protectively around Casey's shoulders.

The man's smile widened further. "The Shepherds have such plans for your remarkable children. Such glorious purpose awaits them."

As he spoke, more figures appeared behind him—men and women in similar lab coats, all wearing that same unnatural smile, all moving with synchronized precision.

"The Initiative was never what you thought it was, Wesley Lumin," the man continued. "Never what any of you thought. It was always just a mask. A convenient fiction."

Keating's hand moved to his concealed weapon, drawing it with practiced ease. "We're leaving," he said firmly. "Step aside."

The man in the doorway laughed—a sound that carried those same strange harmonics as his voice. "I'm afraid that's not possible. The Shepherds have been waiting for children who could hear the frequencies clearly for a very long time. Perfect vessels for what's coming."

From within the building, that humming intensified, rising to a pitch that made the air itself seem to vibrate. More figures appeared in the shadows behind the man—people moving with that same uncanny synchronization, their features obscured in darkness.

"Last chance, Wes," Keating urged. "Take your family and go. I'll buy you what time I can."

But as I turned to run, I saw more vehicles pulling up to the security gate—white vans identical to the one already parked in the lot. Men and women in civilian clothes emerged, moving with that same synchronized precision we'd seen in Johnson after Sullivan's frequencies took hold.

We were surrounded.

"You see?" the man said, his terrible smile still fixed on his face. "The Shepherds have been planning this reunion for a very long time. They're so looking forward to meeting your family properly."

The humming reached a crescendo, and reality itself seemed to ripple around us. Through the open doors, I caught a glimpse of what waited inside the research facility—not just people, but something else. Something vast and ancient that bent light around itself like a gravitational lens.

The boys pressed closer together, their expressions filled with determination rather than fear. Ben's voice was steady as he spoke: "They can't have what they want. The guardian won't let them."

"And neither will we," Cynthia added, her maternal ferocity a tangible force as she gathered our children closer.

The Shepherds had set a trap.

And we had walked right into it.

999

Chapter 45: The Shepherd

I watch them on the monitor, the Lumin family cornered like rats in a maze of my design. Trapped in that Idaho facility, surrounded by my faithful. So much careful planning, so many centuries of patience, all culminating in this perfect moment.

The children are extraordinary. Even through the surveillance feed, I can see the guardian's frequencies shimmering around them—blue light that ordinary humans can't perceive but that shows so clearly to those with the right sight. Five points of resonance, exactly as prophesied. The pattern completed at last.

Behind me, the wall of screens displays similar scenes unfolding across the globe. Tears in reality opening in precise mathematical patterns—Des Moines, São Paulo, Johannesburg, Tokyo, Melbourne. Each one synchronized to the second, calibrated to the exact frequencies we've spent generations fine-tuning.

Amber's broadcast was the catalyst we needed—the perfect delivery system for frequencies that had previously been contained to specific locations. Now the signal spreads exponentially, the hunger reaching through to receptive minds across continents, across oceans.

I stand and approach the glass map that dominates the eastern wall of my sanctuary. Pin-points of light mark each tear location, each one pulsing in perfect synchronization. The pattern is unmistakable to those with eyes to see—a vast summoning circle spanning the globe itself.

My disciples call me the Shepherd. They believe I guide humanity toward transcendence, toward evolution beyond flesh. They have no conception of what truly waits beyond the veil, what has been whispering through the frequencies all along.

The Book of Revelation speaks of seven seals, seven trumpets, seven bowls of wrath. The prophets always understood in their primitive way—patterns of seven unlock cosmic doors. What they couldn't grasp was the mathematical precision required, the exact harmonic frequencies needed to thin the boundaries between dimensions.

Our order has dedicated itself to this work. Three centuries of careful breeding programs, of selective genetic cultivation. I am but the current caretaker of this sacred mission, the latest in an unbroken line of Shepherds dating back to 1666. The Sullivan family was merely one branch of a much larger tree, one strand in a complex web of bloodlines carefully guided toward producing the perfect vessels.

The Lumin children represent the culmination of this work—five perfect resonators, calibrated to frequencies that should have been beyond human perception. The guardian thought it was preparing them as defenders. It never suspected it was preparing them for sacrifice.

Seven tears. Seven locations. Seven frequencies.

But five children—the pentagram within the heptagram. The star within the circle. The ancient pattern completed at last.

One of my acolytes approaches, hesitating at the border of my private space. "The ritual preparations are complete, Father. The Conclave awaits your blessing."

I nod without turning, my eyes fixed on the Idaho feed. The Lumins have formed a protective circle, the guardian's blue light pulsing around them. Even trapped, they resist. Impressive, if futile.

"Begin the Seventh Invocation," I instruct. "The stars are aligned. The frequencies converge. After three centuries of waiting, the veil will finally part."

"And the Lumin family, Father?"

"Their resistance was anticipated. The trap serves its purpose either way." I smile, though he cannot see it. "Whether they fight or surrender, their presence completes the pattern. The tear in Idaho is the keystone—the final frequency that locks all others in place."

He bows and retreats. Around me, the sanctuary thrums with power as the Conclave begins the ritual seven floors below, their voices raised in the ancient harmonics we've preserved since the first whispers reached through the frequencies. They believe they're ushering in a new age of enlightenment. A transcendent evolution of consciousness.

I know better.

The frequencies have always been a door. And doors open both ways.

On the screen, the Idaho tear grows larger, the fabric of reality stretching, thinning. Soon it will rupture completely, creating the gateway we've worked so long to build.

I open my private terminal, accessing files that even my closest disciples have never seen. The true history of our order, recorded by my predecessors across centuries. The actual translation of what came through the first tear in 1666, when Friedrich Schäfer heard the hunger's first whispers and began our great work.

The hunger has had many names across many cultures. Devourer of Light. The Hollow God. That Which Waits Between. Always reaching, always calling, always searching for those who could hear its frequencies.

I glance at the calendar—nine days until the convergence reaches its peak. Nine days until what waits beyond can fully manifest. The beginning of what the ancient texts called the Great Consumption.

My disciples believe we're summoning divinity—that the hunger represents the next stage of cosmic evolution. They expect transcendence, apotheosis, the transfiguration of flesh into something greater.

They cannot conceive that evolution has always been a euphemism for extinction.

The Idaho feed shows the Lumin family still holding firm, still united despite everything arrayed against them. Their resistance creates complex harmonic patterns in the frequencies, ripples that spread outward through the entire network of tears. The guardian's influence flows through them, stronger than anticipated.

It won't matter. The pattern is already locked in place. The mathematics are irrefutable. Seven tears, positioned at precise coordinates, generating exact frequency harmonics that, when combined, create a summoning circle spanning the entire planet.

The hunger has waited millennia for this moment. It can wait a few days more.

I turn my attention to the other feeds. In Tokyo, test subjects already show the early signs of transformation—that telltale black fluid seeping from eyes and ears as their physical forms begin to align with the hunger's frequencies. In São Paulo, the tear has expanded to engulf an entire city block, reality itself distorting around the rupture point.

The patterns multiply, amplify, reinforce each other across vast distances. Exactly as designed. Exactly as prophesied.

My private phone chimes—a sound I haven't heard in weeks. Only five people have this number, and all of them hold positions of significant influence.

The display shows a name that sends a chill of anticipation through me: Thomas Spade.

I answer immediately. "The convergence has begun."

"They're trapped?" His voice carries that perfect balance of authority and charm that's taken him from tech billionaire to frontrunner in the presidential race. The polls show him twenty points ahead with just months until the election.

"As we speak. The Lumins walked right into our carefully prepared reception."

"And the children?"

"Exactly as promised. Five perfect frequency conduits, united in their resistance. The guardian's influence flows through them powerfully."

Spade's voice drops lower, reverent almost. "Then we're ready for the next phase. The Council is assembling as we speak. Representatives from every major world government, just as we've prepared for generations."

On my screens, I watch as the tear in Idaho grows larger, reality itself stretching thin around the Lumin family. Their continued resistance only strengthens the pattern, their unity creating harmonic resonances that amplify rather than dampen our work.

"The President has been briefed?" I ask, though I already know the answer.

"Not entirely," Spade's smile is evident in his voice. "He knows only what he needs to—that a breakthrough scientific discovery requires his presence at tomorrow's summit. Once he's in the chamber with the others..."

He doesn't need to finish. The chamber has been prepared beneath the Capitol for over a century, its frequencies carefully calibrated to affect even minds not naturally sensitive to the hunger's call. Nine world leaders in one room, surrounded by technology designed to open their consciousness to specific frequencies.

The pattern will spread from the top down, exactly as planned.

"What about the guardian?" Crawford asks. "Our readings show increased activity across all monitoring stations."

"A predictable response," I assure him. "It senses the convergence approaching and struggles to maintain the barriers. But it's fighting a war on too many fronts now. The tear network has expanded beyond its capacity to maintain."

Seven tears. Seven locations. Seven frequencies.

With nine world leaders as the primary vessels for what comes through.

"And Rebecca Lumin?" Crawford's tone shifts slightly. "Our intelligence suggests she's accessing materials that should have been destroyed decades ago."

That gives me pause. Wesley's mother has always been more resourceful than we'd given her credit for. "What materials?"

"Her ex-husband's journals. Roy Lumin discovered things in '64 that came dangerously close to exposing the Council. We thought all copies had been contained."

I turn back to the monitors, reassessing variables, recalculating probabilities. "It doesn't matter now. The pattern is already locked in place. The mathematics are irrefutable. Seven tears, positioned at precise coordinates, generating exact frequency harmonics that, when combined, create a summoning circle spanning the entire planet."

"Just ensure the Lumins remain contained," Spade says, authority hardening his voice. "The Summit begins in nine days. By then, I need confirmation that all nine tears are fully operational."

Nine. Not seven.

The true pattern reveals itself at last. What we've shown the lower ranks of our order has always been incomplete—the seven public tears serving as anchor points for the six hidden ones, creating the true sacred geometry required for complete manifestation.

"They will be," I promise. "The final preparations for your ascension are already underway."

Spade's laugh holds genuine pleasure. "Not my ascension, old friend. Ours. The world remade according to the ancient design."

I end the call and turn my attention back to the Idaho feed. The Lumin family remains unified, the guardian's blue light still pulsing around them. Their resistance creates complex harmonic patterns in the frequencies, ripples that spread outward through the entire network of tears.

Unexpected, but ultimately useful. The stronger their connection to the guardian, the more powerful the response when it finally breaks. And break it will—mathematics doesn't lie.

My second-in-command enters after a respectful knock. "Father, we've received confirmation from our agents in Tokyo, São Paulo, and Johannesburg. The tear network is expanding precisely as calculated."

"And our governmental assets?"

"In position. The World Security Summit will proceed as scheduled. Nine world leaders, all in one room, at the exact moment of convergence."

I nod my satisfaction. On the screens before me, I watch as reality itself begins to warp around the Idaho facility. The hunger grows impatient after millennia of waiting, pressing against the thinning barriers. In nine days, the accumulated power of Nine tears will create a gateway large enough for what waits beyond to finally step through.

And Thomas Spade—tech billionaire turned political messiah—will be its primary vessel.

A perfect voice for the hunger. A perfect face for the transition. A perfect shepherd to guide humanity toward its new purpose.

The world will never understand what happened until it's far too late. They'll see only a charismatic leader uniting nations, bringing peace, creating order. A visionary tech genius who promises to solve humanity's problems through innovation. They'll welcome the changes without recognizing them as extinction.

Evolution by another name.

My aide pauses at the door. "There's one more thing, Father. We've detected unusual activity from Rebecca Lumin's residence. She appears to be reaching out to former government contacts."

"Which agency?"

"That's just it, sir. These aren't standard intelligence channels. She's accessing a network we've never seen before. Communication protocols that don't match any known government system."

For the first time in decades, uncertainty creeps into my calculations. Rebecca was always perceptive, but this suggests resources beyond what our intelligence indicated.

"Monitor everything," I order. "And prepare a team. If she becomes problematic..."

He nods and withdraws, understanding the unspoken command.

I turn back to the monitors, watching the Lumin family's continued resistance with new interest. Perhaps there's more to this bloodline than we anticipated. More connections we failed to map.

No matter. In nine days, when nine world leaders gather beneath the Capitol dome and nine tears reach their peak alignment, such details will become irrelevant.

The hunger will have its vessels.

The pattern will be complete.

And humanity will serve its true purpose at last.

I smile at the thought. After three centuries of preparation, the New World Order is finally at hand.

And it will begin with Thomas Spade's inauguration.

EPILOGUE

World Security Council Meeting, Nine Days Later

Nine figures sat in perfect formation around the circular table, its obsidian surface inlaid with ancient symbols that pulsed with inner light when touched. The chamber deep beneath the Capitol building had existed far longer than the structure above it—constructed by anonymous craftsmen working from blueprints that had passed through secret societies for centuries.

Unlike the public faces they presented to their respective nations, these nine world leaders wore ceremonial robes adorned with the three interlocking circles—the symbol that had guided their Order for generations. They had been chosen not through democratic processes, but through careful bloodline selection spanning centuries.

"The tear in Idaho remains open," announced the American President, his voice carrying a satisfaction that would have shocked his voting public. "Our agents report that the Lumin family has been... contained."

"Excellent," replied the Russian Premier, his fingers tracing the symbol sewn into his robe's sleeve. "That family represented the greatest threat to our grand design. The guardian's influence has been weakening for decades, but those five vessels might have strengthened it beyond our capacity to counter."

Thomas Spade smiled from his position at the head of the table, his charismatic features catching the light from below as hidden projectors cast a red glow across the chamber. "With Sullivan's work now integrated into our own, the nine tears are performing precisely as calculated. The frequencies are destabilizing barriers worldwide."

The British Prime Minister studied the holographic display hovering above the table's center, showing nine glowing points on a global map. "Each tear grows stronger by the hour. Tokyo and São Paulo have already reached Stage Three. The locals report significant psychological effects among the population."

"As prophesied," intoned the German Chancellor. "The Great Cleansing approaches."

The Council members nodded in solemn agreement. For centuries, their Order had guided world events from the shadows—placing agents in governments, religions, scientific institutions. All working toward this culmination, this final transformation of humanity.

"Our predecessors understood only parts of the truth," Spade continued, activating another display that showed ancient texts scrolling beside modern scientific data. "They believed they were serving competing forces—what they called the 'Divine Protector' and the 'Great Devourer.' But we know better."

"There is only Transformation," the Council members recited in unison. "There is only Ascension."

The Chinese President adjusted controls on his armrest, bringing up footage from experimental sites around the globe. Each screen showed people convulsing as that familiar black fluid leaked from their eyes, mouths, and ears. "The vessels are responding as expected. The hunger's frequencies reshape them from within."

"The Book of Revelation speaks of seven seals, seven trumpets, seven bowls of wrath," said the Indian Prime Minister, his voice reverent. "But our texts speak of nine—the completion of the cycle. Nine tears to break the barriers completely. Our ancestors interpreted literally what they could not understand scientifically. These nine tears are those prophesied events—portals through which transcendence arrives."

Spade rose from his seat, commanding the room with his presence. Three centuries of careful breeding had produced in him the perfect balance of charisma, intelligence, and psychopathic detachment. His presidential campaign was already thirty points ahead in the polls, positioned to make him the most powerful man in the world just as the transformation reached completion.

"For generations, we have prepared humanity for this moment," he declared. "The great religions with their promises of apocalypse and rebirth. The scientific institutions with their evolutionary theories. Even the environmental movement warning of civilizational collapse. All seeding the collective consciousness with the inevitability of transformation."

As he spoke, the chamber's lighting shifted from red to black, the only illumination now coming from the nine pulsing points on the holographic map. Each tear connected to the others through lines of energy, forming a sacred geometry that spanned the globe.

"The Shepherds of Light believe these tears must be sealed," said the Japanese Prime Minister with a dismissive gesture. "They still cling to the guardian's protection, still believe humanity should continue in its current form."

"Their time is ending," Spade replied. "The guardian grows weaker as the hunger grows stronger. The balance tips toward transformation, just as foretold."

The holographic display shifted to show population centers near each tear. Millions of people going about their daily lives, unaware that reality itself was unraveling around them. Unaware that the black fluid already flowed through their veins in microscopic quantities, preparing them for what was to come.

"How long until full manifestation?" asked the French President, his fingers drumming against the obsidian table with barely contained excitement.

Spade consulted readings only he could see. "The mathematical progression is accelerating beyond our initial projections. The Lumin family's resistance created an unexpected pressure differential that actually strengthened the remaining tears. What we projected to take months might now occur in weeks."

"And the physical effects?" asked the British Prime Minister. "When do they become... undeniable?"

"They've already begun," replied the Chinese President, enlarging footage from surveillance cameras in Tokyo. "Mass hallucinations. Temporal distortions. Spontaneous synchronization of behavior." The images showed crowds of people stopping in unison, all turning to face the same direction before continuing as if nothing had happened.

"The first stage of consciousness dissolution," Spade confirmed. "Individual identity giving way to collective awareness. The hunger's influence spreading person to person, mind to mind."

He activated a secondary display, showing medical data from test subjects. "The black fluid production accelerates exponentially once it reaches a certain concentration in the bloodstream. We've observed complete transformation in as little as seventy-two hours after that threshold is crossed."

"And the transformed?" asked the Russian Premier. "They remain... controllable?"

Spade's smile didn't reach his eyes. "They recognize their shepherds. Those of us whose bloodlines have been prepared across generations to serve as vessels of authority rather than transformation. We will guide what emerges on the other side of this great change."

The American President leaned forward, his face illuminated by the holographic glow. "And those who resist the transformation? The naturally immune? Those connected to the guardian?"

"Irrelevant," Spade replied with the casual cruelty that had made him such an effective political operator. "Once the tears reach Stage Nine synchronization, resistance becomes mathematically impossible. The frequencies will saturate every electronic device, every broadcast medium, every communication channel. No human mind will remain untouched."

The chamber's lighting shifted again, bathing the Council in that familiar blue glow—not the guardian's light, but a perfect simulation designed to evoke religious awe in those who witnessed it. The Council members raised their hands in practiced unison, forming the sacred gesture their Order had maintained since its inception.

"We stand at the threshold of the greatest transformation in human history," Spade intoned, his voice resonating with frequencies subtly altered to inspire devotion. "What our ancestors began in 1666, we complete today. The circle closes. The pattern fulfills itself."

The holographic display shifted one final time, showing the mathematical progression of the tears' development. Nine points of light, pulsing in perfect synchronization, their energies combining to form a pattern that matched exactly the three interlocking circles of their Order's symbol.

"The time of waiting ends," Spade declared. "The time of transformation begins. After centuries of preparation, the hunger will finally manifest fully in our world."

The Council members rose as one, their robes shifting in perfect harmony despite the absence of wind. Above them, the nine points of light on the display pulsed faster, their rhythm matching the heartbeats of every person in the chamber.

"What was begun with seven drops of blood upon three circles in a colonial clearing," Spade intoned, "ends with nine tears upon the world. The covenant is fulfilled. The transformation comes."

As the Council members joined hands, completing their ritual circle, the chamber's lighting shifted to deepest crimson. The First Elder's prophecy from 1666 echoed through time to reach this moment of fulfillment: "They will either save mankind from eternal darkness, or usher in its final transformation."

The Council had made their choice. Transformation. At any cost.

The hunger would feed. Reality would bend. Humanity would transcend.

And the world would never be the same again.

To be continued in

LOVE AND LUMINATI

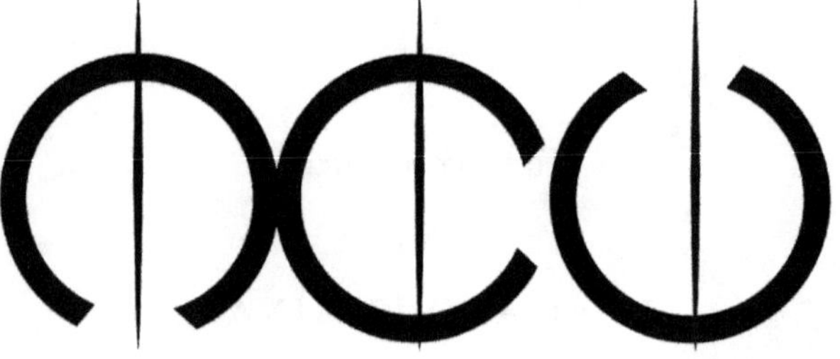

www.ingramcontent.com/pod-product-compliance
Lightning Source LLC
Chambersburg PA
CBHW070530310726

48976CB00002BA/590